# NIGHT
# WRAITH

# ALSO BY ANTHONY M. STRONG

## THE JOHN DECKER SUPERNATURAL THRILLER SERIES

Soul Catcher (prequel) • What Vengeance Comes • Cold Sanctuary
Crimson Deep • Grendel's Labyrinth • Whitechapel Rising
Black Tide • Ghost Canyon • Cryptic Quest • Last Resort
Dark Force • A Ghost of Christmas Past • Deadly Crossing
Final Destiny • Night Wraith • Wolf Haven

## THE CUSP FILES

Deadly Truth • Devil's Forest

## THE REMNANTS SERIES

The Remnants of Yesterday • The Silence of Tomorrow

## STANDALONE BOOKS

The Haunting of Willow House • Crow Song

# NIGHT WRAITH

A John Decker Novel

# ANTHONY M.STRONG

 WEST
STREET

Night Wraith

West Street Publishing

*Cover art and interior design by*
*Bad Dog Media, LLC.*

ISBN: 978-1-942207-52-8

*For Sonya!*

# PROLOGUE

## BOSTON-DECEMBER 1922

HAROLD WAINWRIGHT BANGED on the library door, his fists echoing in tandem with the low chimes of a grandfather clock as it struck midnight yet again.

"Harold, we still have one more place to visit," said a voice from behind him as the clock gave one last ominous rumble that shook through the sprawling house like a heartbeat. And in a way, it was a heartbeat. Because the house was alive. Wainwright was sure of it. A building so entwined with the specters within its walls that it was impossible to separate them. The house and its occupants might as well be one and the same.

"I don't want to go anywhere else with you," Harold wailed. "Please don't make me. I beg of you."

"That isn't my decision to make."

A hand fell to Harold's shoulder. Bony fingers pinched his flesh through his shirt.

He didn't dare to look around, to stare into that dreadful face again. Of the three spirits he had met in this house, this last one was the worst. It filled him with a dread worse than any he had ever felt before. He wished, not for the first time that night, that he had never entered this house. Hadn't let Leona convince him to go inside . . .

---

Harold and Leona had attended two soirées already that evening, where the booze flowed like water despite the iron fist of prohibition pressing down upon the city. It was Christmas after all, and the wealthy socialites and businessmen who made Beantown their home were hardly averse to breaking the law in the name of a good time. Especially when they viewed that law as ridiculous and were safe in the knowledge that they would not be raided thanks to their influence and position.

They were stumbling along Beacon Street toward Harold's brownstone full of holiday cheer when they came across the house sitting on the wide expanse of Boston Common stretching off to their left. Leona noticed it first, her attention drawn by the faint sound of music and laughter within.

The windows were ablaze with light. Faint puffs of smoke curled from the twin chimneys, one at each side of the structure. The music grew louder. It sounded like an orchestra. They were playing the Charleston.

"That's funny," Leona said, her eyes narrowing. "I've never noticed this place before, and I'm sure I would have noticed a house like that right here on Boston Common."

"Me too," Harold agreed, thinking it strange that he didn't recognize the building, given his habit of taking evening walks around Boston Common and the surrounding streets. "Doesn't look new. I can't imagine how we missed it."

"Who cares?" Leona tugged at Harold's hand. "Come on."

"What are you doing?" he asked, his head swimming.

"They're having a party," she replied with a grin even as she tugged him up the front steps toward the door. "It's still early. I don't want to go home yet."

"We don't even know these people. What makes you think they

want us to join their party?" Harold asked, but even as he said the words, the door creaked slowly inward, spilling a square of welcoming yellow light down the frosty steps.

"They opened the door for us to come on in." Leona gripped his hand tighter. "I'd say that's a pretty good invitation, wouldn't you?"

"I'm game. Just so long as they have good gin and better music." Harold stepped across the threshold but soon came to an abrupt halt. Instead of walking into the midst of a roaring holiday celebration, he found himself in an imposing entry hall. A grand staircase swept up to a second-floor balcony. Portraits hung on the walls. Richly hued oil paintings in ornate gilded frames. Dozens of them. Beneath each was a name on a small brass plaque. The signs of the party were gone. Now, only silence swirled around them.

"Where is everyone?" Leona almost bumped into Harold's back. "I swear there was a party going on in here just moments ago."

"There was. We both saw it." Harold walked to the middle of the entrance hall, staring up toward the second floor. It was dark and empty. He went to the portraits hanging on the walls and studied them, reading aloud the names on the brass plaques. He didn't recognize any of them, at least until he came to one particular portrait. "Charles Dickens."

"What?"

"This painting. It's Charles Dickens."

"So what?" Leona stood with her hands on her hips. "Maybe whoever owns this house likes literature. I'm more concerned with where everyone is."

Harold walked back to her. "Maybe we were mistaken. We should go."

"No. This is ridiculous. We both saw the party. Heard the music." Leona turned toward a pair of sliding doors to their right. "Someone must be here."

She took a step forward, was about to open the doors, when a voice broke the silence.

"You won't find anyone in there, I assure you."

Leona gave a small gasp of surprise.

Harold whirled around to see a tall man wearing a black tuxedo. He gripped a polished blackthorn cane with a silver handle in one white-gloved hand.

"We've been waiting for you." The man's lips lifted into a narrow smile, with only the barest hint of teeth showing.

"Us?" Harold glanced at Leona, who was staring at the stranger as if she'd never seen such a creature before. "What could you possibly want with us?"

"Not Leona." The man took a step forward, his cane clacking on the checkerboard marble tiled floor. "Just you, Harold."

"I don't understand." Harold made an instinctive move to put himself between Leona and the odd stranger.

"We thought there was a party," Leona said. "That's the only reason we're here."

"Oh, we're going to have a party." The man's smile faded. His eyes glinted like steel. "In fact, it's all in Harold's honor."

"I think we should go." Leona gripped Harold's arm, her fingers pressing through the jacket into his flesh.

"You're free to leave." The man lifted his cane and pointed toward the door. "In fact, I insist."

"Then that's what we shall do." Leona backed up, pulling Harold along with her.

"Stop." The cane came down, striking the floor with a ringing smack. "Only you. Not Harold. He'll be staying a while."

"What?" A flash of confusion passed across Leona's face. Confusion mixed with fear. "I'm not leaving him in here alone."

"He won't be alone." The man lifted the cane again and brought it down. No sooner had its silver tip struck the floor than a change came over the man, almost as if a veil had been lifted and they could see his true countenance. The tuxedo was now dusty and torn. His face was skeletal, with only the barest hint of flesh clinging to gleaming white bone. His fingers, curled around the cane's handle, were gnarled and twisted. Draping behind him, as if he were shackled to the house, a dozen or more heavy iron chains disappeared into the darkness.

Leona screamed. All Harold could manage was a strangled croak. He took Leona by the shoulders, propelled her toward the door. Bundled her out into the frigid Boston night. He stepped across the threshold, relieved to escape that strange house and the horrors that dwelled within.

But instead of arriving on the sidewalk, he found himself right back where he started, facing the grand staircase in the entrance hall, and surrounded by those strange portraits that watched the proceedings with dead eyes.

Behind him, the front door slammed shut.

His host shambled forward, chains rattling, even as his deathly face creased into a rictus grin.

"We have a long night ahead of us, Harold. A *very* long night." The man, or rather what remained of him, reached out with a bony hand. "Now, let's step into the library and I'll introduce you to the Ghost of All Things Past."

# ONE

YOU LIED TO ME." John Decker fixed the man seated across the desk from him with a glowering stare sufficient to match the tone of his voice. It had been a month since his return from Singer Cay and reunion with Nancy. A month he had spent readjusting to the modern world after almost a year in the past. He had also been pondering the implications of what Mina had told him in her bunker apartment on Singer Cay the day he returned and trying to figure out his future. During that time, he had stayed away from the organization he worked for and had avoided contact with both Adam Hunt and Mina. Only now had he made the trip from the mainland to CUSP's island headquarters with a singular intention. But first, he wanted answers from the person who had recruited him. "All this time, you were playing me for a fool."

"John, I assure you that isn't true." Adam Hunt shifted in his chair and leaned forward, resting his elbows on the desk. His own voice was measured and calm, in stark contrast to Decker's. "I merely withheld information that you could not possibly know without altering the course of future events. In my situation, you would have done the same."

"Shackleton, Alaska," Decker said.

"What about it?"

"You told me you were there to monitor the removal of equipment from the labs under the North Tower. That the break-in by those two men intent on stealing top-secret military technology, and all that followed, was merely coincidence. That wasn't true. No one spends more than a year of their life in a godforsaken place like that just to watch a bunch of decades-old equipment get loaded onto a truck. You were there to guarantee that events progressed in a way that would ensure all that followed. You knew I would show up there, and you were quite happy to let a teenage girl get involved in a life-threatening situation."

"Mina was never in any danger." Hunt shrugged. "How could she be? Her older self was running CUSP and had been doing so since our organization's inception. She already knew the outcome of everything that would happen in her life right up until Celine Rothman appeared at your wedding and we all got thrown back in time to 1942. She was literally witnessing her own past play out before her eyes."

"Which brings me to my next point. Your gracious gift of Singer Cay for our wedding. Colum was right to be suspicious. It was anything but a generous act. You were manipulating me, just like you had since the first day we met. You knew what was going to happen on that island. You could have spared Nancy six months of heartbreak, but you didn't."

"I had no idea what was going to happen on Singer Cay," Hunt said. "You must believe me. Mina took me into her confidence, I admit, but she refused to tell me more than was necessary regarding future events. Most of the time, I knew nothing of the motivation behind the orders she gave me. That was true right from the start, all the way back to Shackleton. The majority of decisions were my own. Just like the idea of providing Singer Cay for the wedding was mine. Mina was confident the timeline would play out correctly without interference because it already had, at least as far as she was concerned. But she also understood that her own knowledge of the future and involvement with CUSP meant that a gentle prod would be necessary once in a while. She called these minor interventions *immutable points in time*. For example, she was the only one who could send me to Shackleton and keep me there for so long. She also suggested that I shouldn't put up more than token resistance to her younger self joining the investigation into Jack the Ripper. Honestly, had I been privy to the same foresight as Mina, I'm not sure I could have resisted the urge to intervene and save you and Nancy from your ordeal."

"Which would have broken the chain of causality."

"And created a paradox that could be resolved only by the timeline splitting. Nothing I did would have made a difference to the reality we inhabit, and you know it."

"Perhaps. Or maybe we have it all wrong. If you had refused to let Mina join the investigation into Jack the Ripper, all the events that came afterward would have happened differently. She would never have traveled back in time to create the Order of St. George. Classified Universal Special Projects would never have come into existence."

"Which means I would not have been in Shackleton," said Hunt.

"Exactly. The timeline would have unraveled. Mina would never have attended college in London. Colum and I would not have been there to stop Abraham Turner. Mina said that altering the events in London would have caused a paradox, but on reflection, I'm not so sure. The only reason any of us were there was because of actions Mina herself took many decades in the past. If we had averted the circumstance that led to her traveling into the past, the timeline would just have unfolded differently."

"The younger Mina would have continued living in Shackleton as a regular young woman, oblivious to the greater destiny that might have awaited her."

"Yes."

"On the other hand, Thomas Finch might have gone on to

create the Order of St. George on his own and set the whole original timeline in motion again. Ergo, a paradox."

Decker grimaced. "We could talk about this all day, and never come to a satisfactory conclusion. Right now, all we can do is accept what happened."

"That works for me." Hunt appeared to relax. "Does this mean you accept my apology?"

"I haven't heard an apology yet, and even if I did, I'm not sure it's enough."

"But you just said—"

"I said we have to accept the past as it stands because we can't change it, and possibly never could. What's done is done. Now I have to think about the future." Decker slipped a hand inside his jacket and removed a white envelope with Adam Hunt's name written on the front. He laid it on the desk and pushed it toward his boss.

"What's this?" Hunt looked at the envelope with wary suspicion.

Decker took a moment to compose himself before he answered. Then he took a deep breath. "It's my resignation."

# TWO

NANCY CASSIDY SAT in the living room of the house she and John Decker shared in Portland, Maine, and sipped Chamomile tea from a fine China cup. It had been a month since Decker reappeared on the doorstep, and they had barely been apart since. Celine, newly independent and living on her own, was more than happy to cover for Nancy at the bakery and had told her to take all the time she needed.

During that month, Decker had told Nancy much about his time trapped in the past, including a harrowing voyage on the Titanic and subsequent encounter in New York City with a golem. It didn't take long for her to realize that she was lucky he had made it back. So much could have gone wrong, leaving him stranded there forever. Decker appeared to feel the same way, and several times she had found him sitting alone, brooding, and lost in thought. Finally, even though he wasn't due back at work until the new year, he had decided to make the trip over to CUSP's headquarters on an island off the Maine coast and pay a visit to Adam Hunt.

Nancy suspected the reason behind his impromptu excursion but didn't press him on the matter, even though she knew that quitting his job would cause some short-term hardship for them. It was his decision to make, and honestly, she looked forward to a life where she wasn't constantly terrified that he would not return. A fear that had become a grim reality for six months after their interrupted wedding. She felt like they had been given a second chance, and wasn't willing to squander it by convincing him to stay.

She placed the cup back on its saucer, her eyes dropping to a book that rested next to it on the narrow end table. It was a rare first edition printing of 'A Christmas Carol' that Decker had purchased while still in 1911 from a London bookseller. Feeling lonely and further away from her than ever, he had sought out the gift as a way to preserve some sense of normalcy. At that point, he wasn't even sure there was a way home or if his gift would ever reach her but had asked Thomas Finch to send it from London to New York after the Titanic sank none-the-less, then carried it with him from the past. When he finally made it home, he presented it to her not as a present to be put under the tree until Christmas morning, but as one from the Christmas he had spent bereft and separated from her.

She loved the book, not only because the story within its covers felt like an old friend, but also because of how it had come into her possession. Yet until now, she had only given the book a cursory inspection, opting instead to make up for lost time with John. Now, with hours on her hands as she awaited his return, she picked it up, laid the book on her lap, and studied it.

It was a thin volume, at least by modern standards, bound in cinnamon-colored cloth with the book title and author's name presented within gilt and blind-stamped holly and ivy wreaths on the spine and front board. The page edges were also gilt. Nancy opened it carefully and browsed the interior, marveling at the wonderful hand-colored plates protected by thin sheets of tissue to stop the color rubbing off. The book was in fantastic condition for its age. But then again, it had skipped a century of wear and tear on its way to her.

She turned to the first page of stave one, careful to touch the edge only lightly lest she leave oil from her fingers on the delicate paper. Again, she noticed the wonderful state of preservation, without a hint of foxing and no creases or tears. Whoever owned this book in the past must have cherished it enough to keep the volume in almost pristine condition.

Her eyes fell to the first line of the story. *Marley was dead: to begin with.* She could not think of a more prophetic opening, considering she had believed John Decker dead only a week before, and now, much like Marley's ghost, he had returned. But this was not some fleeting visit by a chained and miserable specter. Decker was alive and well, and she had every intention of making sure he stayed that way.

Speaking of which . . . Nancy glanced toward the door, wondering how much longer it would be before he returned. John had been gone for over an hour already. The boat journey across to the island took forty-five minutes and a similar amount of time for the return. And who knew how long he would end up stuck at CUSP's headquarters. His visit was unannounced, and there was no guarantee Adam Hunt would quickly receive him. She had at least a couple more hours to wait.

With a sigh, Nancy turned her attention back to the book and started to read, consuming stave one in short order and relishing the Victorian world that sprang up around her. By the time she was halfway through stave two, her throat was dry. She glanced at the empty teacup sitting on the side table and closed the book, intending to lay it down and make another cup. But as she did so, something slipped from between the pages yet to be read. A square of yellowed paper that fluttered to the floor and landed at her feet.

Nancy froze momentarily, taken by surprise. She stared at the slip of paper, wondering at first if the book was in worse condition than she had previously thought. A leaf must have worked loose and fallen out. But she soon ruled it out. The sheet was folded, and there was no discernible printed material on it. Rather than being a part of the book, this was something else that had been placed between its pages. A stowaway across time.

A prickle of anticipation ran through her. She placed the book on the end table and bent down, gently lifting the folded sheet of paper from the floor. It looked old, perhaps as old as the book from which it had come, judging by the discoloration of the paper, that had turned from what must once have been a soft white to a pale shade of ochre with darker brown stains mottling the surface. A faint hint of handwriting in blue ink had bled through to the blank side of the sheet.

Nancy resisted the urge to unfold the slip of paper. Not there, in the living room where it could get damaged. Instead, she rose and walked through the kitchen to a table in the breakfast nook surrounded on three sides by large windows that overlooked Casco Bay. She placed the sheet of paper down and unfolded it once, twice, and held it flat to reveal the handwriting within.

Then she stared in mute disbelief.

# THREE

WHEN DECKER ARRIVED HOME, Nancy was waiting in the living room with a strange look on her face. At first, he thought it was because she had guessed the outcome of his meeting with Adam Hunt, but he soon realized otherwise.

"I have something to show you." Nancy was sitting on the couch, but now she stood and approached him. There was a folded slip of paper in her hand, which she held out. "Look at this."

"What is it?" Decker asked, although he was only faintly interested. The anger that had simmered and grown in the time since his return from the past was still there, and his confrontation with Hunt had done little to ease it. In fact, if anything, he was angrier now than he had been before. He had sensed no remorse in Hunt. Even when he offered his resignation, the man had just sat on the other side of his desk and looked at him with an unreadable face. It left Decker feeling like he had never been a valued member of CUSP but rather an expendable pawn in the bigger game being played by Adam Hunt and the older version of Mina.

"Take it and look." She held the folded sheet of paper gently between thumb and index finger, careful not to crease it. "You won't believe your eyes."

Decker took the sheet and unfolded it to discover that he was holding a letter. It looked old. He gave it a cursory glance, then folded the sheet back up, still preoccupied. "It's an old letter. So what?"

"It's not just an old letter," Nancy said. "It came out of the book you bought me, and it's incredible. You have to read it."

Decker crossed to the couch and sat down, then laid the letter out in front of him on the coffee table. It was only now that he saw what Nancy was talking about. The prose was written in small cursive. The ink was blue, and the paper still retained much of its original brightness. A date at the top of the sheet identified it as being written in February 1844. But it was the flamboyant signature at the bottom that caught his attention.

Charles Dickens.

Decker stared in disbelief. "You found this inside the book I brought back?"

"Yes," Nancy said, her voice trembling with excitement. "What do you think?"

Decker lifted his gaze from the signature and read the letter, studying a line here and there when he stumbled over a word or two. Then he went back to the beginning and read it all over again, just to make sure he understood exactly what was in front of him on the page.

> *My Dear Forster,*
>
> *I send you this copy of A Christmas Carol—a fine first edition for your shelf—even though I know you have read the manuscript already and will find little to surprise you within its pages. Your guidance with the aforementioned work was most gratefully received, as always. I will never come close to repaying your dedication to my prose and unending friendship, which I cherish dearly. But in one small way I can provide at least a down-payment on that impossible task.*

You asked last year, when the manuscript was nearing completion, how I came upon the idea for Scrooge and the ghostly visitors who gave him such an opportunity to reflect upon his life and change his ways.

At the time, I demurred, replying merely that the story occurred to me in a fit of inspiration. That, my dear friend, is not the whole of it, and you deserve a full account. For you see, the terrors that Ebenezer Scrooge endures at the hands of his night wraiths came not so much from my imagination, as personal experience.

You will recall my trip, along with Catherine, to the United States in January of '42. You will also recall my complaints that upon our arrival in Boston, I was besieged and spent a good portion of my time in that city at the mercy of the multitude, who made it their mission to follow me with relentless vigor. As such, I could not do as I wanted, nor see the places I wanted to see. My only respite came late at night, when I could slip from my suite at the Tremont House under the cover of darkness and explore the city unencumbered.

It was during one of these late-night excursions that I had an experience that would later inspire me to write the book you now hold.

I departed the hotel a little before midnight to stretch my legs, turning left at Beacon Street and hurrying away from King's Chapel and its burying ground. It was a night laden with fog. The kind of evening when ghosts and ghouls spring easily to the imagination. Alone and lost in thoughts of all things supernatural, I pressed on toward Boston Common, holding my coat tight to fend off the bitter cold. That, my friend, is when I came across the house.

It stood apart from its surroundings, as if it were not a part of them, but existed despite them. It occupied a spot on the common that I was sure had been nothing but grass earlier in the day. The façade was of stone, with columns holding an imposing port-cochere. Tall windows flanked this, black and soulless. On the second floor, more dark windows gazed upon me.

At that moment, I had the strangest feeling, as if the house was there for me, and me alone. It was a most unusual sensation. I looked away, fearful that the sudden materialization of this house, which I am sure was not standing there previously, might result from a chill brought on by the inclement weather. Or possibly by an undigested bit of beef, or a blot of mustard, as Scrooge would say.

But the house was still there when I turned back. Only now, dear Forster, the windows were aglow with radiant light, and the front door stood open as if beckoning me inside.

Well, you can imagine what I did next.

I took the house up on its offer. After all, it was just an old building, and I was in an exploratory mood.

It was there, inside that ghastly house, that I met the inspiration for what would eventually come to be the specters I put down on paper. For indeed, there were *spirits within, and even a wraith entwined in chains, just like poor old Marley . . .*

*And here I will leave the tale, tantalizing you with only the barest snippet. But fear not, for the next time we meet (which I hope will be soon), we will sit warming ourselves in front of the fire with a tot of brandy as I relate to you the rest of this haunting tale. I warn you now, you may not believe a word of it, dear friend, but it is true. Every word.*

*Until Then, Faithfully Yours*
*Charles Dickens*

When he was finished, Decker folded the letter and looked up at Nancy, who was hovering at his shoulder. All thought of his conversation with Adam Hunt was momentarily lost to his amazement. "Wow!"

"Isn't it crazy?" Nancy sat down next to him. She reached out and touched the letter, picking it up almost reverently. "A first-hand supernatural account of the inspiration for A Christmas Carol."

"Tucked inside a copy of that very same book. It must be the actual volume that Dickens references in the letter to Forster, whoever that is."

"I looked him up," Nancy said. "John Forster was a friend of Charles Dickens and also his biographer. They were very close. Forster read all of Dickens' manuscripts prior to publication."

"He refers to Forster reading the manuscript of A Christmas Carol in this letter," Decker said. "Although that isn't the interesting bit."

"No, it's not." Nancy sounded excited. "If you believe what Dickens says—and it's a stretch—he got the inspiration for the book from a mysterious house full of ghosts that appeared before him while he was taking a late-night walk."

"A house in Boston, of all places," Decker said. "It's a shame he didn't finish the tale. I would love to know exactly what he experienced inside that building and how it relates to the ghosts of Christmas past, present, and future."

"He probably did finish the story," Nancy said. "Just in person, around a roaring fire with a glass of brandy."

"Which means we'll never know the rest of it."

"Unless—" Nancy fell silent for a moment. "You should take this letter to Adam Hunt. Show it to him. If anyone can investigate this and get to the bottom of it, find out what Charles Dickens experienced in that house, it's CUSP."

Now it was Decker's turn to fall silent. Distracted by the letter, the events of the past few hours had slipped from his mind. Now they came roaring back. He cleared his throat and looked at Nancy. "I can't do that."

"Why on earth not? This is exactly the kind of thing that Hunt would be interested in."

"I agree. And under any other circumstances, I would absolutely show Adam Hunt this letter." Decker took a deep breath. "But I couldn't even if I wanted to, because I don't work for Classified Universal Special Projects anymore."

# FOUR

I FIGURED that's why you went over there," Nancy said in a small voice. "I wish you had talked it through with me first."

"What good would that have done?" Decker replied. "It wouldn't change the fact that they used me. Lied to me about everything. Even Mina, who—"

"Mina has always looked up to you," Nancy interrupted. "Thought of you almost as a surrogate father. I can't imagine she meant to cause any harm. Just the opposite. I'm sure everything she did was with the best of intentions."

"You're talking about the Mina I met in Shackleton. The young woman who couldn't wait to see the world. To get out of that place and make a life for herself. She isn't that person anymore. She hasn't been that girl for a hundred and fifty years."

"That doesn't mean—"

"I don't want to talk about it." Decker stood and paced to the window. He stared out across the Portland skyline toward the docks and the gray ocean beyond. "I'm not taking that letter to Adam Hunt, Mina, or anyone else at CUSP."

"John, just stop and think about it." Nancy put the letter down, followed him to the window, and slipped her arms around his waist. She rested her chin on his shoulder. "You found that book in

London and carried it over a hundred years across time just to give to me. You bought it for me even though there was every chance we would never see each other again. That we would be forever separated by not just an ocean but a century. You survived the sinking of the Titanic to find a way back to me."

"I'm not sure what your point is," Decker said.

"The letter. That's my point." Nancy took a step back and folded her arms. "Do you really think it was a coincidence that you pulled that particular book off the shelf out of all the books in the world?"

"That's exactly what I think."

"Or you were always meant to find the book. Maybe that letter is a sign that you were too hasty in quitting your job with CUSP. After all, it must have waited for decades sitting between those pages, undiscovered and unread. What are the odds of that?"

"About a hundred percent, given the circumstances." Decker turned back to her. "It's intriguing, I'll admit. It's a one in a thousand chance that no one found that letter before you. But it's not some kind of sign from the universe that I'm meant to accept what happened and move on. Just forgive everyone."

"Unless it is," Nancy said, apparently unwilling to give up. "Maybe Mina was right: everything that happened from the moment you met her in Shackleton was a timeline set in stone. An immutable series of events. Her becoming a victim of Jack the Ripper, recently freed from a basement tomb that an older version of herself had imprisoned him in. Your disappearance on Singer Cay. Falling back in time. Ending up in Edwardian London. The Titanic. A closed loop that must happen because it always had happened."

"I'm not so sure of that," Decker said. "Maybe Mina or Hunt could have changed all our futures by just choosing a different path and decided not to, or perhaps they *did* try to alter this timeline and failed. But we'll never know because it's impossible to prove either way."

"John, have you ever stopped to consider that Hunt and Mina

were caught up in it just as much as you? Neither of them intended to create the situation. They made the best of their circumstances, just like you were forced to do in London. Finding herself stuck in the past, Mina had no choice but to do what she did. Likewise with Hunt. The older version of Mina was his boss before you ever came on the scene. If anything, they were protecting the timeline rather than trying to hurt you."

"You might be right," Decker conceded. "But it doesn't change the fact that they lied to me. Mina could have revealed herself earlier. Adam Hunt could have told me the truth before we ended up stuck in the past."

"If the timeline really is unchangeable, maybe they did, and it failed. But that's the problem. None of you would have any memory of it in that circumstance. Besides, you did the same thing."

"I don't know what you mean."

"Yes, you do. You could have gone to Celine Rothman and warned her when you found yourself in early 1900s New York, but you chose not to. You didn't tell her to stay away from Singer Cay and the penthouse suite in her husband's hotel there. It would have been easy to do, given your association with Clarence Rothman. But you kept quiet about her fate and let her fall forward in time and end up trapped in the twenty-first century instead. Worse, you used her misfortune to get home."

"That isn't the same."

"Isn't it?"

Decker said nothing.

Nancy pressed her advantage. "And what about the Titanic? You didn't warn anyone aboard that ship of what was about to happen, even though you knew how that crossing would end."

"That really was different. Any intervention would just have split the timeline, leaving the original events to run their course, anyway."

"Which by that definition is exactly what would've happened if

Hunt or Mina had tried to intervene and stop the series of events that led to this moment."

"Maybe you're right." Decker glanced at the letter sitting on the coffee table. "I'm still not asking for my job back, and I'm sure as hell not going to them with that letter. Not right now. I need time to process all this."

"You really don't want to know the rest of the story?" Nancy asked. "What Charles Dickens experienced inside the house?"

"You know I do. But even if I swallow my pride and go to Adam Hunt with the letter, I'm not sure what it will achieve. As far as I know, they don't have a time machine at CUSP, and even if they do, I have no desire to take any more trips into the past. And short of that, I can't for the life of me think how we could ever know what a pair of men who died well over a hundred years ago said to each other in front of a hearth in the 1840s. Unless Charles Dickens wrote a sequel to that letter—and I'm pretty sure he didn't, given the sensational nature of its contents—the details of his supernatural experience in Boston went to the grave with him." Decker pushed his hands into his pockets and met Nancy's gaze. "And that's all there is to it."

# FIVE

THREE HOURS LATER, Decker sat in the small home office he used when he wasn't needed at CUSP's headquarters or on assignment. His time there was normally spent doing research on whatever mysterious event or creature Adam Hunt wanted him to investigate next. But not today. Instead, he was going through files and paperwork, separating personal documents from those related to his former employer.

As he did this, he thought about the letter that Nancy had found in the Dickens' first edition, partly because it intrigued him despite his reluctance to bring it to Adam Hunt, and also because it distracted him from his current circumstances. Yet at the back of his mind, there was a nagging fear.

He was now unemployed with no more prospect of obtaining another job in law enforcement than before he went to work for CUSP. It was that lack of employability that had tipped the scale in favor of working for Adam Hunt in the first place. No police department was going to hire a disgraced former sheriff who claimed to have killed a werewolf, and he could hardly rely on Hunt to back up his claim, or even give him a reference. That was the downside of working for a clandestine organization that operated in the murky world of the supernatural.

And even if he could go back to his old life, he wasn't sure he wanted to. CUSP had introduced him to a wider universe than he could ever have imagined. A universe of monsters, vengeful spirits, time travel, and alternate dimensions. Putting on a small-town sheriff's badge and settling disputes, breaking up bar fights, and pulling people over for driving too fast on Main Street paled in comparison.

Not that it mattered. The only badge he was ever likely to wear was that of a junkyard security guard, and he wasn't even sure he would get that job. His past felt like an anchor weighing him down.

With a sigh, Decker transferred a clutch of folders into his computer's trash. One good thing about the digital age was that he wouldn't have to make a second trip out to the island. Everything related to CUSP was on a local hard drive with encryption that not even the NSA could break, or stored on his erstwhile employer's servers and accessed through a secure connection.

His access to CUSP's servers had already been severed, probably within moments of Adam Hunt accepting his resignation. Now, with a tap of the delete key, the last of his local work files were gone too.

"Hey."

Decker looked up to see Nancy standing in the office doorway.

"You okay in here?" she asked, stepping into the room.

"I'm worried," Decker admitted. "We have money in the bank, but it won't last forever, and I'm hardly the most employable person in the world. All I know is being a cop. I'd be lucky to get a job as a janitor in a police department, let alone an officer." He looked up, daring her to mention going back to CUSP.

She didn't. Instead, she stepped into the room and put her arms around his shoulders. "We'll be fine. We have the bakery, and you'll find something."

"The bakery isn't doing well enough to support both of us. Not yet. Maybe never."

"The margins are thin, but we're in the green. With a little hard work and some—"

"If you're going to say luck, I'd think twice. There hasn't been a lot of that around here lately."

"I beg to differ." Nancy released Decker and perched on the edge of the desk, looking at him with wide eyes. "I consider getting you back from the past to be the luckiest thing that ever happened to us. I thought you were gone forever. I didn't think I would ever see you again."

"That wasn't luck. In fact, just the opposite. If luck was on our side, I would never have ended up there in the first place."

"You're being dramatic." The sympathy gone from Nancy's voice. "The situation we're in now has nothing to do with bad luck. You handed in your resignation—without talking it over with me first, I might add."

"Because I knew what you would say, and I couldn't stay working at that place after what happened. After they lied to me."

"Maybe. But there was no reason for you to rush over there on the spur of the moment. They didn't even expect you back at work until the new year. If you had discussed it with me, I would have told you to wait and think it over until then."

"There was no point," he said. "It wouldn't change my mind."

"Maybe not. But it would have kept a paycheck coming in while you considered what to do next."

Decker had no answer for that. It hadn't even been a consideration in his haste to sever ties with CUSP. On the boat ride back from the island, he had felt liberated. As if a weight lifted from his shoulders. Now he just felt purposeless and adrift. "There's nothing I can do about it now."

"I'm not so sure about that," Nancy said. "But I'm just glad to have you back home, and honestly, it might be better if you're not working for CUSP. At least I won't be terrified of losing you every waking minute."

"You won't lose me." Decker pushed his chair back and stood

up. He pulled Nancy into a tight embrace. "Regardless of where I end up working."

"Promise?"

"I promise." Decker kissed her. "Even if it means getting a job at the local bakery and coffee shop. I'm on favorable terms with the owner."

"You are, huh?" Nancy laughed. "What makes you think she wants you working there?"

"Wow. So that's how it's going to be." Decker stepped back, feigning insult.

At that moment, the doorbell rang.

They both looked back through the living room toward the front of the house.

"Are you going to get that?" Nancy asked after the second ring. "I have a feeling it will be for you."

"I doubt it," Decker said, heading toward the front door. But when he pulled it open, he saw Nancy was right. Mina waited on the other side of the door.

# SIX

WHAT ARE YOU DOING HERE?" Decker asked, before Mina could say a word. "Because if you've come to talk me out of quitting, it's a waste of time."

"I figured you'd say that. Want to let me inside?"

"Not really."

"How about you do it anyway, for old time's sake?"

"You've got five minutes." Decker opened the door wide enough for Mina to enter. "After that, we're done."

"Guess I'd better talk fast then." Mina stepped past Decker into the living room. "This wasn't how I wanted it to end."

"You should've thought of that before you kept me in the dark."

"That wasn't my intention." Mina looked around. "I did what I thought was best for both of us."

Decker wasn't sure what to say, so he said nothing.

Mina had no such problem. "I'm the same woman you saved from Abraham Turner in London. The same woman who barely survived the Titanic. I thought we settled our differences on Singer Cay when you first arrived back. Was I mistaken?"

"I wasn't sure what to think back then. I gave you the benefit of the doubt. But I've had a month to reflect on what happened and I keep coming back to the same conclusion. I was nothing but a means to an end. My involvement was necessary to keep the timeline intact, and nothing more. I was only a member of Classified Universal Special Projects because without me, the dominoes wouldn't fall in the correct sequence."

"That's not true." A shadow passed across Mina's face. Decker couldn't tell if it was sorrow or frustration.

"I want to believe you," he said. "But no matter how much I think about it, nothing changes. The only reason Adam Hunt recruited me into CUSP was because you told him to. You needed me to make sure history played out the way you wanted. That you would come face-to-face with Jack the Ripper in modern London and inherit his abilities. That you would fall back in time to meet Thomas Finch and have a daughter with him. Start The Order of St. George. Imprison Abraham Turner in that cellar so that he would be in the right place at the right time for your confrontation over a century later. Am I missing anything?"

"No. I agree. You were necessary to the timeline. But no more necessary than me, or Hunt, or even Nancy. Singling yourself out as nothing but a pawn is a narrow-minded view. By your definition, we were all pawns. I truly believe we are trapped in this timeline, regardless of our efforts to alter it. For all you know, I tried to avert what happened and change the course of events. Maybe I never sent Adam Hunt to Alaska. Then I would never end up in London and we wouldn't have recruited you to CUSP. Maybe I told him not to offer you Singer Cay as the venue for your wedding, thus avoiding our trip back to 1942 and everything that followed. But here's the kicker. We'll never know, because those events would split off from this timeline, and we would have no memory of them. You can't blame me for something I couldn't alter even if I wanted to."

"That's not what I'm doing."

"Are you sure about that?" Mina asked. "Because from where I'm standing . . ."

Decker shook his head. "Look, we can go around in circles

forever arguing about whether I could have changed the timeline, and like you said, we'll never know which of us is right. But it doesn't change the real issue. You didn't hire me for my experience, or because I brought any unique skills to the table. You hired me to keep the timeline intact. That's why I quit. I've served my purpose, and you don't need me anymore."

"Ah. You're feeling sorry for yourself."

"That's not what I said."

"But it's the truth. You don't feel appreciated."

Decker shrugged.

"But here's the real truth. You *do* bring skills to the table. Look at everything you've achieved at CUSP. You defeated Grendel and his mother. You're one of the few people on earth who know the true identity of Jack the Ripper and what he really was. Without you, he'd still be out there killing people. You freed all those sailors on that U-boat from an eternity stuck in a parallel dimension. Do I need to go on?"

"No. But you're also making a good argument for why I shouldn't return to CUSP. The work I do is dangerous. I've almost died several times. Hell, Nancy believed I was dead for months after we got stuck in the past. And on our wedding day. She doesn't deserve any of that."

"That's one argument I can't refute, but it doesn't alter the fact that you were one of the best operatives we've ever had, in the present or the past. You would've ended up working for us regardless of timelines or anything else. We'll miss you." Mina fell silent for a moment. "*I'll* miss you."

"You'll do just fine without me, just like you did for over a hundred years when you took the long way back from 1912. And anyway, you can still drop into the bakery once in a while and say hello, even if I don't work for you anymore."

"I'm going to do more than that," Mina said. "You're not getting rid of me that easily."

"I figured as much." Decker thought for a moment, then he grinned. "Speaking of the present and the past—I've technically been in your employ since Thomas Finch hired me to work at the Order of St. George. I only quit this morning, which means I'm owed a mountain of back pay. About a century's worth."

"Huh." Mina rubbed her chin, then she grinned too. "You have a point. Adjusted for inflation, that would come to several million dollars."

"At least ten million by my calculation," Decker said. "And more if you include raises and end-of-year bonuses."

"Of course, you didn't actually show up to work for most of that time, which I figure makes us about even."

"I was hoping you wouldn't realize that."

"You think I was born yesterday?"

Decker laughed. "That's one thing I don't think."

# SEVEN

AFTER MINA LEFT, Nancy stepped into the living room. "I heard what you said. You don't need to quit CUSP because of me. I don't want that responsibility."

"That isn't the only reason I resigned, and you know it."

"But it is partly because of me."

"You were a consideration," Decker admitted. "And you already said that you won't miss the worry when I'm away on assignments. This is best for both of us."

"I don't want to be the reason—"

"I'm not going back to CUSP. All my life I've put myself first. I took the job at CUSP because I missed being a cop, and it felt like the next best thing. It never occurred to me how working there would affect you or Taylor. I was putting myself first when I ran from Wolf Haven and left you behind when we were teenagers. I was being selfish. Just like when—" Decker stopped abruptly, his throat tightening.

"Just like what?" Nancy asked.

"When I let my mother die in the woods."

"John, you can't possibly blame yourself for that. You were a 10-year-old boy. You weren't even there, and if even if you had been—"

"You don't understand. There are things I haven't told you about that day. Things my father didn't even know."

"Like what?"

"Like that I'm the reason she died. She wouldn't even have been in the woods if it wasn't for me. I could have saved her, Nance."

Nancy was silent for a moment. "I don't believe that for a second."

"It's true."

"An animal attacked your mother."

Decker nodded. "That was the medical examiner's conclusion. But after what happened to us in Wolf Haven, I don't believe that anymore. I think it was the loup-garou. My father thought the same thing. I know because I went through his papers."

"Okay. But that still doesn't explain why you feel responsible."

"Because she was looking for me when she died." Decker crossed the couch and sat down. "I was never allowed in the woods as a kid. My parents were adamant that I stay out of them, although they never told me why. Just said it was dangerous. I couldn't believe that because my friends played in the woods all the time, and nothing happened to them, so I used to sneak out and go into the woods, anyway. That's what happened the day my mother died. I asked her if I could go fishing down at Pinewood Creek. She said no. But I still snuck out and did it. They found her body that evening close to the creek. I guess she must've gone looking for me and ran into her killer."

"You don't know she was out there because of you. I remember your house. The woods were right out back. Did you see anything out of the ordinary? Hear anything?"

"Honestly, I don't remember much about that day after I went into the woods. My first recollection after leaving the house with my fishing pole is of being in the coroner's office waiting room and seeing my mother dead on the mortuary table through a crack in the door. I guess I must've blocked it out because of the trauma."

"Hey. You really don't know if she was there looking for you or not. And even if she was, it wasn't your fault. Just like leaving Wolf Haven wasn't your fault. You were dealing with so much at home. Your father was crazy by then. I remember what he was like. It was no wonder you wanted to get away from there. To run as far away as you could."

"I should have asked you to go with me."

"Maybe. But who knows if I would have said yes." A shadow passed across Nancy's face. It told Decker that regardless of what she said, Nancy would have gone with him, and even after all these years, she still harbored the pain of being left behind.

"You know, I—" Decker almost blurted something out that he had never told her. Something that might have changed the trajectory of both their lives had it gone differently. But he didn't because he was afraid it would only make her feel worse. Instead, he pushed the maudlin feelings back down, and picked up the letter written by Charles Dickens. "This could be worth a fortune, especially considering the subject matter."

"No!" Nancy shook her head.

"No, what?"

"Were not selling that letter. It was inside the book you bought for me last year as a Christmas present. I don't care how much they're worth. We're not selling either of them."

"That wasn't what I was suggesting." Decker took a minute to read the letter again. "Must have been some conversation they had around that hearth."

"It's hard to stop thinking about, huh?"

"Yeah. I have to admit, a small part of me wanted to tell Mina about this. To get CUSP involved, just to see what they could find out."

Nancy sat down next to Decker. "You could have done that, even if you don't want to go back and work for them."

"I know. But I'm not sure I could stay out of it if I did. You know me. I don't like standing on the sidelines." Decker ruminated on the contents of the letter in silence. What exactly had Charles Dickens experienced inside the house that inspired him to write A Christmas Carol? Had he really come face-to-face with a shackled ghost who became the inspiration for Marley? Did he see the past, or maybe his future? The letter came to a frustratingly unsatisfying conclusion. "Of course, not telling Mina about it means we'll never know the truth."

"Not necessarily." Nancy put her arm around Decker's shoulder and looked down at the letter. "There *is* one thing we can do. We can go to Boston and see if we can find that house for ourselves."

# EIGHT

ABSOLUTELY NOT," Decker said with a shake of his head. "The last thing I want to do is go looking for more trouble. Don't you think we've had enough of that?"

"But it's Charles Dickens," Nancy pleaded. "You said it yourself. You want to know the rest of the story."

"Not that badly. These things have a habit of spiraling out of control. Trust me."

"Then we won't let it." Nancy took a deep breath. "And anyway, the chances are we won't find anything. I mean, come on. A house that materializes out of thin air? Ghosts wearing chains?"

"Haven't you had enough adventure for one lifetime?"

"It's a few days in Boston, not some trek into an unexplored jungle full of monsters." Nancy wasn't giving up. "It will be good for us. We'll go down there and explore the city. Take in the sights. Visit a couple of museums. And in the evenings, we can snuggle up together with a bottle of wine and make plans for our wedding —which will be as far away from Singer Cay as we can get this time."

"And look for that house."

"Come on. You know you want to do it. I can see it in your eyes. And besides, it's not like you have anything better to do."

"You don't need to rub it in." Decker was all too aware of his employment situation. He had no idea what to do next, and might even be unemployable, at least in any field he wanted to work in. And that was another concern. "Even if I agree, we don't have the money."

"Things might be a little tight right now but we're not *that* broke. And honestly, I think we both need it. You haven't exactly been yourself since you returned, and I'm not sure I've fully processed everything that's happened yet. I thought you were dead. I spent six months mourning you. I think the least you could do is take me on a romantic weekend getaway."

"And hunt some Victorian ghosts in the process."

Nancy shrugged. "Only if you insist."

Decker threw his arms up in mock defeat. "I'm not going to win this argument, am I?"

"Nope." Nancy grinned. "But if you want to keep arguing a while longer to soothe your manly ego, I'm good with that. We've got all night."

"My manly ego will cope just fine. If you really want to go to Boston, then let's do it."

"Yay." Nancy clapped her hands together. "I knew you couldn't resist."

"But there's a condition attached. We play it safe. If Charles Dickens really encountered something supernatural on his visit to Boston, it might very well still be there. It could also be dangerous. I'm not willing to risk our lives over some old letter. If we find that house—and it's a huge if—then we proceed with caution, and you do as I say."

"Don't I always?" Nancy said with mock subservience.

"I mean it. The supernatural isn't something to take lightly. I should know. I've been there."

"Hey, lighten up. I agree. We'll be careful, okay? Even if we find the house, we don't have to go inside. We can turn around and walk the other way if we want to. No pressure."

"Okay."

"Then we're going to do this?" Nancy couldn't keep the glee from her voice.

"Sure." Decker hoped he wasn't agreeing to something he would regret later. "We're doing this."

# NINE

CHARLES DICKENS STAYED at the Tremont House back in 1842," Decker said, as he and Nancy made their way along Tremont Street past Boston Common around midnight on a wintry November evening ten days after Nancy had first found the letter. "It stood on the corner of Beacon Street, but it's not there anymore. They tore it down over a hundred years ago, but we can use the location as a starting point to retrace the author's route on the night he encountered the phantom house."

"Dickens wrote that he left the hotel and went as far as Beacon Street before turning left and circling back around to the other side of Boston Common," Nancy said. As they walked, she consulted a photograph of the letter on her phone. "If I'm reading it correctly, the house must have been on the left side of the street—literally on the common where there have never been any buildings, at least according to what I read online."

"Dickens never said exactly where on the common the house appeared to him," Decker said. "But we can assume it fronted the road, given his description."

"Makes sense," Nancy agreed. "He never mentioned entering Boston Common or walking its interior."

"The letter just says he was on Beacon Street."

"That still amounts to a considerable stretch of land all the way to Charles Street and the Public Garden." Decker studied the vast open space ahead of them as they crossed over Park Street.

Beyond its wrought-iron railings, Boston Common was swathed in darkness, with only scattered lamp posts at intervals lighting the footpaths within. This was the second time that day he and Nancy had come here, the first being earlier in the afternoon while it was still daylight to acquaint themselves with the area.

It looked different under the blanket of night.

The sidewalks were mostly deserted. The street vendors selling souvenir baseball caps and T-shirts had all gone home. It must have looked very much like this to Dickens on that fateful night, Decker thought, except the electric lighting would have been oil lamps, and horse-drawn carriages would have filled the streets instead of automobiles.

"Dickens made it sound like the house appeared out of thin air, which is almost too fantastical to be true," Nancy said, echoing a thought that had already occurred to Decker. "Especially since it supposedly manifested itself in a well-trafficked area populated for hundreds of years. Surely someone else would have noticed the house by now if it was so easy to find. Which begs the question, why did it appear only to him?"

"Maybe it didn't. It could be like you said, and the letter was just a fanciful ruse to get his friend to pay a visit. Nothing but another ghoulish fiction from a master storyteller."

"Do you believe that?"

"I think it's plausible," Decker replied. "But I'm also not willing to write off the account as a product of Dickens' overactive imagination. Not just yet. If my time at CUSP taught me anything, it's that there are weirder things in this world than you would ever expect."

"You mean like finding out that werewolves are real, coming face-to-face with a prehistoric alligator in middle-of-nowhere Florida, or traveling back in time and ending up as a passenger on the Titanic?"

"That's only the half of it." Decker put an arm around Nancy's waist as they approached the intersection of Charles Street, where Boston Common became the Public Garden. "But I'd rather not talk about any of that if it's all the same to you. Weird ghost house full of Christmas spirits or not, we're on vacation. We're supposed to be getting away from our troubles, not obsessing over them."

"That wasn't what I was doing." Nancy sidled close to him.

"I know." Decker came to a halt. "We've gone the entire length of Boston Common and all I saw was a homeless guy looking for a park bench to sleep on and a bunch of taxicabs. I think we've entertained Charles Dickens' fantasy long enough. Want to go back to the room, open a bottle of wine, and run a bath for two in the soaking tub?"

"That sounds heavenly." Nancy kissed him lightly on the cheek.

They started off again, strolling back along the perimeter of the vast park toward their hotel. If Nancy was disappointed that the phantom house amounted to nothing more than fiction, she didn't show it. And perhaps she had never really believed they would find it, Decker thought. Maybe this had all been a way to get him away from Portland and the feelings of betrayal at the hands of Adam Hunt and Mina that he couldn't quite put aside despite his best efforts.

They proceeded in silence, content to share each other's company. There was no need for small talk. After all that they had been through, the turmoil of the last year, being together was enough.

At least until Nancy came to an abrupt halt.

She squeezed his arm. "John, do you feel that?"

"Feel what?" Decker glanced around and at first saw nothing amiss. But then he noticed the wind. Or rather, the lack of it. They had been walking with their heads bent low against a frigid breeze that whistled down the street and stung their faces and hands. But now it had vanished. The air was calm as a millpond. There was something else too. The steady stream of traffic moving up and down Beacon Street was gone. The road was uncharacteristically empty.

"This is so weird," Nancy whispered under her breath as if she were afraid to disturb the silence. Or maybe draw unwanted attention to them. "Where did everyone go?"

"Beats me." Decker looked around, trying to locate the homeless man who had crossed their path before shuffling off into the common. Now he was nowhere in sight. Which was impossible, given his lazy gait and the shopping cart full of what looked like old rags and cardboard boxes that he was pushing.

"I don't like this." Nancy inched closer to Decker, pressing her body against his. "Maybe it wasn't such a good idea to come here, after all."

"I think you might be right," Decker said grimly. Because ahead of them, sitting on what had been an empty patch of grass only moments before, was an imposing Gothic structure that would have looked more at home in a horror movie than one of the most famous public parks in the country.

# TEN

THE HOUSE SAT BACK from the road, as out of place on Boston Common as an alligator would be in the Arctic. It was a two-story structure with a steep gabled roof and a brick turret at one end that extended above the main building's roofline. A porch with a covered balcony above ran from the turret around the front and one side of the house. Twin chimneys, one on each side of the building, reached toward the leaden sky like skeletal arms. A narrow path from the road ran to a set of steps that led up to the porch and the front door. The windows were dark and cold, with no signs of life within.

Decker could feel Nancy pressing against him. She was shivering. He tore his eyes away from the phantom structure. "Just ignore it and keep on walking."

"Oh, thank God." Nancy visibly slumped with relief. "For a second there, I thought you might suggest that we go inside."

"I'm not so sure that would be a good idea," Decker said, keeping watch on the house from the corner of his eye as they hurried past. "I'm not so sure I want to know what Charles Dickens encountered inside that building anymore."

"Me either." Nancy quickened her pace. "I just want to get the hell out of here. Whatever was I thinking?"

"Good question." Decker took long strides to keep pace and held onto her arm, positioning himself between his fiancée and the house until they were clear. When he saw the wide-open space of Boston Common appear to his right, he relaxed his grip. "Just keep walking and don't look back."

"I don't think we're safe yet," Nancy said. "The air is so calm, and there are still no cars on the road. It's like we're the only people left in the world."

"We must be inside whatever reality the house occupies. If we walk far enough, we'll come out the other side safe and sound."

"You sure about that?" There was a tremble in Nancy's voice.

"Not entirely." Decker reached for his phone, slipped it out of his pocket. He might not work for CUSP anymore, but he still had friends inside the organization. People who knew all about things like this. And right now, he wanted to talk to one person in particular who just might understand their predicament. Rory McCormick. The man possessed a deep knowledge of all things metaphysical, despite being an archaeologist by trade. If anyone could get them out of this, it would be him. But when Decker tried to place the call, it wouldn't go through. He had no service. Which he now realized was not surprising, given his suspicion that they were no longer on their own plane of existence.

Frustrated, he put the phone back in his pocket and urged Nancy to keep going. He could tell she was scared but figured that once they got past the boundary of the common, which was not far ahead now, they would be free.

Except that the house appeared to have other ideas. The buildings surrounding Boston Common had previously been visible in stark relief against the dark night sky but were now fading as if being wiped from existence. The culprit, he realized, was a rolling wall of fog that crept down Beacon Street and blotted out the city, swallowing everything as it went.

"John!"

"I see it." Decker came to a halt and looked over his shoulder. Behind them was another wall of fog that inched across the public garden, devouring streetlights, benches, and even the road itself. More fog encroached to their left and right, inching across the common and weaving over the roofs of the buildings on the other side of the street.

"Come on." Decker grabbed Nancy's hand and pulled her forward, heading toward the swiftly approaching fog bank that lay in their path.

"What are you doing?" Nancy faltered, tried to pull back.

"There's only one way to get out of here. We have to go through it. With any luck, the real Boston is right on the other side."

"What if you're wrong? We don't know what's in there."

"True. But we know *exactly* what's in here." Decker turned and pointed. "That house. And I have a nasty feeling it doesn't want us to leave."

"Then what makes you think that walking into the fog will help the situation?"

"I have no idea if it will help or not," Decker said. "But it's closing in around us, anyway. We either go into the fog, or we face whatever's inside the house. Which would you rather do?"

"When you put it like that, I'll take the fog."

"I figured that's what you'd say. Whatever happens, don't let go of me." Decker gave Nancy's hand a reassuring squeeze and started toward the looming fog. It rose above them like a drifting, white tsunami. Tendrils reached out, curling around lampposts and railings like slithering eels.

As they drew close, Nancy recoiled. "John."

"Yes?"

"I love you."

Decker nodded. "I love you too." Then he stepped past the wall of swirling nothingness and into the unknown, with Nancy right behind.

# ELEVEN

ONE MOMENT they were on Beacon Street, and the next, they were surrounded by a featureless expanse. Smoky wisps of white mist curled and probed, as if looking for some solid object to latch onto. Permeating this vast nothingness was an ethereal radiance that appeared to come from all directions at the same time. It bathed them in a shadowless light and forced them to squint against the glare as they pressed forward.

It was as disorientating as it was frightening.

Holding Nancy's hand, Decker kept going, half expecting some grotesque creature from his worst nightmares to lunge toward them out of the mist, mouth agape and claws extended. Until just as quickly as it engulfed them, the mist parted, and the world came back into view. But to Decker's dismay, they were not on the other side of Boston Common surrounded by late-night traffic and the occasional pedestrian hurrying back from some bar or restaurant. Instead, they ended up back on the sidewalk and looking at the house they were trying to escape. Its windows were now ablaze with yellow light in stark contrast to the swirling monotone fog surrounding them. A faint sound of music pulsed from somewhere within the building.

Then the front door opened slowly inward.

"Looks like someone wants us to go inside," Decker said, staring at the door.

"Hell, no." Nancy took a step back. "I don't know how we ended up back here, but there's no way I'm stepping into the house."

"I couldn't agree more." Decker turned away from the house and led Nancy back toward the shifting fog at a brisk pace. "Let's try this one more time."

With that, he stepped back into the fog—only to reappear a moment later in the same spot as before, right in front of the house. The door still stood open, spilling a patch of warm yellow light down the front steps.

Nancy gasped. "It didn't work."

"I can see that."

"What are we going to do?"

"Try again," Decker said, striding toward the wall of fog with a look of grim determination on his face. But as before, they ended up right back in front of the house.

"This is hopeless." Nancy sagged against Decker's shoulder. "There has to be a way out of here."

"I can only see one option left to us," Decker said, looking at the open door.

"Still not going in there." Nancy shook her head.

"We might not have a choice," Decker replied, because he had noticed something. The fog was on the move again. It was closing around them like a noose, forcing them closer and closer to the front steps of the house. Their only alternative was to be engulfed by the stirring mist. And since they clearly weren't able to walk through it and out the other side, he was afraid that once the small pocket of reality they currently inhabited closed, they would end up lost within the drifting void forever.

Unless they entered the house.

Decker suspected that once they stepped through that door, the fog would stop its advance. Something wanted them to enter. They were being herded closer and closer to their only means of escape, although what they were escaping into, he could only guess.

It looked like they were about to find out.

His foot bumped the bottom step.

Snaking tendrils of smokey mist lapped at their heels.

Decker went in the only direction left open. He took Nancy's hand and climbed the steps toward the front door.

Fingers of mist curled over the steps and threaded themselves around the railings.

They reached the porch even as the fog devoured the steps behind them.

Another few seconds and it would claim them forever. He couldn't explain how he knew that with such certainty, but Decker was sure that if they went back into the fog, they would never come out.

Without giving himself time to think, he pulled Nancy forward and stepped over the threshold and into the unknown.

# TWELVE

NO SOONER HAD they entered the house, then the door slammed behind them with a resounding thud.

Nancy grabbed the door handle and tugged. "It won't open. We're trapped."

"I'm not sure we'd have anywhere left to go, even if we could open it," Decker told her, studying his surroundings. They were in a wide entrance hall facing a sweeping staircase that flowed up to a second-floor landing. Portraits hung on the walls all around them, rich oil paintings within ornate frames. Doors varnished to a deep mahogany led off to their left and right. A chandelier hung from the ceiling and lit the space in a soft glow. Long shadows crept across the marble tiled floor from the corners of the entrance hall and the gloom beyond the stairs.

"Look." Nancy approached one of the portraits. "It's Charles Dickens. Why would there be a portrait of Dickens here?"

Decker stepped forward, his eyes alighting on the brass plaque beneath the portrait. There was a date under the author's name. January 1842. He examined the other portraits hanging nearby. There were other names, each with their own date.

Emily Pendleton—December 1854.

Andrew Worthington—November 1877.

Harold Wainwright—December 1922.

Lynette Babbage—January 1931.

And it went on. At least twenty portraits hanging alongside that of the famous wordsmith. On the other wall, beyond the staircase, hung more paintings, no doubt with more names and dates.

"I don't recognize any of the other people here," Decker said, stepping back. "But the logical conclusion, given that the date under Dickens' portrait matches the details in the letter you found, is that each of these people were unwilling guests in this house."

"So many of them." Nancy turned her attention from the portrait of Dickens and looked at the other paintings.

"And all of them around Christmas," Decker said. "November, December, or January. I don't see any other dates."

"I guess we came at the right time, then."

"Lucky us." There was no humor in Decker's reply. He turned and walked to the other wall, his gaze flitting from painting to painting. Then he stiffened. "Nancy. Come here. You need to see this."

"Did you find something?" She crossed the foyer, her footsteps ringing on the tiles.

"You could say that." Decker nodded, directing Nancy's gaze to a pair of paintings hanging near one of the doors.

"Oh my God," Nancy said with a sharp intake of breath. "That's us."

"Yes, it is." Decker's eyes dropped to the brass plaques underneath each painting. Plaques engraved with their names and the date.

"I don't like this." Nancy cast a nervous glance toward the front door, as if she hoped it had miraculously opened again all on its own.

It remained stubbornly closed.

Decker suspected that if they tried the handle, they would have about as much success opening the door now as they had before. He looked back up at the creepy paintings. "We need to find another way out of here."

"I'm afraid there is no way out," said a voice to their rear.

Decker spun around to find a slender man in a black tuxedo standing at the top of the stairs and looking down at them. A man with silver slicked back hair, gaunt features, and deathly pale skin. His steel-gray eyes glinted like diamonds in the light from the chandelier. He gripped a silver tipped cane in one hand, the tip of which rested on the floor.

Nancy let out a small gasp. She gripped Decker's arm. "John?"

"I see him." Decker stepped in front of Nancy, shielding her. "Who are you, and what do you want with us?"

"Oh dear. There appears to have been some sort of misunderstanding. It was *you* who came looking for me, not the other way around."

"We were looking for the house," Decker said.

"And you found it." The man started down the stairs, his cane making a small tapping noise on each one as he went.

"Then we thought it best to leave without exploring further. But I guess you had other ideas."

"Me?" The man laughed, the sound dry and brittle. "None of this is my doing. If you're here, it's because you want relief from the chains that shackle your tortured souls."

"What is he talking about?" Nancy asked in a trembling voice.

"I don't know, and I don't care." Decker never let his gaze stray from the unsettling stranger. "You never answered my question. Who are you?"

"Who I am is not important." The man lifted his cane. "You should be more concerned about what I am."

He brought the cane down onto the floor with a sharp crack, and his true nature was revealed. A skeletal face with clumps of hair clinging to his skull like wiry, desiccated islands. A tattered and water-stained tuxedo, submerged with the dust of the grave. Behind him, heavy chains that trailed off into the shadows behind the stairs, their links corroded and flaking.

Nancy screamed.

She backed away, then turned and fled toward the closest door.

"Wait." Decker made a futile attempt to stop her.

But Nancy was already at the door. Flinging it open, she rushed headlong into the room beyond.

Decker turned and raced after her. He half expected the door to slam shut and separate them. He was thankful when it didn't. But when he entered the room he came to a skidding halt, because even though there were no other doors through which she could have fled, Nancy was nowhere in sight.

She was simply gone.

# THIRTEEN

THE ROOM WAS A LIBRARY. Bookcases filled with volumes rose on all four walls from floor-to-ceiling. There was a leather sofa in the middle of the room, along with a reading table and two chairs, all arranged on an Oriental rug that covered most of the floor.

The one thing Decker didn't see was Nancy.

He looked around, frantic, then turned back toward the door. The chained apparition blocked his path.

He fixed it with a glowering stare. "Where is she? What have you done with her?"

"She's fine, I assure you. Safe and sound in her own version of the library." The specter shuffled forward, dragging his chains along the floor behind him. They scraped and clanked as he moved.

"What does that mean?" A chill ran down Decker's spine.

"In this house, everyone has their own library." The ghost lifted his cane and brought it down onto the floor again. In an instant, he transformed back to the dapper gentleman who had greeted them when they entered. His chains vanished. The skeletal face regained its flesh. The tuxedo was smart and crisp. He stepped further into the room, moving with ease now his shackles were gone, and gestured toward the bookshelves with a flourish. "This one is yours."

"I still don't understand." Decker hadn't paid much attention to the books on the shelves, but now he noticed something strange. They all looked identical. Thousands of thick volumes with black spines and gold lettering. He approached the closest bookshelf and read the spines, his sense of unease growing when he saw that each one bore his own name, along with a date. He reached out tentatively, almost took one down, then withdrew his hand. "What is this?"

"I think you've already guessed." The specter watched him with narrowed eyes. "Each of these books represents a single day in your life. From birth until this very moment, everything you've ever done has been recorded here, from the smallest act to the greatest achievement. All of your hopes and dreams. Every decision you ever made, and its consequences."

"Then what are you, my biographer?" Decker stepped toward the apparition.

"Me? Goodness, no. You wrote these books yourself second by second and minute by minute. As did Nancy, in her own library."

Decker bristled at the mention of Nancy. It was his responsibility to keep her safe and now she was gone. He wanted her back. "This can't be real. It's nothing but an illusion. Tell me where she is."

"I did, already. I can't help it if you don't believe me."

"Right. She's in some supernatural library of her own making. A library that started magically filling its shelves with books on the day she was born."

"Oh, there were plenty of books on the shelves before she was born. This isn't just a chronicle of your life. It's also a record of how you came to be. All the actions and decisions that led to your birth —because those events ripple forward through your entire life." The apparition motioned to a set of shelves on his left. "For example, these shelves hold a selection of volumes written by your father. On the shelves below are those your mother created. Everything they thought, or said, or did, that has affected your existence in even the smallest way has been catalogued in this library."

Decker stared at the rows of books, almost too stunned to comprehend. And then he saw it, his mother's name stamped on the spine of a thick volume in gold foil. And beneath it, a date he recognized all too well. The day of her death.

He reached out with trembling hands and took the volume down. He opened it to a blank page. Flicking through the volume, he discovered that all the other pages were also blank. "There's nothing in here. The book is empty."

"It's all there, I promise," his ghostly companion said. "Every moment of that day is there, recorded in exquisite detail. You just can't see any of it."

"That's ridiculous." Decker returned the book to the shelf and turned on his unwelcome host. "If this library is the story of my life, why wouldn't I be able to read the books?"

"Because they aren't meant for you." The specter in the tuxedo clasped his hands together.

"Then who are they meant for?"

"The ghosts, of course." The apparition moved back to the library door.

Decker followed, his frustration growing. "What ghosts?"

The apparition smiled. "Those of your past, present, and future."

"You mean like in the Dickens book?"

"That I couldn't say. Not a big reader."

"Yet you have a library."

"I already told you; this isn't for me." The specter waved an arm around. "I can't read the contents of these books any more than you can. Only the ghosts can do that. Don't worry, you'll be meeting them soon enough."

"Maybe I don't want to meet them."

"That isn't your choice. Not anymore. You came looking for the house and you found it. You obviously need to be here. Only those with unresolved turmoil grace our walls."

"And Nancy?"

"She has her own demons to confront."

"Not good enough." Decker stepped toward the apparition. "Bring her back. Right now."

"That's not in my power, I'm afraid. I'm just here to greet you. Our time is up. You have other places to be." The specter turned and moved back into the foyer.

"Wait. I'm not finished with you."

"Yes, you are." The apparition turned back toward him and raised his arm. He clicked his fingers, the sound sharp and hollow.

Then the library door slammed closed, trapping him before Decker could do anything about it.

# FOURTEEN

DECKER RACED FOR THE DOOR, reaching it a moment after it thudded closed. He tried the handle. Locked.

"Hey. Let me out of here." He slammed his fist against the unyielding wood.

There was no reply from the other side of the door. If the apparition in the tuxedo was still there, he was silent.

Decker tried the handle again, rattling it to no avail. Frustrated, he slumped against the door. He was trapped in a spectral house on what appeared to be another plane of existence. Nancy was who knew where, probably locked in another library just like this one. Except that the books lining the shelves would tell the story of her life, not his. Now he understood where Charles Dickens had found inspiration for his ghost story, A Christmas Carol.

Decker's only hope was that Dickens had obviously escaped this house after undergoing whatever ordeal the spirits had in mind for him. Of the other people who found themselves here—those men and women in the portraits hanging on the walls of the foyer—he had no idea. Maybe they all walked out of this house alive . . . Or maybe they didn't. It was impossible to tell. All Decker knew was that he wasn't going anywhere, anytime soon. Not that he had any intention of leaving without Nancy.

Giving up on the door, he stepped back into the center of the room and sat on the sofa to wait for whatever would happen next. There was no point in looking at any of the books. The pages would be blank, just like the volume he had already examined. He was sure of that.

He buried his head in his hands, thinking of Nancy. After being stuck in the past and separated from her for so long, he had sworn they would never be parted again. He even quit his job at CUSP. Not only because he felt betrayed—which he did—but also because he didn't want Nancy to ever again worry that he would go on an assignment and not come back. Now, less than two weeks later, they were trapped and separated in a supernatural realm, and he had no way to find her.

"Dammit." Decker cursed aloud. He stood up and paced to the library door, trying one more time. It still didn't open. Then, as he turned back toward the center of the room, the chandelier hanging from the ceiling above him flickered. Then it went out completely.

For a moment, nothing happened.

Decker stood rooted to the spot, afraid to move. For all he knew, the library was now gone, and he was in some other place entirely. Somewhere worse. But then the light came back on.

He was still in the library. Except now he wasn't alone.

A figure stood in the center of the room, near the reading desk. It was a woman. She was slim and tall, with a pale complexion and cascading blonde hair that fell around her shoulders. She wore a white dress with a hem that touched the ground. When she looked at Decker, her eyes shone a sparkling green.

He stepped toward her cautiously. "Let me guess. The Ghost of Christmas Past?"

"Not just Christmas. I'm the ghost of *all things* past." The woman smiled. "But you're not the first to ask that question. It's a common mistake. Ever since Mr. Dickens wrote that book, people have been leaping to conclusions."

"You know about the book?" Decker thought back to the

specter that greeted them, and his claim not to know anything about the novel.

"Of course. We know everything about those we have crossed paths with. The sum of Mr. Dickens' existence is contained within his library. Everything he did before we met him, and the life he lived after. He didn't quite get the details right, which I shall attribute to poetic license, but it was an engaging yarn."

"But you showed him his past, present, and future?"

"We showed him what he needed to see. Some of it happened before he was born. Some took place after he died. The only requirement is that everything we show you must affect your life in one way or another."

"So that's why you've us trapped here. To live out the pages of an old ghost story."

"If that's how you want to think of it." Then, as if reading Decker's mind, she said, "You needn't worry about Nancy. She will be fine. Right now, she's taking a trip into her own past. There are things she needs to see in order to let go of the doubt she's been carrying since you went to college and left her behind in Wolf Haven."

"She still thinks about that?" Decker thought their past was behind them. Obviously, he had been wrong.

"Not all the time, but it's there." The spirit moved toward him, although it was more of a gliding motion than a walk. Her dress billowed out behind her as if caught in a breeze. "Would you like to observe?"

"You'll take me to her?"

The ghost nodded. "It's your past too."

"What do I need to do?" Decker had no idea what to expect, but it would reunite him with Nancy, and that was all he cared about.

"You don't need to do anything." The ghost went to the shelves, selected a book, and took it down. "But be warned, you will be able to see her, but she won't be able to see or hear you anymore than the shadows of the past can see or hear her. To them, she might as well not exist. She is nothing but a silent observer. A phantom, invisible to their gaze. To her, you are the same."

"You mean I won't be able to—" but it was too late. The ghost had opened the book. Meanwhile, from somewhere else in the house, a clock struck midnight. The sound echoed, deep and sonorous. Then, as the clock kept chiming, the world around Decker pulsed, faded, and was soon replaced by another time and place. One that he recognized all too well.

It was Cassidy's Diner in Wolf Haven.

Only it wasn't the diner he knew from his days as sheriff. This was an earlier time that he recognized all too well. It was nine months after he left for college, and three months after his father died. Decker was nineteen back then. An angry and confused young man who had finally decided to do the right thing.

He glanced sideways and saw Nancy—his Nancy from the present—standing a few steps away watching the scene playing out in front of them with a look of anguish on her face. She also knew exactly what day this was. And judging by the tear that rolled down her cheek, she understood the missed opportunity as clearly as he did. An opportunity that would have brought them back together many years earlier had things played out in a different way.

"I'm sorry," Decker whispered. "I should have tried harder."

But his words fell on deaf ears.

"I told you already, she can't hear you," said the ghost to his right. "Now watch."

# FIFTEEN

NINETEEN-YEAR-OLD JOHN DECKER stood on Main Street outside Cassidy's Diner with a bunch of flowers clutched in his hand, plucking up the courage to go inside. He hadn't been back to Wolf Haven since leaving for college nine months before, and he wasn't sure if he'd made a mistake in returning now.

The day he left was seared into his mind. A day he would never forget. His father had been out in the woods as usual, tromping around looking for answers he would never find. He was the town sheriff, although by then it had become more of an honorary title than anything else because the mayor was reluctant to strip him of it.

He was a man obsessed. And that obsession was with finding whatever killed his wife. Everything else came in a distant second. In his absence, the deputy sheriff—a man named Eddie Franks—picked up the slack and kept the department running smoothly. It was a suitable situation for the mayor, who hardly relished firing a man still locked in the throes of grief for his dead wife. But it didn't help his son, who he ignored with the same fervor as his job.

Even when John told him about the college applications, about being accepted to a small school in New York to pursue a criminal justice degree, his father barely noticed. There were no congratulations. Just the usual lip service from a man barely paying attention to anything but his own fevered delusion. A delusion catalogued in the notebooks filled with crazy theories about the wild animal that killed his mother. Not that John had ever read them. His father kept the books under lock and key in his study, which in reality was a spare bedroom at the back of the house with a deadbolt installed on the door.

It was to this room that Sheriff Robbie Decker had gone after coming in from his daily search of the woods. John had been waiting for him, because he wasn't entirely sure that his father realized he was leaving for college that day.

He knocked on the study door, hoping his father would answer, but all he received was a gruff, "Go away. I'm busy."

He tried again, balling his hand into a fist, and slamming it against the door three times, hard enough that it rattled in the frame. It was an act of rebellion born from months of feeling neglected. His father was hardly ever at home, and when he was there, he holed up in his study and obsessed about his wife's death. Meanwhile, the younger Decker fended for himself. He was even paying the bills—writing checks and sending them off—because his father was so wrapped up in his own head that they would end up sitting in the dark otherwise.

The door had flown open. His father stood there, face flushed red with anger. "There had better be a mighty good reason for this interruption, boy. Now what is it?"

It was college. Something the elder Decker should already have known.

When John told him he was leaving, his father's face had creased into a scowl.

"That's what you wanted to bother me with?" Robbie Decker gripped the door with one hand. The other rested on the service weapon that he wore all the time, even when he was at home. "You're leaving for college? Well, what are you waiting for? Go ahead then. Get the hell out and leave me alone. I don't need you."

Then he slammed the door.

John had left.

Six months later, his grief and paranoia having apparently spiraled to new lows, Sheriff Robbie Decker swallowed a bottle of pills and died. In the time between, he had answered none of his son's calls or responded to his emails. Returning the favor, John skipped the funeral.

Now, three months later, John was back. The official reason was to sign paperwork with the lawyer handling his father's estate, meager as it was. A few thousand bucks in the bank and the family house, which probably wasn't even worth selling in a backwoods town like Wolf Haven. But the real reason was more important.

Nancy. The girl he'd thought he would marry until life got in the way. She was always there when he needed her. Always ready to listen when it got too much at home. When living with his father became intolerable. But the blackness that consumed his soul had urged him to run, and that was what he'd done, leaving her behind heartbroken and confused.

Until he realized his dreadful mistake.

Which was why, after months of soul-searching, he left New York for Louisiana, driving through the night and most of the next day and only pulling over to catch an hour of sleep on the side of a road somewhere in Tennessee.

Now he was back in town and standing outside Cassidy's Diner, the restaurant owned by her mother, and staring through the window at the dining room beyond. It was evening, and the restaurant glowed with red and yellow neon lights that set the chromed counter and stools alight with reflected twinkles. Music pulsed from the retro jukebox next to the door. It was Saturday night, so most of the booths were full. Servers in red checkered uniforms hurried back and forth. It was just like he remembered it.

And then he saw her.

Nancy came out of the kitchen, laughter creasing her face. She wasn't working. Instead of a uniform, she wore a halter top and knee-length skirt. Her hair was pulled back into a ponytail that bobbed when she walked.

His heart swelled.

At first, he thought she was leaving the diner, but instead of walking toward the entrance, she turned in the other direction and started toward the counter. He would rather have surprised her outside, but he couldn't wait.

He opened the door and stepped inside, ignoring the tingle of apprehension in his stomach. Nancy was at the counter now, facing in the other direction.

She hadn't seen him.

He could imagine her surprise when he walked up and tapped her on the shoulder, gave her the flowers and told her how much he'd missed her. Asked her to come to New York with him. It was what they had talked about so often, and now he intended to make it right.

Except her attention was on someone else. Tommy Broussard, onetime quarterback of the Wolf Haven High Wildcats.

His eyes met John's, and a smug grin flashed across his face. Then his gaze shifted to Nancy. He took her in his arms, sliding them around her waist and pulling her close.

And then they kissed.

Tommy's hands slid lower. They strayed from the small of her back to the swell of her rump, even as he made eye contact with John a second time.

It was a message the younger Decker received loud and clear. He had waited too long. Nancy had moved on.

With a heavy heart, John Decker turned and left the restaurant before Nancy even knew he was there. On the way back to his car, he dumped the flowers in a trashcan. Then he drove back to New York and tried to forget the only girl he would ever love.

# SIXTEEN

I DIDN'T KNOW," Nancy said under her breath, watching the college-age John Decker retreat from the diner. Inside, beyond the window, the younger Nancy and Tommy Broussard were still locked in a tight embrace. "All these years, I never realized you came back."

"It's okay," said Decker, standing next to her at the window. "I should have tried harder."

"She can't hear you," the ghost said.

"I know." Decker wanted to take Nancy into his arms, to comfort her. But it was impossible. She had no idea he was standing there, just as their younger counterparts didn't know they were being observed.

He stepped aside as his younger self left the diner and walked toward his car, throwing the flowers into a trashcan along the way.

Decker could still remember that day. He had driven back to New York with a mixture of disappointment and resentment twisting his gut. Watching those events from long ago play out from a third person perspective reminded him just how much he had lost. It would be almost twenty years before they reunited, during which Nancy had married, had a child, and divorced. She had also taken over the diner. Decker had moved on with his life in the Big Apple, working first as a beat cop and ending up as a detective in the homicide division before everything came crashing down when his partner tried to kill him. He couldn't help but wonder where they would be now if Nancy had only turned around on that fateful day instead of embracing Tommy Broussard. If she had seen him, their lives might have been very different.

Nancy apparently felt the same way. She stood with her hand pressed against the window, as if she could reach out and somehow influence the events that had torn them apart for so long.

"Damn it John, you should have told me you were back in town," she said in a voice that carried an almost wistful tone. She lowered her hand from the window. More tears were flowing now. "You should have done more. I still loved you."

"I loved you too," Decker said, even though he knew she couldn't hear him. Not that it mattered. Because the scene was fading, becoming translucent.

Decker reached out to Nancy. Said her name. But his hand found only empty air as she vanished from sight.

Then they were back in the library.

"What did you do with her?" Decker asked, turning toward the Ghost of All Things Past. "Where is she?"

"Nancy has other places to be," the ghost replied. "As do you."

"What places?" He and Nancy had confronted the missed opportunity that kept them apart for so long. As far as he was concerned, they were done. "You showed us our mistake."

"There's so much more." The ghost reached for another volume and pulled it from the shelf. "Are you ready to meet your past?"

"Wait." Decker was staring at the book's spine because his name wasn't on it. Instead, it bore his father's name, and a date years before Decker was born. "That isn't my past."

"No," replied the ghost. "But it's where everything began. Where the guilt you've carried for so long has its origins."

"Guilt? I don't understand."

"The guilt of your mother's death, of course." Then the ghost opened the book.

The library faded and they were back in Wolf Haven, standing outside Cassidy's diner, just like before.

Except it wasn't.

The cars. The clothes. Even the diner itself. Everything looked . . . old-fashioned.

Standing outside the diner, looking in through the window just as Nancy had on their previous visit, was a scrawny-looking teenage girl with limp black hair that fell to her shoulders. Next to her, leaning against the wall, was a bicycle. The girl looked around, as if she were afraid someone would stop her, then opened the diner door and slipped inside.

There was something familiar about the girl, but he couldn't place it. Was she why the ghost had brought him there? He was about to ask, but then he caught movement from the corner of his eye. A group of boys were horsing around and jostling each other the way teenagers do as they strolled along the sidewalk.

And now he understood.

Because walking toward the diner was someone Decker knew all too well. He was younger, for sure, but there was no doubt of his identity.

A chill ran up Decker's spine. He took a step forward even as a single word escaped his lips. "Dad?"

# SEVENTEEN

ANNIE DOUCET LEANED her bike against the wall outside Cassidy's diner and peered through the window. She watched a waitress behind the counter squirt a tall column of whipped cream onto a milkshake before depositing a ruby-red glistening cherry on top.

Her envious gaze followed the waitress as she brought the strawberry concoction, along with two straws, to a young couple sitting in a booth near the jukebox with bench seats as red as the cherry. On her way back to the counter, the waitress noticed Annie on the other side of the window and smiled.

Annie returned the smile, the phantom taste of the milkshake already in her mouth. How many times had she stood at this window on trips into town, wishing she could summon the nerve to enter? But it was always too busy. Annie was not a popular girl. She lived with her mother two miles outside of Wolf Haven in a shack surrounded by swamps. Annie was an outsider. She had no school friends and could not wait until she turned eighteen—six months away—when she could escape that dreadful place forever.

She would start her senior year soon, but she doubted she would finish it. The diner was another matter. She yearned to step foot inside, had almost done so a couple of times. Except that it was bad enough being teased at school. She didn't need to be teased just for wanting a milkshake. Now, though, the diner was uncharacteristically empty. The only customers, the milkshake couple, were strangers. They were also engrossed in each other, heads bent close. They would pay her no heed, she was sure.

Annie left her bike propped against the wall and edged toward the door. Was she really going to do this?

She reached out and touched the door handle, hand shaking. In her pocket was a small purse that contained the week's grocery money. Her mother had stopped coming into town as soon as Annie was old enough to make the trip alone, and it had fallen to her daughter to take care of the shopping ever since. The all-American meal—hamburger, fries, and a milkshake—cost thirty-five cents. Annie knew this because she had memorized the menu board over the last two years. Just because she hadn't ever entered the diner didn't mean she couldn't fantasize about it. Top of her list, the things she dreamed about most when she was alone in her bed at night, was the All-American meal. If she was careful with the grocery money, Annie could just about eek out the cost of that meal. She would need to be more thrifty than usual, but it could be done. Laying aside the last of her fears, Annie pushed the door open and stepped across the threshold into Cassidy's Diner.

The air inside the restaurant was redolent, full of the fragrances of onion rings and hamburgers and key lime pie. Annie paused inside the doorway, soaking up the heady aromas and the atmosphere of the place that she had yearned to enter for so long. She put her hand in her pocket, fingers closing around the small purse. In that moment she didn't care how much it cost, or whether she would have enough money left for the groceries her mother expected her to bring home. All she cared about were the delights waiting for her at the counter.

Annie took a step forward, then another. She approached the counter and climbed onto one of the stools. She perched on the red vinyl seat and reached for a menu even though she knew what she was going to order. She wanted to savor every second of this forbidden delight.

"What can I get you, hon?" The waitress who had smiled at her through the window breezed up, a notepad and pen clutched in her hands.

"Gosh, I . . . I don't know." Because now Annie wasn't sure if she should get a strawberry shake, or a chocolate shake. She wanted them both, and a vanilla shake to boot. But she had to pick because she couldn't afford all three, let alone drink that much milkshake. She looked up from the menu, and in a moment of clarity, made her choice. "Chocolate. I'll have the All-American with the chocolate shake."

"Ooh. Nice choice. That's my favorite," said the waitress. Her name was Cindy according to her name tag. "You want everything on your burger?"

"I don't know." Annie had no idea what came on the burger.

"Pickles ketchup and onion. You like all of those?"

"Yes." Annie nodded her agreement.

"Coming right up." The waitress turned and left, ripping a hastily scrawled order from her notepad as she went and slipping it through a hatch in the back wall to the kitchen.

Annie leaned on the counter and closed her eyes for a moment. She could hardly believe she was here. When she heard the door open and the sounds of raucous laughter, she opened her eyes and looked around. Her heart fell. Walking in, like they hadn't a care in the world, were a group of boys she recognized from the high school football team.

They had seen her too.

"Well, if it isn't Swampy Annie." One boy, who she recognized as Travis Cox, Wolf Haven High's star quarterback, twisted his face into a leering sneer. "They'll let anyone in this place."

Another boy spoke up. "You know there's no alligator on the menu here, right?" The boy laughed. "That's what they eat in the swamps. Alligators. When they're not eating raccoons or snakes."

"I heard it was the other way around. The alligator ate her father." This elicited another round of laughter.

Annie felt her cheeks redden. She glanced down toward the floor. "My father wasn't eaten by an alligator. It attacked him while he was out hunting in the swamp, and he died."

"Dang. He wasn't even tasty enough for the gator to eat him." This was the quarterback again. "Poor little Swampy Annie. Lives alone in a shack with her mother because her daddy lost a fight with an alligator."

Annie turned away from the cluster of boys. She glanced up at the menu, her eyes settling on the All-American meal, the one they were preparing for her right now in the kitchen and which she knew she would never eat. With a heavy heart, she slid down off the stool and turned toward the door.

"Hey, where are you going, Swampy?" Travis sneered.

Annie glanced toward the door. The boys were standing between her and freedom. If she wanted to escape, she would have to push through them. She took a deep breath and steeled herself. But then, to her surprise, a new voice spoke up.

"Come on guys, leave her alone." This was a boy to Travis's right. Annie recognized him as Robbie Decker. She'd seen him around school. He was not traditionally handsome but had those unconventional good looks that ensured he was never short of a date. Now his blue eyes fixed on her. He stepped away from the group and motioned toward the stool. "Why don't you sit back down and have your food."

"I think I should go."

The boys watched this fresh development with a combination of annoyance and mirth, then they turned, grumbling, and made their way toward a booth, leaving Robbie alone with Annie.

"Don't be silly." Robbie flashed a white-toothed smile. "You shouldn't let what other people think worry you so much. It's not worth it." He nodded toward the counter and the waitress who was approaching with Annie's milkshake. "You can't leave without drinking that milkshake, it would be a crime."

Annie wavered a moment, caught between her desire to flee and her surprise, then she turned and hopped back on the stool.

# EIGHTEEN

ROBBIE LEANED on the counter and watched as Annie sucked her milkshake up through the straw. "How come you haven't come in here before?" He asked.

"I don't know," Annie replied even though she knew all too well what had kept her out of Cassidy's for so long. She glanced sideways at Robbie and couldn't help wondering why he was talking to her.

"It doesn't matter what anyone thinks," Robbie said. "If you want to do something, you should just do it."

"That's easy for you to say." The waitress was bringing Annie's food now. She looked down at the plate, not sure if she wanted to eat in front of this boy. "You're on the football team. People like you. No one likes me."

"You just need to give people a chance." Robbie reached out and stole one of her fries. He popped it in his mouth, eyes twinkling with mischief.

"It's more that people won't give me a chance." Annie took a fry and ate it, her courage bolstered by Robbie's brazen theft. "I'm not like the other girls at school."

"So what?" Robbie took a second fry. "Do you have to be like everyone else?"

"It would help."

"What's it like?"

"What's what like?" Annie shook her head, confused.

"Living out in the swamps. It must be scary."

"Not really. I've lived there all my life." Annie nodded toward the hamburger. "You want to share this with me? Its bigger than I thought it would be."

"Sure."

Annie cut the burger in half with her knife and pushed the plate between them. She waited for Robbie to pick his share up before she dove into hers. They ate in silence for a few moments, polishing off the burger and most of the fries.

"Aren't you afraid of alligators?" Robbie asked when he was done eating. "Being surrounded by them all the time."

"Why would I be afraid?" Annie replied. "They mostly stay away from us."

"They didn't stay away from your dad." The jovial look on Robbie's face dropped away instantly as he spoke the words. "Sorry. I didn't mean it like that."

"That's okay. My dad died a long time ago. I never knew him." Annie pushed the empty plate away and sucked up the last of her milkshake.

"I can't imagine being bitten by a gator. I bet it's scary."

"Probably. I try not to think about that."

"It must be lonely out there, just the two of you. Why don't you move into town?"

"I like living in the swamp." This was a lie. Annie had dreamed about living in town, but even if they had the money, which they didn't, her mother would never move. Emmylou Doucet, while not quite a shut-in, was hardly a social butterfly. Annie studied her empty milkshake glass and decided it was time to change the subject. "Did you know the county fair is coming to town?"

"Doesn't everyone?" Robbie's smile was back now. "It's the best part of summer."

"I saw them setting up at the state fairground when I was

cycling into town. They have a Ferris wheel, a tilt-a-whirl, and bumper cars. It looks like so much fun."

"Are you going?" Robbie asked.

"Probably not." Annie shook her head. Even if she wanted to go, she had no money. Not that she could imagine her mother letting her attend anyway. Fun fairs were for other people. Normal people. They weren't for folk like her. "I don't have anyone to go with and its no fun going alone."

"There must be someone you can go with." Robbie raised an eyebrow. "Have you ever even been to the fair?"

"No." Annie's head dropped, and she stared at the floor.

"You've never been to the fair?" The look on Robbie's face made it obvious that he didn't believe her. "You're almost eighteen and no one has ever taken you?"

"Why is that so hard for you to believe?" Annie squirmed on the stool, uncomfortable. She glanced toward the door and contemplated making a quick escape.

"I'm not saying I don't believe you," Robbie said. "It's just that . . ."

"It's just that you've never seen anyone quite this uncool?"

"That isn't what I meant." Robbie folded his arms. "There's nothing else for it. I'll take you to the fair."

"What?" Annie felt a tingle run up her spine. She couldn't tell if it was shock or excitement. "Why would you want to do something like that?"

"You make it sound like a chore."

"No one's ever wanted to take me anywhere before."

"There's a first time for everything. You can't hide out in that cabin in the swamp forever. What do you say?"

"I don't think it would be a good idea." She could imagine what her mother would say. Not only going to the county fair but doing it with a boy. Regardless, she couldn't help feeling a pang of disappointment. "Thank you for asking, though."

"Come to the fair with me," Robbie said. "I won't ask again."

"I don't know . . ." Annie wanted to say yes so badly. "Why me? You could take any girl at school."

"I know. But you're the girl I'm asking. Well, what do you say?"

"I thought you weren't going to ask again."

Robbie shrugged. "Figured I'd give it one more try. Since you're playing hard to get."

"I'm not playing—" Annie blushed. "I just—"

"Hey. Calm down. Take a breath and say yes."

Annie did as she was told. She took a breath. Then she looked at Robbie and said yes.

She was going to the fair.

# NINETEEN

ROBBIE DECKER WATCHED Annie Doucet leave Cassidy's, and then he joined his friends in a booth near the window.

"What the Sam Hill was all that about?" Travis Cox asked, looking bemused. "You got a hankering for a walk on the wild side?"

This comment was met with raucous laughter.

"Leave her alone. Annie's not so bad." Robbie slipped into the booth. "She's shy, that's all."

"Annie? You're on first-name terms with her now?" Travis snorted and picked at his fries. "You'll be telling us the two of you are going steady next."

"I'm not going steady." Robbie slapped Travis on the arm. "It's not like that. But I am taking her to the county fair tomorrow night."

"Seriously?" Travis shook his head. "Aw, come on man, you can do better than that. Swampy Annie?"

"You shouldn't call her that. It's not nice."

"Yeah, but it's true. If you're taking her to the fair, you can steer clear of us. You might not care who you hang around with, but we do." Travis leaned back in the booth, his mouth curling up into a sneering smile. "Man. I can't believe you're dating Swampy Annie. Swampy *freaking* Annie."

"I told you already. I'm not dating her. I feel sorry for the girl, that's all. She doesn't have any friends, and everyone makes fun of her."

"She lives in a swamp surrounded by alligators."

"So what? You live on the edge of town next to a junkyard. No one makes fun of you. They don't call you Junk Yard Travis" Robbie glared at his friend. "You don't have to be so mean."

"My family ain't poor. We own that junkyard, moron." Travis was on the defensive. "And anyway, I heard that Annie hunts for food in the swamp. Goes right out there and catches snakes and mice."

"Mice don't live in swamps, and even if they did, she doesn't eat them. She was in town getting groceries. Geez, it's no wonder she doesn't want to come in here with people like you hanging around and poking fun at her."

"What, like you've never made fun of her?" Travis cupped his hands behind his head.

"I might have said some stuff once in a while. But I was wrong. We have it easy. Everyone likes us. We're popular. Imagine what it's like for her."

"I'd rather not. If she doesn't want us to make fun of her, she shouldn't be so weird."

"And poor," said one of the other boys, Clayton Bradley.

"Cut it out," Robbie snapped. "You don't even know anything about her. None of you. Who cares if I take her to the fair?"

"Hey, if you want to ruin your night that's up to you." Travis shrugged. "You just better hope she doesn't get all doe eyed and fall in love with you."

There was another titter of laughter from around the table.

"That's not going to happen," Robbie said. "She knows we're going as friends."

"You sure about that?" Travis smirked. "Because the way she was looking at you over there . . . Man, I'd say you've got yourself a girlfriend."

# TWENTY

## BACK IN THE LIBRARY

DECKER GASPED.

One minute he was in the diner watching his father flirting, and the next he was back in the library at the house Charles Dickens had used as inspiration for his famous Christmas ghost story. The same house he and Nancy had gone searching for on Beacon Street in Boston, and unfortunately found.

"That girl in Cassidy's Diner," he said, turning to his ghostly companion. "It was Annie Doucet."

"Yes." The ghost nodded.

"And my father knew her back in the seventies because they were in school together?"

Again, the ghost nodded.

Decker sat down on the library sofa, trying to process this new information. The murderous old woman he had killed in the high school a few years before—a woman who had turned herself into a vicious Cajun werewolf to wreak vengeance on the town for taking her land against her will to build a highway interchange—barely resembled the innocent teenager his father asked out to the fair.

He did some quick math and figured that she must have been

around sixty-eight when she was terrorizing Wolf Haven as the loup-garou, which surprised him. Annie Doucet had seemed ancient even when Decker was growing up. It had never occurred to him that the old woman who lived in the swamp was only the same age as his parents. If asked, he would have pegged her as at least a decade and a half older. Maybe that was what living in a run-down cabin out in the swamps did for you. She had led a hard life, for sure.

Or maybe it was something else entirely.

There had always been rumors around town, whispers that she was a witch, even back when he was a kid. All the local children were afraid of her. Those seemingly tall tales—which the adult John Decker had dismissed as nothing more than ridiculous town gossip spread by superstitious town folk—had turned out to be true. He discovered that the hard way when she went on her killing spree that left several residents of Wolf Haven dead, including the boyfriend of Nancy's daughter. Was it possible that her use of magic took a physical toll on her?

This brought up another question in Decker's mind. How many times *had* Annie Doucet turned into the loup-garou over the years? It didn't strike him as logical that she used her ability to transform into the wolf only after the town tried to take her land. He thought back to the days after their confrontation in the high school when he and his deputy, Chad, were going through Annie Doucet's cabin. They had found all sorts of interesting things. Like a spell book, cauldron, candles, and a variety of strange ingredients stored in jars. Some of those ingredients could have been found in any Louisiana kitchen. Paprika. Pepper. Garlic powder. But others were more exotic. The dried and shredded skin of toads and frogs. Venom from a variety of snakes including the deadly water moccasin. Indigo milk mushrooms.

Some of it, like the mushrooms, had been recently acquired. But the contents of other jars looked more like ingredients the old woman kept on hand all the time, which told Decker that Annie had been practicing her witchcraft for much longer than the few days it took for her to exact bloody revenge on those who wanted her land and cabin.

None of this explained why the ghost was showing him events so far back in his father's past, though. He looked up at the ghost. "I don't get it. You said the books in this library—the ones about my parents—tell of events before I was born that had an impact on my life."

"That is correct."

"What possible impact could my father going to the fair with Annie Doucet have had on me?"

"A big one," the ghost replied, taking another book down from the shelf and opening it. "We just haven't gotten that far yet."

Wait—" Decker jumped up. He still had more questions.

But it was too late. The library blinked out of existence, and Decker was back in the past again. But this time it wasn't the diner. Instead, he was standing in Annie Doucet's cabin. And he wasn't alone. Sitting in a chair facing the door, was a woman he hadn't seen in a very long time. It was Annie's mother, Emmylou Doucet. And she didn't look happy. Not happy at all.

# TWENTY-ONE

## WOLF HAVEN, AUGUST 1972

ANNIE DOUCET CYCLED home in a daze, her wheels barely touching the ground despite the heavy grocery bags in the basket attached to her handlebars. It hardly seemed real. Robbie Decker, tight end on the football team and one of the most popular boys in school, and she was going to the county fair with him. Then she remembered her mother, and the dream crashed down around her. By the time she arrived home, her euphoria had turned to dread, which only deepened when she entered the cabin.

Emmylou Doucet was sitting in her favorite chair in the front room, her eyes fixed on the door. When Annie entered, her mother jumped up.

"Where have you been?" Emmylou asked in a sharp tone. She speared her daughter with a glowering stare. "You should have been back an hour ago."

"It was busy at the store," Annie lied. She stood in the doorway holding the bags of groceries and wished she could shrink behind them and disappear. "I had to wait in line to check out."

"Wait in line?" Emmylou Doucet clearly did not believe her daughter. "You've never taken this long in town before."

"I stopped to talk to a friend outside of the store." Annie could imagine what her mother would say if she mentioned the diner, and the All-American meal. That was a conversation she did not wish to have.

"Friend. What friend?"

"Someone I know from school, that's all." Annie wished her mother would just drop the subject. It was going to be impossible to get permission to attend the fair if this turned into an argument.

"You don't have any friends at school. You don't have any friends at all. You're lying to me, girl."

"I'm not lying. I really was talking to someone." This much was true, and Annie was grateful for some speck of honesty in what was fast becoming an untenable situation.

"Who was it, then?" Emmylou pressed ahead with her questioning, clearly under the belief she had talked her daughter into a corner.

"It was just a boy." Annie said the words before she realized her mistake. It would have been better to invent a friend than admit this. But she was committed now. "He goes to my school."

"So now the truth comes out." Emmylou pressed her lips together. "I knew you were up to no good."

"You don't need to make a big deal out of it," Annie said. The grocery bags were getting heavy in her arms. She walked through the cramped front room and into the tiny space that served as a kitchen. She dropped the bags on the floor with relief. When she turned around again, her mother was right there. "I wasn't doing anything wrong."

"I was wondering when you'd start up with the boys. I suppose I'm lucky you've stayed away from them for as long as you have. You know they only want one thing."

"Mom, please. Nothing happened. I told you already. I was just talking."

"That's how it always begins. That's how I ended up with you. They say they just want to talk and before you know it, they're doing a lot more than talking."

"Mom, don't talk about dad like that." Annie hated it when her mother started badmouthing her father. She knew they hadn't had an easy relationship, but Emmylou had, in her own way, loved her husband. The anger, Annie suspected, came from the fact that her dad had gotten himself killed and left her alone.

"I'll talk about him any way I want. My life would've been different if it wasn't for him."

"Mom, please . . ."

"You don't know the half of it." Emmylou started taking items out of the grocery bags, inspecting them one by one, as if she expected her daughter to have messed up. "But we're not talking about me, we're talking about you. You're too young to be taking up with boys."

"I'm almost eighteen." Despite her protestations of adulthood, Annie could feel tears welling up at the corners of her eyes. Her mother had, as usual, smashed away any joy that her daughter felt. "It's not right that you treat me like this."

"Not right? I gave birth to you. I have every right." Emmylou put a gallon of milk in the old refrigerator that stood as one of the few electrical appliances in the entire cabin. "What did this boy want, anyway?"

"He asked me to go to the county fair with him tomorrow evening." Annie had hoped she could delay mentioning this but could see little point in avoiding the truth. One way or the other, her mother was going to find out. "It's not a big deal, just an hour or two."

"Why would a boy want to take you anywhere?" Emmylou looked her daughter up and down. "You're all skin and bones. Scrawny. Surely he could do better."

"I don't know, I guess he likes me." Now the tears began. Annie choked back a sob and wondered why her mother was so cruel. "I won't stay out late, I promise."

"You won't stay out at all. You're not going."

"Why not?" Annie rarely spoke back to her mother, but today unusual courage possessed her. Perhaps it was the attention

Robbie Decker had lavished upon her, or perhaps she just felt emboldened by the realization that someone, anyone, could find her attractive. "You can't keep me locked up in this cabin forever."

"Watch me." Emmylou had finished putting the meager haul of groceries away now. If she noticed they were light a pound of potatoes or missing a few smaller items thanks to Annie's splurge on the hamburger and milkshake, she said nothing. "While you're under my roof, you obey my rules."

"I always obey your rules." Annie pleaded. "Why can't you let me have some fun, just once. It's not like I get asked out every day."

"There's plenty of time for fun when you have the maturity to handle it." Emmylou Doucet reached out and took her daughter's hand. "I'm just looking out for you. I want to keep you safe. We're not like the folks in town."

"I know that." Annie pulled her hand away. "I wish we were like the rest of the town, then I wouldn't be so unhappy all the time. Maybe they wouldn't tease me. Maybe they wouldn't call me Swampy Annie."

"That's exactly why you shouldn't go with this boy. He's using you."

"No, he's not. He's different." Annie backed away toward the kitchen door. She glared at her mother. "I hate my life." And then she turned and fled toward the small lean-to on the side of the house that passed as her bedroom.

# TWENTY-TWO

ON SATURDAY EVENING, Annie Doucet put on the best dress she owned, a white cotton outfit with embroidered purple flowers, and pulled her hair back into a ponytail. From the other side of her bedroom door, she could hear her mother moving around, probably tending to the liquor still behind the cabin where she made her moonshine because it was cheaper than buying alcohol in town. If the liquor was ready, she would start in on it, no doubt.

Annie usually hated her mother getting drunk, but today she was counting on it. She would be able to slip away easier if the woman was half-cut. Even if they argued, it was unlikely her mother would remember much about it the next day.

When she left her bedroom, however, Emmylou Doucet was anything but drunk.

"Why are you dressed like that?" she asked, fixing Annie with an accusing stare. "If you think you're going to the fair and seeing that boy, you can put that idea out of your head right this minute."

"It's only for a few hours, Mama. I'll be back early, I promise."

"You're not going anywhere. Get back in your room and take that dress off right now." Emmylou's voice trembled when she spoke, the anger shining through.

"I won't." Annie wondered where this defiance was coming from.

Emmylou took a step forward, her arm raised as if she was going to slap her daughter, but instead she gripped Annie's arm and pushed her backwards toward the bedroom. "Do as I say, girl. I'm still your mother and I know what's best."

"No, you don't." Annie twisted free of her mother's grip and skirted around her toward the cabin's front door. "This is what's best for me. Leading a normal life. Going out."

"Everyone will make fun of you." Her mother was advancing again now, closing the gap between them. "You're not like other girls. We are not like other families. You need to understand that."

"I understand well enough. The only reason we're not like other folk is because you won't let us be." Annie backed up toward the door. It would only take a few more steps to escape. Yet a part of her didn't want to flee. She wanted her mother's blessing to go out and have a night of fun. She wanted to be normal.

"Annie." The tone of her mother's voice changed from angry to pleading. "I'm begging you not to go. It's a mistake. If you meet this boy, you'll regret it."

"Why do you think it's a mistake?" Annie asked, unable to understand her mother's concern.

"Because I know boys. I know what they want. You might think this one is different to the others, but he isn't. He'll use you and hurt you. That's what men do."

"Robbie isn't like that." Annie blurted his name out before she could stop herself. "He's not like dad."

"Ah. The boy has a name. Robbie."

"Yes. And he's nice. A gentleman."

"Don't make me laugh. He's a man, no better than any of them. All he wants is one thing. I won't let you do this." Emmylou darted forward, her arm outstretched to take ahold of her daughter and stop her from leaving.

"No." Annie sidestepped the clumsy assault with ease and

pushed the front door open. She stepped outside and ran to her bicycle, before turning back to see if her mother was giving chase.

Emmylou Doucet stood in the doorway, her hands at her sides, a pained expression on her face. She watched her daughter for a moment before she spoke again. "I'm giving you one last chance. Come back into the house and we'll talk about this."

"No." Annie shook her head and gripped the bicycle's handlebars. She wheeled it away from the tree onto the dirt path that led away from the cabin and towards the road. "I'm going to the fair and there's nothing you can do to stop me."

"Why are you doing this to me?" Her mother's voice drifted on the swirling breeze that moved across the swamp. "Haven't I always tried to do my best by you?"

Annie didn't answer this because she didn't want to lie, and she was loath to hurt her mother further by telling the truth. Instead, she glanced backwards and said, "I'll be back in a couple of hours, I promise. Don't worry. Robbie's not like other boys."

Emmylou said nothing in return. She just stood in the doorway and watched as Annie mounted the bicycle.

Annie slipped her feet onto the pedals, then gave one last glance back. She had defied her mother for the first time in her life, and strangely, it felt good. A couple of miles down the road, on the outskirts of town, Robbie was waiting for her at the state fairgrounds. Annie took a deep breath to quell her trembling nerves, and peddled away from the cabin, aware of her mother watching as she went. But Annie didn't care. Robbie liked her, and that was all that mattered. Emmylou was wrong. After tonight, she would be Robbie's girlfriend, and no one would tease her ever again.

# TWENTY-THREE

ANNIE CYCLED like crazy toward town, and the county fair, overcome by a mixture of elation and trepidation. She had done what she wanted, instead of doing as her mother told her. There would be hell to pay later. Annie didn't care. All she could think about was the evening ahead of her, and Robbie Decker.

She arrived at the fairgrounds and hopped off her bike, wheeling it through the gates and past the parking area, already packed with cars. A band was playing somewhere, their jangling music competing with the rival tunes emanating from the various rides and sideshows. She wasn't even inside yet, and already she could smell the odor of hot dogs, cotton candy, and fried dough. Children ran around darting between the cars, their excited cries rising into the air as they waited for their parents to lead them toward the wonderland beyond the turnstiles.

Annie wheeled her bike to a rack and parked it before turning her attention to the fair's entrance. A small crush of people waited to pay their dollar admission fee, moving past the ticket booth one by one as they collected their ride tickets. She stopped, realizing with a sinking heart that she didn't have a dollar for admission. It hadn't occurred to her that she would need to pay just to get inside the fair. She had assumed that each ride would charge its own fee.

Annie only had fifty cents on her, a meager amount scraped together over the last few months and hidden in a tin box in her dresser. She had figured it would be enough to pay for some rides, and maybe a hot dog.

Now her heart fell.

She couldn't even get onto the midway.

She bit her lip and tried not to cry in disappointment. This was awful. How could she meet Robbie now, without even the money to pay the entrance fee? She turned to walk back to her bicycle, intending to cycle back home where she would have to endure hours of her mother harping on about being right. That she hadn't even met her date would not matter. But then, before she had even moved a single step, a voice called out.

"Hey, Annie."

Annie stopped and turned around. There, standing near a powder blue Mustang, was Robbie. She felt her heart pounding inside her chest. She would be embarrassed now, either way. Staying meant she would have to admit she couldn't afford the entry fee, but if she fled, he would think her crazy. She forced a smile. "Hi, Robbie."

"You look nice tonight." Robbie walked toward her, hands on his hips. His blue eyes sparkled in the late evening sunlight. The breeze ran gentle through his hair. "Are you ready to go in?"

"I . . ." Annie searched for the right words. "I don't have enough money. I thought it would be free to enter."

Robbie shrugged. "I figured. I've got this." He pulled some dollar bills from his pocket. "I have enough for cotton candy too."

"It's too much money. I can't let you pay for me."

"Don't be silly. I asked you to come with me. Naturally, I'm going to pay." Robbie put a hand on her back and steered her toward the fairgrounds. "I hope you haven't eaten yet. They have this awesome funnel cake that they make right in front of you. You have to try it."

"I've never had funnel cake." Annie felt herself relaxing. Robbie's hand on her back felt strange, but in a nice way. He was standing so close that she could smell his aftershave. At that moment, she didn't care if she went in there or not. Just being with Robbie was good enough.

The line moved forward, and soon they were at the ticket booth. Robbie handed over the dollar bills. Then they were inside the fair, standing at the edge of the midway, their senses assaulted by a cacophony of noises, bright lights, and mouthwatering odors. Annie gazed at the scene before her with a mixture of awe and excitement. This was so much better than she had imagined. The midway was packed with people, a throng of bodies that weaved in all directions. A few of them she recognized from high school. Many she did not.

"What do you think?" Robbie glanced her way.

"I think it's wonderful," Annie breathed, soaking in the sights and sounds.

"What would you like to do first?"

"All of it." How could she choose just one thing? "I want to do it all."

# TWENTY-FOUR

THE FIRST PLACE Robbie took her was a shooting gallery with rifles connected to the booth by chains. On the back wall were a row of targets and above this on shelves that lined the rest of the booth, plush toys of various sizes with tickets on them denoting the number of hits it would require to win one. The carny was quick to take Robbie's ticket and watched with a bemused smile as the young man attempted to win a prize. Robbie was a superb marksman, and scored close to the bull's-eye on three of his four shots, the gun's pellets leaving small round tears in the paper target. Only the first shot went wide. The carny, no longer amused, grudgingly handed over a twelve-inch-tall plush bear.

"If I'd nailed that first shot, I could've won you the big bear." Robbie looked wistfully up at the largest of the prizes, three times the size of the one he now offered to Annie.

"This one is perfect," Annie said, taking the prize with glee. No one had ever won anything for her before. She wasn't sure what to think. "It's fantastic. I'll keep it forever."

"They rig the games." Robbie didn't bother lowering his voice, which elicited a narrow-eyed glare from the booth operator. "My dad used to bring me to the fair all the time and showed me how to win. The trick is to figure out how the gun is weighted with the first try, then adjust. My rifle pulled to the left and high, so I just needed to aim down to the right of the bull's-eye. Most people don't take any notice of that, and all their shots miss."

"That's so clever," Annie beamed. "I never would've been able to figure that out."

"Sure you would." Robbie nodded across the midway to a food vendor where a short line of revelers waited to pick up a fair-ground snack. "Let's get the funnel cake, then we'll go on one of the rides."

"Okay." Annie agreed. She had never tasted funnel cake before and wasn't even sure exactly what it was made from, but Robbie said it was good and that was enough for her.

They joined the back of the line and a few minutes later they were walking away with the fried delicacy sitting on a cardboard tray in their hands.

Finding a bench, they sat down and picked at the hot crispy batter, dropping powdered sugar which Annie wiped away as quickly as it touched her dress.

Afterward, when the sweet treat was no more, they strolled the midway toward the bumper cars. It was then that Annie noticed the group of teens up ahead and her heart fell. There were eight of them, four boys and four girls, all of whom Annie recognized from high school. Two of them had been in Cassidy's the previous day. She still remembered their taunts, how they'd called her Swampy Annie, and their cruel laughter. The girls were on the cheerleading squad. Karen Leroux, blonde, petite, and a total bitch, would not hesitate to crush Annie under her foot. She had, in fact, done so many times in the past and appeared to enjoy it. Annie had no desire to get humiliated in front of Robbie for the second time in two days, especially now that he was paying attention to her. She did not want to ruin this. She slowed, tensing.

Robbie, walking next to her, sensed her unease. His eyes darted toward the group, then back to Annie, then he took her hand in his and turned them around.

"Come on, we don't have to go on the bumper cars right now."

Annie let out a sigh of relief. It was bad enough that he knew she was afraid of being taunted, but the alternative would've been so much worse. It was then that she realized they were holding hands, and suddenly she forgot all about Robbie's friends. This was proof positive. He liked her. She glanced sideways toward him as they walked, overcome with a sudden sense that her life was about to change. She wanted to squeeze his hand tighter, but she was afraid to draw attention to it, lest he pull away. Instead, she smiled at him. "This is nice."

"Good. I'm glad you're having fun." Robbie shot her a quick look, then turned to frontward again. "What would you like to do now?"

"Anything." She didn't care what they did next, as long as they did it together. "Whatever you want to do is fine."

"How about the Ferris wheel?" Robbie pointed toward the tall spinning disc that dominated the fairgrounds, festooned with thousands of bulbs that blinked and flashed in a dazzling choreographed display that was visible even though it wasn't dark yet. "I heard that when you get to the top, you can see all the way to Lake Pontchartrain."

"That doesn't sound right," Annie said before she could stop herself. She moved closer to Robbie so that their arms were against each other. "But I think we should find out."

"Awesome." Robbie led her through the crowds, zigzagging back and forth past clusters of excited teenagers, kids holding puffs of cotton candy as big as their heads, and young couples turning an innocuous activity into a romantic evening. And this was how Annie felt at that moment. Happier than she ever had before, and more than a little dreamy. She didn't care about the argument that surely waited when she got home, or her mother's unforgiving attitude. All she cared about was being here with Robbie. When they climbed on the ride, squeezing into the small gondola that was barely wide enough for the two of them to sit down, she felt a flutter of excitement. As the restraining bar came down over their waists and the ride took its first shuddering movements, she closed her eyes, held Robbie's hand tight, and wished the evening would never end.

After a few minutes they reached the top of the ride, and Annie looked out over the fairground and the throngs of fair-goers crawling through the wide central alley, their excited cries sounding thin and far away as they mixed with the jangle of music, and thrum of the generators that powered the temporary city of pleasure. She forgot all about Robbie's friends and her previous nervousness. When the ride started on its downward trajectory, she felt a glimmer of disappointment at its brevity. If only they could have stayed up there, head in the clouds, just the two of them.

When the gondola reached ground-level once more Robbie stepped off and held the door open for her to exit. They rejoined the milling throng and when they made their way to the bumper cars this time, there was no sign of Robbie's friends. Ride by ride, they worked their way along the midway, Annie clutching the bear that Robbie had won for her through every ride. After another hour passed, she told him she must go home.

"Are you sure?"

"Yes." Annie wished that she could stay but knew that she was pushing her luck. It was bad enough she had fled the cabin in defiance of her mother's orders. It would be worse if she stayed out late. As it was, trouble was surely waiting for her when she arrived home.

She allowed Robbie to walk her to the Fair's entrance. Here they paused. She wasn't sure what was supposed to happen next, and she lapsed into a shy silence.

Robbie watched her for a moment, then spoke. "I can walk you to your bike if you like."

"You don't need to do that." Annie sensed that he didn't want to leave the fair, and if he accompanied her through the gates, he might not get back in. "I enjoyed the evening though. It was nice."

"I'm glad you enjoyed it," Robbie said. "I had fun too."

Annie smiled and looked up at Robbie, their eyes meeting. In that moment, she knew what she was supposed to do next. She stood up on tiptoe and leaned in, planting a kiss on his cheek. Then she whirled and ran from the fair towards the parking lot, overcome by a mixture of excitement and coy embarrassment. On the other side of the ticket booth, she turned and glanced back toward Robbie. He was standing where she'd left him, watching her with a surprised look on his face. She grinned and waved, then made her way to the bicycle. When she looked around again, Robbie was gone.

# TWENTY-FIVE

ROBBIE WAITED at the ticket booth until he was sure Annie was safely on her way home, then he turned and strolled back up the midway to find his friends. He wasn't sure what to do. Travis had been right. Annie thought there was more to their relationship than friendship. She had kissed him. It was only a peck on the cheek, but for someone like her that was enough. He should never have gotten involved in this to begin with. Now there was surely going to be an uncomfortable conversation in his future. The worst of it was that he liked Annie. Behind the shy inexperience and odd mannerisms lay a sweet, if socially awkward girl. She wasn't actually that bad looking either, even if the dress she'd worn to the fair was a little frumpy. None of that mattered, though. Robbie couldn't date her even if he wanted to. There was a social hierarchy in high school, and he was at the top of it. He was on the football team. He was good-looking. He was popular. Annie would be a lead weight pulling him down to her level at the bottom of the pecking order. He didn't want to hurt her, but he also didn't want to end up a social pariah. A laughingstock. His father had a poster hanging in the garage above his workbench. It read no good deed goes unpunished. For the first time in his life, Robbie thought he understood what that meant.

Robbie found his friends waiting to board the Scrambler, a ride that featured clusters of cars suspended from arms branching out from a central pivot. When the ride whipped around, the cars spun in the other direction. Robbie had already ridden it once with Annie. He remembered her screams as the cars hurtled in ever faster circles, making them dizzy. When they'd stumbled off the ride she was laughing, something he'd never seen her do before. Now he joined his friends and waited for his second go around of the night.

"How was your date with Swampy?" Travis asked.

A burst of laughter erupted from the group.

"Lay off." Robbie had little interest in discussing his evening, especially since it was so obviously hilarious to his friends.

"Did you make out on the Ferris wheel?" This was Jonny Foster. "What was she like?"

"Hey, cut it out." The line inched forward. It wasn't moving fast enough for Robbie. He started to wish that he'd left with Annie and done the chivalrous thing by escorting her home. That's what he would've done with any other date. He certainly wouldn't have abandoned them to go meet his friends. Of course, he'd have been looking for more than a peck on the cheek with any other girl.

"Take it easy, we're just messing with you." Travis grinned and punched him on the arm. "You'd do the same if the situation was reversed."

"Yeah," Robbie said. "I guess I would."

"Not like that would ever happen." Travis laughed again. "I wouldn't be caught dead with Swampy Annie."

"I was just being nice, guys." Robbie pushed his hands into his pockets. "I felt sorry for her. I bet this is the first date she's ever even been on."

"That ain't your problem." Johnny rolled his eyes. "Geez, you are such a pushover. What you need is a real girlfriend."

"Yeah?" Robbie said. "And who's gonna find her for me. You?"

"Maybe." Johnny pointed across the midway toward the hot dog stand. "See that girl over there? What do you think of her?"

Robbie followed Johnny's gaze and saw a petite blonde girl wearing a white sleeveless blouse and yellow taffeta midi skirt. "Who's that?"

"Lily Colston." Travis leaned close to Robbie. "She's the daughter of the new English teacher. They moved to town a few weeks ago."

"And how do you know this? School hasn't even started yet."

"She joined the cheerleading squad," Karen Leroux said. "We started practice last week, and she was there. She's sweet, and she doesn't live in a swamp."

"I thought we agreed to drop this."

"I never agreed to drop it." Karen flicked a stray hair from her face and grinned. "I have a reputation to maintain, and I don't need you fouling it up."

"Nice." Robbie shook his head. "For the last time, I was just trying to make her feel better about herself."

"Forget about Swampy Annie. You'll feel better about yourself if you have a decent girl on your arm," Travis said. "Just talk to Lily. That's all I'm asking."

"Fine. If we run into each other, I'll talk to her." Robbie rolled his eyes. "Happy now?"

"Yup." Travis grinned. "In fact, you can talk to her right now."

"What?" Robbie looked back toward the hot dog stand. Lily was handing over a dollar bill. She waited for the change and then scooped up a hot dog in a paper tray. She turned in their direction, walking toward them. "She's coming over here."

"Well, duh." Now it was Karen's turn to roll her eyes. "Like I said, she's on the cheerleading squad. She's one of us."

"You could've mentioned that before," Robbie said. But he wasn't mad, because as Lily drew closer, he felt a tingle run up his spine. She was gorgeous. And when she arrived at the group, hot dog in hand, and turned to him with a smile, he smiled back. By the time the introductions were over, he'd forgotten all about Annie Doucet.

# TWENTY-SIX

ANNIE CYCLED HOME IN A DAZE. The sky was darkening now, the last rays of the sun turning the horizon into a fiery kaleidoscope of red and orange and yellow colors. She cycled slowly, wanting to prolong the feeling of euphoria, and knowing that once she arrived home, an argument would undoubtedly ensue. Annie didn't want to ruin her mood.

By the time she arrived at the cabin, the sun had sunk low enough that the dazzling display of colors had mutated into a deep blue, almost black, sky. The moon was not up yet, and the swamp was dark and foreboding beyond the fragile cabin that sat alone at the edge of the wilderness. It was a marked contrast to the bustle a short distance down the road in Wolf Haven. It might as well have been another planet.

Annie leaned her bike against a tree at the entrance to the property and made her way up the dirt path toward the cabin, then mounted the steps onto the front porch. She hesitated at the door, wary of what lay beyond and her mother's wrath. She could not loiter outside forever though, and with a heavy heart, Annie pushed the door open and stepped into the humid and claustrophobic cabin.

The front room was empty, the cabin unusually quiet. This was not what she expected. After their spat earlier in the day, Annie expected her mother to be sitting in the frayed armchair facing the door with a glowering look upon her face.

"Mom?" Annie called out, even though she preferred the unusual quietude to the alternative.

There was a rustle of movement from her mother's bedroom at the back of the cabin, and then Emmylou Doucet appeared in the doorway with a harrowed look upon her face. "You need to go to your bedroom and pack a bag."

"What? Why?" A creeping unease replaced Annie's fear of an argument. Emmylou Doucet went nowhere voluntarily. The cabin was her world. "Why do I need to pack a bag?"

"A messenger came while you were out cavorting." Emmylou turned and disappeared back into the bedroom, talking over her shoulder as she went. "Your aunt is sick."

"Sick?" Annie stood in the bedroom doorway and watched her mother throw clothing into an old suitcase that hadn't been outside the cabin's four walls in at least a decade. "Are you talking about Aunt Babette?"

"Do you have another aunt?" Emmylou snapped the words as she slammed the suitcase shut and clicked the latches.

"How is she sick?" Annie had never met her aunt, although she had heard about her often enough from her mother. The two did not talk, having fallen out many years previous. Annie didn't know what had caused the rift, only that it kept the sole living members of her family apart.

"What do you mean, how is she sick? She's ill. That's all there is to it." Emmylou heaved the suitcase off the bed and moved it toward the door.

Annie stepped aside to allow her mother passage and then trailed behind her. "Do you mean we have to go there and look after her?"

"Well, she can't look after herself." Emmylou dropped the bag by the door. "Now go pack that bag. I want to be out of here at first light, and I don't need you giving me trouble. We have a long drive ahead of us."

"What should I take?" Annie assumed it would be a brief trip. Her mother hated straying too far from the cabin. That she was willing to drive across the state to her sister's house on the outskirts of Shreveport spoke volumes to the seriousness of the affair. It also occurred to her it might be a ruse to keep her away from Robbie, but her mother hadn't mentioned that, so Annie kept quiet about it. "How long will we be gone?"

"A week. Maybe two. Hopefully, we'll be back before school starts."

"That long?" Annie's heart fell. There was less than three weeks until the start of the new school year. She had hoped to spend more time with Robbie during those lazy, carefree last days of summer. How could she do that if she was hundreds of miles away? And maybe that was the point.

"We'll be there until your aunt gets better. Stop prevaricating and gather your clothes."

"You don't even like Aunt Babette. You always say she thinks she's too good for us." Annie had no desire to take off for parts unknown just when her life was coming together.

"She's family. This might be my last chance to see her."

"I thought you said we were only going there until she got better?"

"Or until she dies." Emmylou retreated toward the kitchen. "I'm going to make sandwiches for the road. By the time I'm done, I expect your suitcase to be packed."

Annie wanted to protest further, but she could see it would do no good. Her mother had made her mind up and whether she was trying to keep Annie away from her new boyfriend, or wanted to reconnect with her sister before it was too late, made little difference. They were leaving town and Annie had no say in the matter. She could only hope that Robbie would still be there for her when she got back.

# TWENTY-SEVEN

THEY LEFT the next morning as the sun rose. Emmylou Doucet had a station wagon, which she kept on a patch of high ground behind the cabin. It was an old clunker that she'd bought a decade before and barely used. Annie couldn't remember the last time her mother had driven, yet miraculously the battery was not dead. After a couple of false starts, the engine roared to life. They threw their bags in the back and climbed in. The interior of the car smelled musty, and a layer of dust had accumulated on the dashboard. Emmylou wiped it away with the palm of a hand, sending the particles billowing into the air. She pulled away from the cabin without bothering to fasten her seatbelt and turned onto the road that fronted their property, heading in the opposite direction and away from Wolf Haven.

Shreveport was a four-hour drive.

Annie settled into the front passenger seat with a grudging acceptance of her fate. Every mile further from town was another stab at the joy of Annie's fledgling relationship. She hadn't even been able to tell Robbie that she was leaving. They didn't have a telephone–they barely had electricity–and even if they did; she didn't know his number. The unfairness of her situation weighed upon her.

Half an hour passed before her mother finally spoke. "There are some things you need to know about your Aunt Babette before we arrive in Shreveport. Important things."

"Like what?" Annie asked, allowing her intrigue to get the better of her annoyance at being dragged away from Robbie.

"Your aunt ain't like us," Emmylou said. "She holds with some wild beliefs. You would do well not to listen to her ramblings during our time there."

"Is that why you don't talk to her?"

"Your aunt and I fell out many years before you were born. If she weren't likely on her deathbed, I would not be going to see her now. Babette is a tortured soul who has strayed far from the path."

"What does that mean?"

"You'll find out soon enough," Emmylou said. "You should be mindful not to put too much stock in what you see and hear at your aunt's house. I wouldn't say that she's suffering from madness, but I also wouldn't say she's entirely sane. Even when we were growing up, she was possessed with dangerous ideas and dark thoughts."

"Like what?" Annie sat up straight. She felt a tingle of unease. If her mother thought Babette to be bad, how awful must she be? Emmylou was hardly a pillar of the community.

"Never you mind. I've gone and said more than I should. If I could've left you back at the cabin while I deal with this, I would have."

"I could have stayed." Annie sensed an opportunity missed, but maybe it wasn't too late. "I'm almost eighteen. I'm not a child anymore."

"Is that why you disobeyed me last night and went to meet a boy? Heaven knows what you got up to with him."

"I didn't get up to nothing." And there it was. Annie had been expecting her mother to bring this up and was surprised it had taken so long. The irony of it was that her mother was basing her daughter's lack of maturity on the fact that Annie wanted to lead her own life. "Why don't you trust me?"

"How can I trust a girl who won't listen to a word I say?" Emmylou glanced sideways, her eyes nothing more than slits, before looking back at the road ahead. "And don't you tell me that nothing happened last night because I don't believe a word of it. I saw that glow on your face when you came in."

"We just kissed, that's all." The words slipped out before Annie realized what she'd done. She smacked her lips shut, surprised at her own indiscretion.

"Now the truth comes out."

"It was just a peck on the cheek."

"This is precisely why I can't leave you home. You'd be inviting that boy over the moment I was out of sight. You'd probably be pregnant by the time I got back."

"Mom! For goodness' sake. What's wrong with me having a boyfriend?"

"You poor child. He doesn't want you, at least not for his girl-friend. There's only one thing young men like him want from folk like us, and the sooner you learn that the better."

"You're saying that he can't like me for who I am?" Annie felt the anger boiling up inside of her, but she bit her lip and swal-lowed it. The last thing she wanted was a screaming match with her mother in the car's confined space.

"I'm saying that you're naïve. You've led a sheltered life. It's my fault for not telling you about this stuff earlier, but there's not much I can do about that now." Emmylou shook her head. "The only way I can protect you, is to keep you close."

"And what if I don't want to be kept close? What if I want to see Robbie Decker? Why can't you let me make my own mistakes?" Annie's lip trembled. She felt the walls of her mother's stifling love closing in around her, pressing close on all sides and denying her the life she so desperately wanted. Was it even love that drove her mother? Annie wasn't sure, but she suspected that somewhere, deep down, her mother harbored a desperate fear of Annie striking out on her own and finding happiness, because then she would be forced to confront her own abject failures in life.

# TWENTY-EIGHT

THEY SPENT the next ninety minutes riding in silence. Annie fell into a depressed funk. Was her mother ever going to let her go? The most annoying part of it was that she could have stayed back at the cabin. It was only her mother's emotionally suffocating attitude and lack of trust that had prevented her from staying home and further fanning the flames of her fledgling relationship with Robbie. It was all so unfair. Emmylou, for her part, appeared to sense her daughter's frustration and made no attempt at conversation.

As they approached the northern part of the state and drew closer to Shreveport, the sky darkened and soon they were amid a mighty thunderstorm. Emmylou slowed the car, hunched over the steering wheel, and peered through the windshield as rain lashed across the glass, the aging wipers unable to keep up with the torrent. The dreadful weather further deepened Annie's foul mood. She folded her arms in the passenger seat and tried not to think about the relationship she was riding away from.

After a longer journey than she expected, they finally arrived at Babette's shotgun house on the outskirts of Shreveport. It was still raining, but the downpour had eased up enough for Annie to see a strange sight as they approached the property. Attached to the railings that skirted the front porch, was a large hand-painted sign that provided her first clue regarding the odd behavior her mother had warned Annie about. She leaned forward and read the sign.

*Tarot Readings. Palmistry.*
*Tea Leaves. Love Potions.*
*All are welcome. No appointment necessary.*

Annie stared at the words with a mix of disbelief and surprise. Aunt Babette, it appeared, was a fortune teller. Was this what her mother was so worried about? It was odd, but innocuous. Hardly something that would lead her astray. But when they pulled up and approached the house, Annie saw something else. On the front door, hanging on a nail, was a rusting pentagram made of metal.

Her mother lifted the welcome mat to reveal a key. She unlocked the door, pushing it inward with a creak of rusty hinges. Annie was relieved to step inside, away from the pentagram. It was creepy, and she didn't like it. The shotgun cabin's interior, however, was not much better.

It was gloomy and dark inside the house. Curtains were drawn across the front windows. The only illumination came from a floor lamp sitting against the opposite wall. A round table sat in the middle of the room, covered by a black cloth. Upon the table stood a crystal ball. A set of tarot cards lay upon a green velvet cloth next to a candle which had burned halfway down, the wax dripping onto the table and hardening there. A painting dominated the far wall, a depiction of a goat-headed man sitting cross-legged with a pentagram on his chest and his hand raised. It reminded Annie of a religious painting, yet the subject was anything but. She resisted the urge to run back to the car, hop in, and lock the door. Instead, she looked around, wondering where her aunt was.

"Emmylou." A disembodied voice floated out of the gloom. It was thin and croaky, full of phlegm. "Is that you?"

"Yes." Annie's mother answered. "It's me."

There was a groaning sound, a shuffle of feet, and then a hunched figure appeared from the darkness across the room. Now that Annie looked closer, she saw the outline of an easy chair in the corner. Her aunt had been sitting there the whole time, even though Annie had thought the room empty.

"Who's this?" Aunt Babette shuffled forward, leaning heavily on a cane made of carved ash. "You must be Annie. I've wanted to meet you for so long."

Annie recoiled as her aunt drew closer. She couldn't have been much older than her mother, but she looked ancient. Whatever disease was ravaging Aunt Babette's body had caved in upon itself and left her a walking husk, leathery skin pulled taut over wasted muscle and brittle bones. Her hair, which was as long as Annie's own, fell over her shoulders and down her back in a cascade of white. "Nice to meet you," Annie said, forcing the words out.

Babette raised an arm, reaching toward Annie, but at that moment a cough wracked her body. She shuddered and wheezed, leaning heavily on the cane.

Emmylou stepped around Annie and took her sister by the shoulders. "Come along, Babette, let's get you back to your chair, and then I'll make you a cup of tea." Emmylou led her sister back across the room.

After she sat down, she looked at Annie. "I'm glad you're here, girl. I wasn't sure your mother would bring you."

"I'm pleased to meet you too, Aunt Babette," Annie lied. "My mother has told me so much about you."

"Don't fib, girl." Aunt Babette leaned her cane against the side of the chair and rested her head back with obvious relief. "Your mother's hardly spoken of me, I'll wager, and anything she said was surely not good."

"There's no need to talk like that," Emmylou said. "I've not spoken ill of you, regardless of what you think. Besides, you know very well the reason we haven't spoken in so long."

"I know," Aunt Babette replied. "But what we did, we did together, and you can't hide from that."

"What we did was wrong. A mistake, at least on my part."

"What he did was wrong."

"That's enough." Emmylou shot her sister an angry glance. "Not in front of Annie."

"You haven't told her." Aunt Babette stared past her sister toward Annie, her face folding into a look of sadness. "All these years, and she doesn't know the truth."

# TWENTY-NINE

LATER THAT DAY, when her aunt was resting in her bedroom at the back of the house, laying under the covers with pillows propping her head up, Annie asked her mother about the cryptic comment she had overheard earlier.

"What was Aunt Babette talking about when she said I didn't know the truth?" Annie watched her mother preparing the evening meal, a stew with beef, potatoes, and vegetables.

"Never you mind about that," Emmylou said. "Your aunt was rambling, that's all."

"It didn't sound like she was rambling." Annie had seen the look on her mother's face when Aunt Babette spoke. "What happened between the two of you?"

"I said leave it alone. What happened is in the past, and it's between me and Babette. I don't have to explain myself to you."

"I'm not asking you to explain yourself, but if there's something you're not telling me, I want to know. Is it to do with dad?"

"Babette is a sick woman. The fever has rotted her brain." Emmylou continued chopping vegetables and throwing them into a large pot on the stove. "Now leave me alone so that I can make dinner, your aunt needs to eat to keep her strength up."

"Why won't you tell me?" Annie asked, desperate to know the truth.

"Stop this, right now." Emmylou whirled upon her daughter, chopping knife in hand. Her eyes were wild with anger. She waved the knife. "Don't you dare talk back at me."

"Okay. Fine." Annie knew when to back off. Her mother had a wicked temper and the last thing she wanted to do was start yet another screaming match. Especially here, in a strange environment, with a family member who was practically a stranger in the next room. "I'm sorry."

"As you should be." Emmylou Doucet turned back to the stove and carried on preparing the ingredients for her stew. After a while, possibly fed up with Annie lingering in the kitchen, she turned back to her daughter. "Why don't you go and check on your aunt and make sure she's okay. She'll need to take her medicine soon anyway, so I don't want her falling asleep."

Annie nodded and retreated from the kitchen. The shotgun house was laid out with all the rooms in a row, starting with the living room at the front, then the kitchen, the front bedroom where Annie and her mother would sleep, and finally her aunt's bedroom at the rear. The house derived its architectural name from the fact that you could open all the doors and if you fired a shotgun, the blast would pass all the way through the building and out of the back door without hitting an obstruction. It was a clever way to pass a breeze through the house and keep it cool during the stifling Louisiana summer. Right now, all the doors stood open, but when they had arrived, the rooms were oppressive and hot. Annie wondered how long it had been since a breeze touched the interior of this building before their arrival earlier that day.

Annie passed through the front bedroom and into the back one. Aunt Babette was awake, sitting up in bed with a book on her lap. When Annie entered, she looked up.

"Your mother sent you away, huh?" A thin smile touched the woman's face.

"Something like that." Annie edged toward the bed. Now that

she had gotten used to her aunt's appearance, she wasn't as afraid of her anymore. She wanted to ask her aunt about the cryptic comment but having been rebuked once already, was hesitant to bring the subject up again.

Aunt Babette sensed this. She sucked in a rattling breath and spoke, her voice low and rasping. "You want to know what happened between me and your mother."

Annie nodded. She was afraid to speak lest her mother overhear and grow angry yet again.

"I'll tell you, all in good time." Her aunt pushed herself up with considerable effort and sank back with her head against the wall. "Now is not that time though. There are things that you don't know about our family. Secrets. Your mother won't tell you, but you'll find out soon enough."

"Tell me now," Annie whispered, glancing over her shoulder to make sure that Emmylou was nowhere in sight. "I want to know."

"No." Her aunt almost shouted the word despite her frail condition. "It can wait."

"But-"

"No buts. I can see that you are your mother's daughter. You have that same look in your eyes when you talk back. When the time is right, you shall know the truth. Until then, you are going to have to wait. Do you understand?"

"Yes." Annie nodded, disappointed. She didn't understand, but she also knew she wouldn't get anywhere. Not today. She turned to leave, but then remembered her mother's instructions. "Mama says you have to take your medicine."

"She does, huh?" Aunt Babette raised an eyebrow. "She's only been here for one afternoon and she's already lording it over the place."

"I'm just passing on the message," Annie said.

"I know." Her aunt raised a bony finger and pointed toward the nightstand. "There's a pill bottle in the drawer. Get two pills and give them to me, then get me a glass of water."

Annie went to the kitchen and poured a glass of water, then

returned. She opened the drawer and shook two small blue tablets from the pill bottle, then passed them to her aunt, along with the water. Her chore complete, Annie turned to leave.

Aunt Babette reached out with surprising speed and grabbed her niece's arm, preventing her from departing. Her fingernails dug into Annie's skin. "Listen to me, child. Whatever your mother says about me, it isn't true. I loved her. I still do. Anything I did was to help her."

Annie stood frozen in place for a moment, unsure how to react. Then she leaned close to her aunt. "What did you do?"

Her aunt smiled to reveal yellowed teeth and cracked lips. "In time, my child. In time."

# THIRTY

THE NEXT WEEK passed at a snail's pace. Babette was growing weaker by the day, her illness spreading at an alarming rate. On the third day she had taken entirely to her bed. Annie spent most of her time either sitting with her aunt in the shotgun's cramped bedroom or helping her mother prepare meals, clean, and wash bedsheets. She tried to extract information from her aunt on several occasions, but to no avail. Babette remained tight-lipped regarding what had transpired so many years ago. Annie didn't have the nerve to ask her mother and hoped that Aunt Babette would eventually capitulate and tell Annie what she wanted to know.

On the Friday following their arrival in Shreveport, the shotgun received its one and only visitor. It was the landlord, looking for his monthly rent. Annie lingered in the bedroom doorway and listened to her mother conversing with him. Aunt Babette had, apparently, fallen behind in her monthly payments, no doubt because she was not offering tarot readings or fortunes anymore. Her mother listened to the landlord's demands and then gave him a wad of cash that covered half the amount due and informed him that this was all Babette had set aside. The landlord was not happy and threatened to return the following week with eviction papers.

If Emmylou Doucet cared about this turn of events, she did not show it, and given Babette's rapid decline, Annie doubted there would be anyone to serve papers to by the following week.

Annie's hunch proved correct.

By the next Wednesday, her aunt was fading. Where she had been lucid when they had arrived, she now spent most of her time in a feverish state, her grip on reality slipping away. It was during one of her increasingly brief periods of awareness that Annie finally received the answer she was looking for.

Emmylou Doucet had taken their beat-up old car and driven to a convenience store to pick up groceries. Annie was left alone with her aunt and took up her usual station sitting on a dining room chair that had been placed next to the bed. No sooner had her mother departed than Babette heaved herself into a semi-upright position with much exertion. For a moment she said nothing, drawing in deep wheezing breaths, but then she spoke.

"What I'm about to tell you, you must not repeat."

Annie nodded. "I understand." She felt a tingle of anticipation.

"And you must especially keep this a secret from your mother." Babette turned her head to meet her niece's gaze. "This is between me and you."

Again, Annie nodded. She pulled the chair closer to the bed and leaned in toward her aunt so that she would not miss any words.

"Has your mother told you anything about how you were born?" Babette coughed, the sound hollow and dry. "Has she ever mentioned your father?"

"Not really." Annie wondered what that had to do with anything. "Only that he died in a hunting accident. A gator attacked him."

"That he was. But whether it was an accident, I really don't know." A thin smile touched Babette's lips. "Your father was not a nice man. Emmylou met him two years before you were born, and they dated for a while. But I never liked him."

"You don't think my father's death was accidental?" Annie

could hardly believe what she was hearing. Her mother had mentioned none of this.

"Like I said, I have no idea. All I know is that your father led your mother on and got her pregnant, then refused to accept responsibility. She wanted him to marry her. She was so in love. But he would have none of it. When he found out she was pregnant with you he hightailed it out of there."

"What does that have to do with his accident?" Annie asked.

"After he left her, your mother was beside herself. That's when she came to me for help." Babette licked her lips and motioned for Annie to pass her the glass of water sitting on her nightstand. She drank deeply and then handed the glass back.

"What did she ask you to do?"

"She asked me to curse him." Babette laughed, but it was barely more than a thin cackle. "So that's what I did, with her help."

"You cursed him?" Annie didn't understand.

"We did. Emmylou was so angry and afraid. She felt used. She knew I had the gift, so she came to me. She asked me to use it on Clay Doucet, your father."

"The gift?" Annie leaned closer, thinking perhaps she had misheard her aunt. "What's the gift?"

"Witchcraft. If you don't have the gift, it won't work."

"There's no such thing as witchcraft." Annie wondered if the fever was addling her aunt's mind. "It's not real."

"You don't believe in witchcraft? Well, you should. The magic is strong in you. As strong as it was in me when I was young. I can feel it like a pent-up tide. Your mother had a touch of it too, but not like us. That's why she came to me. That's why we did it together."

"What did you do together?" Annie felt a tingle of dread.

"We placed a hex on your father. Cursed him to never succeed, for bad luck to hound him, night and day. It would appear we went too far. A few weeks after we placed the curse, the accident happened. He was in the swamps pulling a gator into his boat. He thought it was dead, but it wasn't. It ripped his arm clean off at the shoulder. He bled out before they could get him back to civilization."

Annie felt the color drain from her face. She knew an alligator had killed her father but had never heard the full story. That her mother and aunt believed it resulted from a curse placed upon him surprised and frightened her. "You really think witchcraft caused his death?"

"Maybe. Maybe not. No one will ever know. Even so, your mother swore off the supernatural after that. She wanted nothing to do with witchcraft, and when I refused to give it up, we fell out. We didn't speak for almost two decades. I'm surprised that she came here now."

"She's still your sister. And I find it hard to believe that you have hexed my father to death, whatever the two of you may think. This is the twentieth century, not the Middle Ages."

"You believe what you want, girl. You'll find out the truth of what lays within you soon enough." Aunt Babette settled back down into the bed and closed her eyes with an audible sigh. "You have the gift. Your mother passed it on. I only hope you handle your powers better than we did."

# THIRTY-ONE

BABETTE DIED THE NEXT DAY. There was no drama, no fuss. She merely slipped away in her sleep during the afternoon hours. If Emmylou Doucet felt any sorrow at her sister's passing, she did not show it. She watched Babette leave the shotgun for the last time in a black bag atop a gurney and then turned back to the house and retreated inside as if nothing had happened.

Annie watched the ambulance drive away, torn between feelings of relief and sorrow. She hadn't known her aunt well, but knowing she was out there, another kindred spirit, was comforting. Now it was just the two of them. If anything happened to her mother, she would be alone.

They spent the next three days going through her aunt's possessions. They cleared the living room by the end of the first day. They placed the crystal ball, tarot cards, and other fortune telling paraphernalia into a box which they sealed with packing tape and stacked near the front door. They split up on the second day. Emmylou handled the kitchen. Annie took the bedrooms. She stripped her aunt's bed and pushed the linens into a black trash bag, which she then deposited outside of the back door next to the trash can. Three more bags followed. Items not worth saving, including her aunt's clothes. Once the closet was bare of all but a few empty wire hangers, Annie emptied the nightstand. She dragged it out to the curb along with the other furniture not worth selling, then returned to the shotgun and went to work on the bed, dragging the mattress aside and then the box spring. When she got down to the bed frame, she made a discovery.

Her aunt had tucked a cardboard box under the bed. Upon it, written in a shaky hand, was her name. She kneeled down and opened it. Inside was a leather-bound volume, several inches thick, with gilt-edged pages. On top of this was a note in the same shaky hand.

*Annie, this is for you.*
*It is your heritage.*
*You will know what to do with it,*
*but you must keep it hidden.*
*Your mother will not understand.*

Annie lifted the book out and examined it. There was no title on the front, no sign of what lay within. She glanced toward the bedroom door. Her mother was still in the kitchen. She could hear her clattering around. Annie opened the book. Inside were strange passages written in flowing lettering. And there were drawings. Strange symbols and sketches of plants and animals. At first Annie thought it was an old textbook. But then she realized what she held in her hands. This was her aunt's spell book.

She almost dropped it in revulsion.

This was the very book that had cursed her father and killed him.

She slammed the volume and placed it on the floor, unsure what to do. The book frightened her, yet her aunt had wanted her to have it. And even though she didn't believe in the supernatural, she couldn't deny the strange sense of power she felt when she handled it. It was like a magnetic attraction that pulled them together even as she wanted to push the book far away. Which meant she could not let her mother see it.

She scooped up the book and climbed to her feet before hurrying into the other bedroom. She unzipped her bag and pulled the clothes out, then placed the book inside, careful not to damage its frail bindings. Then she placed the clothes back on top and pushed them around it. When she heaved the backpack onto the floor it was much heavier, but it was unlikely that her mother would notice even if she picked it up. That done, Annie went back into her aunt's bedroom and ripped up the note, before discarding it in a trash bag along with the flattened box. And just in the nick of time. When she turned around, her mother was standing in the doorway.

"Aren't you finished in here yet?"

"Almost," Annie said. She picked up the trash bag that contained the note and went to the rear door. She placed the bag along with the others next to the trash and returned to the bedroom. "I've emptied the closet already. There's nothing left except the bed."

"Good." Her mother nodded. "Let's get it to the curb and then we can load the car. I want to be out of here first thing in the morning."

# THIRTY-TWO

## BACK IN THE LIBRARY

IN AN INSTANT, the scene faded, and Decker found himself back in the library. He stumbled and reached out, leaning on the reading table for support. The frequent changes of location as they followed Annie Doucet to the fair, then home, and finally to Babette's house had left him feeling unsteady on his feet. Almost like he was suffering from vertigo, although he knew that wasn't the case. He wondered if it was a side effect of whatever supernatural power the ghost was using to move them between locations.

As the strange sensation faded, his thoughts turned to the last place they had visited. Aunt Babette had given the young Annie Doucet a book. Decker recognized that book all too well, because he had found it in the older Annie's cabin during his investigation after the wolf version of her rampaged through the high school and tried to kill Nancy's daughter. It was the spell book she had used to transform from human to beast.

Right now, it was stored in the evidence locker at the Wolf Haven sheriff's office. Assuming Chad, who had taken over Decker's job, hadn't disposed of it.

"That's how she learned to turn into the loup-garou," he said. "Annie Doucet's aunt was a witch."

"Yes. She gave Annie the book," replied the ghost. "Although I'm sure she didn't expect her niece to use it for such dark magic."

"What does any of this have to do with my father?"

"We haven't gotten that far yet."

"Then what are we waiting for?" Decker had often wondered about Annie Doucet, and how she ended up the way she did. All that pent up rage must have come from somewhere, and he found it hard to believe she just erupted and became a killer because the town was taking her land, bad as that was. For her to turn into the beast and kill so many people in such a brutal fashion—including Taylor's teenage boyfriend, Jake, who had done nothing to earn such a terrible end—her heart must already have been hardened. "Show me the rest."

"As you wish." The ghost opened the book again. Then they were back in the past once more.

# THIRTY-THREE

## WOLF HAVEN, AUGUST 1972

ANNIE and her mother returned home the next day. They left early and arrived in Wolf Haven late in the afternoon. Annie was excited to reconnect with Robbie, but she dared not bring the subject up. Annie could only imagine the argument that would ensue if she tried to leave so soon after getting back. Instead, resigned to the reality of her situation, Annie helped her mother lug the boxes containing her aunt's possessions, or at least those which they had kept, into the cabin. They stacked the boxes in the cramped front room. Annie didn't care about most of the items taken from her aunt's house, but she couldn't help being curious about the contents of one particular box, within which lay the crystal ball and tarot cards. When she went near the box however, her mother swiftly intervened.

"You stay away from that box, young lady." Emmylou watched her with beady eyes. "That fortune telling mumbo-jumbo is dangerous."

That settled it. Annie would not be exploring her aunt's legacy anytime soon. With one exception. Her mother did not know about the spell book hidden at the bottom of her travel bag. Annie went to her room and once there, she opened her bag and delved inside for the book, throwing her clothes across the bed. She went to the door and peeked out, but her mother was nowhere to be seen, most likely unpacking her own bag in the other bedroom. Satisfied that she wouldn't be disturbed, Annie went back to the bed and jumped up on it, sitting with her back against the wall and a pillow propped behind her. She leaned the book on her knees and opened it up. She spent the next two hours engrossed in the strange writings contained within the volume and couldn't help wondering why her aunt deemed it so important to pass on to her. The book's contents, at first glance, appeared nonsensical. They were also dark. There were no love potions, or incantations that would grant her fame and wealth. Instead, the book leaned in a more ominous direction. There were spells for revenge and for death. There were spells to bring misfortune, from financial to personal, or render impotence and sickness. Toward the back she found the most disturbing material. Spells to conjure demons and wake the dead, or transform oneself into a beast. She did not linger on these, instead closing the book and sitting with it on her lap for a while, her head filled with the possibilities contained within. Did her aunt really believe that the words within the old leather-bound volume possessed the ability to influence lives and kill? The rational side of Annie's mind told her it was impossible, yet she wasn't sure. She could feel the book's power like a subtle hum that vibrated through her body and somewhere deep within, she knew it was calling to her.

# THIRTY-FOUR

ANNIE REMAINED imprisoned inside the cabin for the rest of that day and a good portion of the next. It wasn't until the following afternoon that she escaped her mother's watchful gaze. They had been away for almost two weeks and had barely any groceries in the house. This provided a valid excuse for Annie to head into town. She took her bicycle and pedaled toward Wolf Haven as fast as she could, tearing along at a reckless pace to glean as many minutes of freedom as possible. Her mother would be watching for her return, and that didn't leave much time to find Robbie and tell him that she was back. Not that he even knew she had gone anywhere since there was no way for her to get a message to him prior to their departure for Shreveport. She could only hope that her prolonged absence hadn't been taken as disinterest. Luckily, she knew where he would be. It was Friday afternoon, which meant he would be at football practice. School was starting the following Monday, but the Wolf Haven Wildcats would already be hard at work preparing for the upcoming Fall football season.

When she reached town, Annie headed directly to the high school and propped her bike against the back of the bleachers before making her way to a bench a few rows up. She couldn't stay until practice finished, but maybe she could at least catch Robbie's eye and sneak a few words with him on the sideline during a break.

The team was already on the field, in the middle of warm-ups. Travis Cox was lobbing fast balls down the field to a sprinting wide receiver who leaped in the air and dragged them down with ease. There were only a few people in the stands, all of them students. There was only one other person in Annie's row, an attractive girl she did not recognize who sported a white T-shirt with the words Wildcat Cheer Squad across the front of it. When Annie sat down, she turned and smiled.

"Aren't they great," she said, eyeing the players. "Much better than my last school. Those guys couldn't catch a ball if it had glue on it."

"I really don't know that much about football," Annie said, wondering why a cheerleader was talking to her. In the hierarchy of senior high, cheerleaders were the top of the pile, and Annie was the bottom. "You must be new in town."

"My mom's the new English teacher. We moved here a few weeks ago. It's such a great place, everyone is so friendly."

"Sure. Friendly." Annie marveled at how easy it was for some people to fit in. If only Annie could move to a new town, then maybe she would be accepted too. Not that it would ever happen. Her mother would never leave the cabin. Even the brief stay outside Shreveport had stretched Emmylou Doucet's nerves to breaking point.

"I'm Lily."

"Annie."

"Pleased to meet you, Annie."

"You too." Annie eyed the T-shirt. "You must have tried out for the squad."

"I did. It was so much fun. Have you ever tried out?"

Annie found herself momentarily speechless. That this girl, slim and attractive, with perfect skin and flowing hair, could believe that Annie, scrawny, unliked, and constantly ridiculed, would ever have the nerve to show up at cheerleading tryouts, was unbelievable. She felt a stab of panic as she realized that Lily was waiting for a reply. She stumbled to find the right words, afraid to lose this momentary camaraderie with the new girl. Before she could speak however, reality intruded in the form of Karen Leroux and her gaggle of toady friends, who appeared from the parking lot and started up the bleacher's steps.

"Well, if it isn't Swampy Annie," Karen said as she reached their row and started along it. "You're looking as bedraggled as ever. Whatever gave you the idea to come here? Shouldn't you be feeding the alligators or something?"

"I'm not doing anything wrong," Annie said, a tremble in her voice. "I'm just watching football practice."

"You're watching the boys, more like." Karen's lips curled up into a vicious smile. "Or one boy in particular."

Annie felt her face redden. "I just stopped on the way into town to pick up groceries, that's all. It's my school too."

"We might allow you into class, but that doesn't make it your school. What do you ever contribute? You're not a cheerleader. You're not on the school Council. You're not even one of those geeky band girls. You're a nobody, and nobody likes you."

Annie didn't know what to say. She wished she were any of those things, but even if she found the nerve to join a social activity, she knew girls like Karen would never accept her.

As if to prove this, Karen threw one more jab as she and her entourage pushed past Annie and took a seat next to Lily. "Why don't you run along and get your groceries, swamp girl. No one wants you here."

Lily had been quiet throughout the exchange so far, but now she fixed Karen with a withering stare. "Why don't you just let her be, she's not doing any harm."

Karen looked momentarily shocked at this act of sedition from one of her own. "You're new to the school, Lily, so I'll let it pass this time, but you should really think about who you want to be associated with."

Lily was unfazed. She reached over and touched Annie's knee. "You stay as long as you want, okay?"

"Yes, you stay just as long as you want," Karen said, mimicking Lily's voice. "Maybe we can even make you head of the cheerleading squad."

"Karen, you don't need to be so mean." Lily was uncomfortable.

"But I really do. You're forgetting this is Swampy Annie. She was born to be the butt of our jokes. Isn't that right, Swampy?"

Annie felt herself choking up. She didn't know what to say. She could see Robbie down on the field, catching balls and sprinting about. She wished he would look her way so she could at least wave to him and let him know that she was back, but he was engrossed in practice. She stood up, realizing that staying any longer would only result in more taunting.

Lily glanced toward her. "Don't let these girls drive you away. If you want to stay and watch football practice, you do that."

"It's okay," Annie said. "I need to get back home, anyway. Mama will wonder where I got to."

"See, she knows her place," Karen said, with a look of smug satisfaction. "Bye-bye, Swampy. Don't let a gator get you on the way home, like it did your daddy."

Annie felt the tears coming. She didn't want to cry in front of Karen and give her the satisfaction. She also didn't want to cry in front of Lily, but for different reasons. Without saying another word, she turned and fled the bleachers.

# THIRTY-FIVE

ANNIE WAS STILL upset when she arrived back at the cabin over an hour later. She dropped her bike to the ground near the front steps and heaved the bags of groceries inside, depositing them in the kitchen. That done she turned and made her way to her bedroom. Thankfully, her mother, apparently worn out from the trip to Shreveport, was sequestered in her own bedroom. Annie could hear her deep snores as she took an afternoon nap and was grateful for small mercies. The last thing she wanted was another questioning regarding the time she'd taken to purchase the week's provisions.

Still trembling from the abuse at the hands of Karen Leroux, Annie closed her bedroom door and flopped down on the bed. She wondered why people were so mean. It wasn't like she had ever done anything to any of those girls. It wasn't even that she had gone on a date with Robbie. They had been picking on her ever since middle school. Thinking of Robbie made her tear up all over again. She'd been looking forward to seeing him and even hoped he might trot to the sideline to talk to her. In reality, he hadn't even noticed her. Perhaps if she'd stayed longer things would've been different, but Karen had made sure that would not happen. She wished that for once Karen could get a taste of her own medicine. Maybe then she wouldn't be so quick to dole out the insults.

That was when Annie remembered the spell book.

She rolled over on the bed and lay on her back looking up at the ceiling, a strange feeling overcoming her. She no longer felt like crying. Now she felt like getting even. There were incantations in that book that would certainly do the trick. Except that it felt foolish to pin her hopes on such superstitious mumbo-jumbo. But her aunt had believed in it. She said that Annie had the gift, whatever that was. But Annie thought she knew what it was, because she'd felt it when she'd held the book in her lap the previous evening. It was like a door opening within her. A switch being turned on. The book had reacted to Annie's touch. It had come alive in her hands.

Annie rolled over and hung off the edge of the bed, reaching underneath the mattress for the place where she'd stashed the spell book to prevent her mother from finding it. She pulled it out and scooted into a sitting position with her back against the wall, just like she had done the day before.

The book felt warm in her hands, the gentle heat surprising and comforting at the same time. She opened the ancient tome, and felt the pages rejoice as she turned them. After a moment, she came to one particular page and smiled. This would be perfect. Not too subtle, but not enough to cause her nemesis permanent damage. She began to read, and as she did so the flowery, scrolling text seemed to come alive under her gaze. She would need to collect some items, but she had the entire weekend to do that. School started again on Monday, and then Karen would discover the cost of messing with Annie Doucet.

# THIRTY-SIX

THE WEEKEND PASSED in a blur of chores. Saturday was spent dragging rugs out onto the back deck that overlooked the swamp and beating the dust from them with a stick. A vacuum cleaner would be easier, but this was a luxury they did not possess. The floors were swept, and cobwebs pulled from the corners of the ceiling with a broom. On Sunday they placed rat traps in the crawlspace beneath the cabin and up in the attic. In the afternoon Annie chopped logs and stacked them in the woodshed in anticipation of the approaching winter. Even in Louisiana it could get cold in December and January, and the cabin had no other form of heat. This yearly Fall prep usually happened around October, but this year her mother moved the annual event up a few months, no doubt to keep her daughter busy and stop Annie getting any ideas in her head about seeing Robbie.

Despite all this, Annie still found time to gather the items required to bring about the downfall of Karen Leroux. By Monday morning, as she cycled to school, Annie was in a state of nervous excitement. In her bag was a small doll fashioned from the root of a Tupelo tree that had fallen at the edge of the swamp. Around the rough piece of wood, she'd wrapped loops of twine. A lump of coal, lashed to the root with that same twine, served as the doll's head. The effigy, known as a Poppet, according to the spell book, served as a crude representation of Karen Leroux. If the incantation she'd muttered over the dark object worked, she would have her revenge. She just needed to bide her time.

But there were other things on Annie's mind, not least of which was Robbie Decker. She still hadn't connected with him since their kiss at the fair and she was eager to rekindle their dormant relationship. The first thing she did after arriving at school was go to her locker and deposit her bag, removing the doll and slipping it into her pocket before heading to homeroom. Robbie would not be there because he was not in her class, but she still looked for him in the corridors as she went about her morning routine. It wasn't until later that she would run into him, as the bell rang to signify the end of second period. She was leaving algebra II, and there he was, stepping into the hallway two classrooms down.

Her heart skipped a beat.

She started toward him giddy with excitement, was about to call his name, but then he turned back toward the door. He smiled, but not at Annie. He hadn't even noticed her. The gesture of warm affection wasn't meant for her, but for Lily, who now stepped into the corridor next to him. She wound an arm around his waist, and he pulled her tight. Their lips met in a brief kiss and then they were walking away in the other direction, soon to be lost in the milling throng of students.

Annie stood frozen in the corridor, disappointment laying like a rock in her stomach. She barely noticed as people weaved around her, some shooting her frustrated glares as they stepped out of her way.

Then she heard a snigger of laughter.

She turned to find Travis Cox standing behind her. Next to him, her arm on his shoulder, was Karen Leroux.

"Aw. Isn't young love just so special." Travis grinned, the gesture creasing his face into a sarcastic mask.

"I bet Robbie's over the moon that Swampy Annie is crushing on him." Now it was Karen's turn to laugh, the sound mirthless and cruel. "Did you think he liked you just because you went to the fair together?"

"He did like me," Annie replied, unwilling to admit that there could be any other explanation for their date, at least to Karen. "We kissed."

This was greeted with a fresh burst of laughter.

"More like you tried to kiss him. He told us all about it," Karen said. "Did you actually believe he could like someone who lives in a swamp? I bet you thought he was going to go steady with you. Take you to the movies on Saturday nights. Did you think he'd show you off at the Kickoff Kegger on Friday night? His queen of the swamps."

Annie flinched, felt her throat tighten. The Kickoff Kegger was held every year after the first football game of the season. It wasn't an official event, but rather a raucous gathering in a woodland clearing outside of town. While not sanctioned by the school, and even frowned upon by some, it was generally accepted as a rite of passage that had been going on for over a quarter century. To that end, most of the parents involved looked the other way–mainly because many of them had either attended in their own youth or desperately wanted to. And if you weren't part of the top echelon of the school hierarchy-or more accurately, associated with the football team-you were not invited.

"Poor thing," Karen cooed, shaking her head. "Sad, deluded, Swampy Annie."

"Leave me alone," Annie said through clenched jaws.

"With pleasure," Travis replied. "Even trigonometry class is better than talking to you."

"We can actually smell the swamp on your clothes. It's gross." Karen took Travis's hand and they started toward their next class. As they went Karen bumped a shoulder into Annie, pushing her aside.

Annie gritted her teeth, was about to say something else, but then she realized that this was the opportunity she'd been waiting for. She reached into her pocket and took out the doll.

Then she stepped up behind Karen and slipped the doll into her bag.

"Hey. What are you doing, bitch?" Karen exclaimed, sensing Annie close behind her.

"Nothing," Annie replied. She slowed and let Travis and Karen pull ahead, then hurried to her own class, thoughts of Karen's downfall swirling in her mind.

# THIRTY-SEVEN

ANNIE SAT through the last class of the morning wrapped in a sense of achievement she'd never felt before. It was done. The Poppet had been placed upon the person of her victim, which was what the spell book demanded. Now, apparently, all she had to do was wait for the doll to do its job. So far, though, she had no proof that the spell had worked. She didn't share any classes with Karen, so if the doll had done its job, she would not know until lunch.

When lunchtime rolled around however, Annie was disheartened to see Karen strolling into the cafeteria without a care in the world, Travis by her side as usual. She joked and laughed as she passed Annie, who was already seated with her food tray on the table in front of her. If Karen noticed Annie, she did not register it, but merely joined the back of the line to get her own lunch.

Annie watched the line inch forward out of the corner of her eye, while simultaneously playing with her food with a fork. The Monday menu of meatloaf, carrot sticks, and mashed potato was not her favorite. Even on a good day she would be slow to eat the bland fare, looking forward only to the square of raisin bread provided as a dessert. This particular Monday was worse than most, mainly thanks to Karen and Travis. Not to mention Robbie, who occupied a seat several tables away, his attention still fixed on Lily. That her heart was breaking was compounded by the lack of progress in giving Karen her comeuppance. She wondered if the doll was nothing more than a useless twig wrapped in some old twine, rather than a potent symbol of witchcraft. The book had been specific on what to do, and how to do it, but if any ill luck had befallen her nemesis, Annie had yet to see it. She felt foolish for believing that such things as witchcraft existed. She should never have listened to her crazy aunt, whose mind was probably addled by disease and her own imminent demise. The spell book was probably nothing more than a curiosity penned in a time when superstition dictated the everyday lives of the population. That her aunt genuinely believed some magical power lurked within its pages said more about her aunt's obvious madness than it did about the existence of the supernatural. Annie resigned herself to the fact that her efforts had been for naught. It was all a stupid fantasy born out of a desire for revenge that she could never fulfill. Even so, when Karen strolled past her table, tray in hand, with Travis trailing behind, Annie couldn't help entertaining a fleeting thought of the precocious cheerleader falling flat on her face in front of everyone. A suitably embarrassing mishap for a girl who prided herself on presenting a prim and proper appearance. But it was all a fantasy. Karen was past the table now and heading toward her own seat. Another moment and she would be happily delving into her plate of meatloaf, blissfully unaware of the fate she had avoided.

Except that wasn't what happened.

No sooner had Karen passed by Annie than she stumbled, lurching forward like some invisible hand had pushed her in the back. She let out a surprised screech and tried to steady herself, the tray of food flipping from her hands in the process and clattering to the floor. For a moment it looked like she would regain her balance, but then she was tumbling forward into the tray of waiting food that had somehow landed upright on the floor. As she fell, her skirt lifted as if tugged by a fleeting breeze, the fabric flapping around her waist to reveal a pair of red panties trimmed in lace. Then she was on the floor, skirt bunched around her waist, buttocks on display for the entire room to see. When she sat up, meatloaf and mashed potato smeared the front of her blouse.

After a moment of shocked silence, the entire cafeteria erupted into raucous laughter.

Travis stood motionless behind her, his mouth open in an expression of mute horror. He stared at his girlfriend, who only now realized that she was exposing herself to the entire room.

A wail of embarrassed anguish erupted from her lips as she climbed to her feet, pulling her skirt back down. She looked around, unsure what to do, as the laughter gave way to excited chatter. Her cheeks burned red. Her eyes were moist with tears. Then she turned and barged past her boyfriend and fled from the room, dripping gravy and mashed potatoes on the floor as she went. Travis hesitated, unsure what his next move should be, then ran after her.

Annie stared at Karen's discarded tray in disbelief. No sooner had she thought about Karen tripping and spilling her food, than it had occurred. And only moments after the thought crossed her mind. Annie felt a swelling of satisfaction. The doll had done its job. The spell book was real. More to the point, her aunt had been correct, Annie actually had supernatural powers.

The student body's glee at the downfall of one of their own had subsided now, and the cafeteria was returning to normal. Annie glanced around to see if anyone had realized that it was her who caused Karen's mishap, but no one was paying any attention to the unpopular girl who lived in the swamp.

Except for Robbie Decker.

As she scanned the room packed with students, her eyes found his table and lingered there. As if he could feel the weight of her stare, Robbie glanced up. He smiled and raised a hand in greeting.

Annie returned the gesture, her heart skipping a beat despite

Lily's presence in the seat next to Robbie. He still liked her. Otherwise, why would he have smiled? As she turned toward her meatloaf and broke off a piece with her fork, Annie marveled at how a day that had started so badly, could now be so good.

# THIRTY-EIGHT

ANNIE SPENT the rest of the day in a state of euphoria. She could hardly wait to get home and examine the spell book. Maybe there were other spells in there that could help her. She briefly considered making another doll and dropping it into Lily's purse, but quickly abandoned the idea. It felt too cruel, especially since Lily had done nothing except date Robbie, and she could hardly blame the girl for that. Annie had been off the scene for two weeks, leading Robbie to believe that their relationship was over, and that she didn't like him. After catching her eye in the cafeteria, Robbie now knew better. Besides, rather than tease Annie, Lily had actually been kind to her. And she was sure that Robbie would ditch the attractive new cheerleader now that he was aware Annie's affections had not waned. She would give it a few days and see what transpired, and then, if her hunch proved correct, it would be she and not Lily that Robbie took to the Kickoff Kegger. She could hardly wait to see Karen's face when that happened.

The next few days rushed by. By Friday morning, when Robbie hadn't sought her out, Annie grew nervous. She knew he was at school because she'd seen him a few times from a distance, either lingering next to his locker with Lily, or heading to class. She didn't, however, see him in the cafeteria, and assumed that he had either dined earlier than her or arrived after she left. She also didn't see Karen again until Friday lunchtime, since she had taken several days off sick. Annie suspected that the phantom illness was more likely embarrassment than any real ailment. This just made her revenge feel even sweeter.

As Friday afternoon came, Annie wondered if she had misinterpreted Robbie's smile on Monday. Maybe there wasn't a connection between them after all. Then, when she arrived at her locker during afternoon recess, she discovered otherwise. Robbie had left her a note, slipped between the metal door and the locker's frame. She took it and hurried down the corridor to the girl's bathroom, her spine tingling with excitement. She found an empty stall and locked the door behind her, then opened the note.

*My sweet Annie,*

*I can't help thinking about you. Our date at the fair was one of the happiest evenings of my life, especially when we kissed. I now realize that I want nothing more than to be with you. Meet me after school. I'll be waiting at Sullivan's Pond.*

*Love, Robbie.*

She felt a surge of elation. He loved her. And later this afternoon, before the first football game of the season took place that evening, he would be at Sullivan's Pond to prove it. She felt sorry for Lily, who would be heartbroken, but that didn't matter, because Robbie and Annie were a couple. For once in her life, Annie had come out the winner.

# THIRTY-NINE

THE REST of the afternoon passed in a blur of fevered anticipation. When the last bell rang, Annie all but ran from the school building and arrived breathless at her bicycle. She was supposed to go straight home, but there was no way she was missing her date with Robbie. If her mother asked why she was late home, Annie could just say that she was helping the art teacher with a class project. She doubted her mother would believe it, but also knew she would not have enough motivation to check the veracity of her daughter's story.

It would take a good fifteen minutes to get to Sullivan's Pond, a well-known make out spot. Annie could cycle most of the way, but when she reached the small parking lot at the bottom of the trail leading to the pond, she would have to leave her bike behind and walk. She looked down at her clothing and wished she had time to run home and change into an outfit more suited to meeting her new boyfriend. That was out of the question, though. Not only was Sullivan's Pond in the wrong direction, there was no way she was going to go back to the cabin and risk being unable to leave again. The art project cover story, and the clothes she now wore, would have to suffice.

When Annie reached the parking lot, she leaned the bike

against a tree and made her way to the trail. It was hot, the sun beating mercilessly down, and she started to sweat as she made her way up the winding dirt path to the pond. She had left her book bag back at the school, safely stowed in her locker, which meant she didn't have to lug it up the trail, but even so she was winded when she arrived at the clearing, in the middle of which sat the crystal-clear swimming hole with trees pressing in on three sides. Where the trail ended a sandy beach sloped down to the water.

Annie was pleased to see that the clearing was empty. They would have it all to themselves. Ahead of her, a blanket was laid out on the sandy bank near the water's edge. She smiled and walked toward it, expecting to see Robbie at any moment, but he was nowhere in sight. When she reached the blanket, she found out why. A note waited for her, held in place by a smooth pebble. She kneeled down on the blanket and brushed the pebble aside, then picked up the note. As expected, it was from Robbie. Her heart fluttered as she read it, a smile creasing her lips.

*Annie my love,*

*I knew you'd come. Our love burns like the sun. It shines like the pale glowing moon on a cloudless night. I've wanted to be alone with you for so long. My lips ache to kiss yours. I have something special planned for us. I'm waiting for you in the water on the other side of the pond. I know you didn't bring a bathing suit, but that's okay. This place is private, I promise, so you needn't be shy. After you undress, come into the water and I'll be waiting. Don't be afraid, I know you will do this because you love me as much as I love you.*

*Your darling,*

*Robbie*

*xxx*

．　．　．

The smile faltered on Annie's lips. She read the note a second time. Could this be real? Robbie wanted her to go skinny dipping with him. She felt scared and excited, all at the same time. She glanced out over the water but could not see him. There were some small inlets around the pond, and it was possible that he was out of sight, obscured by the dense overgrowth that crowded the water's edge.

She placed the note back on the blanket and put the pebble on top again, then stood up. Was she really going to do this? She knew immediately that the answer was yes because Robbie had asked her to, and she couldn't disappoint him.

She slipped her shoes off and then, with trembling hands, she reached up and unhooked the top button of her blouse. She worked her way down until the garment was open at the front and then slipped it off her shoulders and dropped it to the blanket. She looked around again, making sure no one was there, before wriggling out of her skirt.

She stood in her underwear; sand pushing between her toes. Now came the hard part. Butterflies swarmed in her stomach as she reached back, unclasped her bra, and slipped the straps off her shoulders. She kept a shielding hand over her chest and dropped the bra. There was only one thing left to remove, but now she hesitated.

"Annie." A far away voice drifted on the breeze.

She glanced around, ignoring a flutter of embarrassment that tickled her stomach, but didn't see anyone. "Robbie, is that you?"

"It's me." The answer sounded further away now. She couldn't tell where it was coming from. "Finish undressing and come into the water. I can't wait to be with you."

"I don't know . . ." Annie reached down with one hand, touched the hem of her panties, then drew her fingers away as if scorched.

"I'm waiting for you. Please hurry."

"I can't." Annie shook her head. "It's too embarrassing."

"That's what makes it so much fun," Robbie cooed. "Do it for me. Please?"

"For you." Annie dropped her arms, ignoring the heat that blossomed across her cheeks. She took a deep breath, slipped her fingers into the waistband of her panties, and slid them down and off.

It felt weird to be naked outdoors. Even weirder to be so exposed in a public place. The breeze tickled her skin, causing goosebumps to rise. There was still no sign of Robbie, so she padded to the water's edge and waded in, gasping when the frigid spring-fed water touched her bare legs. She continued in up to her knees and stopped, expecting Robbie to appear at any moment and come to her.

"Robbie?" She called his name, expecting him to answer.

The butterflies were still swarming in her stomach.

"Robbie, where are you?" She wondered if he was hiding in the bushes at the edge of the pond, embarrassed to reveal his own nudity. "You can come out. I did what you asked. I . . . I want to see you."

From somewhere behind her, came a giggle. She spun around expecting to see Robbie standing on the shore, but he wasn't there. Instead, she saw Karen Leroux and Travis Cox standing at the water's edge with leering, wicked smiles on their faces.

# FORTY

ANNIE LET OUT A STARTLED YELP.

For a moment she couldn't comprehend what was going on, and then it clicked into place. Robbie wasn't the one who sent those notes. Karen and Travis had written them. She had fallen prey to a vicious practical joke. Now she was standing in the water without a stitch of clothing while they ogled her and laughed.

Worse, there were more figures emerging from the woods. She recognized them as members of the football team, and also a few of Karen's cheerleader friends. They formed a line at the edge of the pond, blocking any chance of escape. Thankfully, neither Robbie nor Lily appeared to be among them, but that was little consolation.

"Look what we've found," Travis said, as he looked her up and down with wide eyes. "It's Swampy Annie in her native habitat."

Annie's hands flew to cover her nakedness. Tears pushed at the corners of her eyes. Her cheeks burned with embarrassment.

"Come into the water, I need you." Travis did a fine imitation of Robbie. "I love you."

He bent over laughing.

"It was you?" Annie could hardly believe what was happening.

"Who else did you think it would be?" Travis said between guffaws. "Your boyfriend, Robbie?"

"I . . ." Annie's lips trembled. "I thought—"

"We know what you thought. Now put your arms at your sides." Karen Leroux barked the order as if she were directing one of her cheerleading squad practices. "Let everyone see you."

"No." Annie shook her head and shrank back. Water sloshed around her calves, raising goosebumps across her bare flesh. "I can't."

"Do what I tell you." Karen sounded annoyed. "Now."

"Please don't make me," Annie begged. "I'll do anything else, but don't make me do that."

"You can either do as I say, or Travis and the boys will do it for you. I'm sure they'll get a kick out of that."

Annie didn't want those boys anywhere near her. Their nasty hands grabbing her. Touching her in places no boy ever had. She lowered her arms, forced them to her sides, as a dozen pairs of eyes invaded every part of her nakedness.

Eventually, after what felt like hours, but had probably only been a minute, Travis motioned to his friends. "Come on, let's get out of here. I'm not sure how much longer I can stare at that scrawny body. We have a football game to play." He stepped from the water's edge, then looked back at her. "You know what, Swampy, if you're bored later and want to give us another show, drop by the kegger. We could do with a little more entertainment. Maybe we'll even get a little dance next time."

Travis turned and walked away. The others fell in behind him. As he passed near the blanket, Travis bent down and scooped it up, and her discarded clothes along with it. He tucked the bundle under his arm and kept on toward the trail.

Karen still lingered at the water's edge. She reached into her pocket and pulled out a familiar object. It was the Poppet doll that Annie had dropped into her bag the previous Monday. The doll that had caused Karen's shame in the cafeteria.

"I believe this is yours." She threw the doll onto the sand at the water's edge. "Maybe next time you'll think twice before you want to make a fool of me."

She stood a moment longer, relishing Annie's discomfort, then turned away. As she left the clearing, Karen shouted one last message over her shoulder, the words growing fainter the further away she got. "If you think this makes us even, you're wrong. We're not even close. No one screws with me and gets away with it. I'll see you at school on Monday. If you dare show your face again, that is."

# FORTY-ONE

ANNIE STOOD FROZEN to the spot and listened to the receding laughter. Once she was sure they had gone, she splashed back to shore. The doll lay at the water's edge, a grim reminder of her shaming. She had no idea how Karen had put the pieces together and concluded that Annie was responsible for her mishap in the cafeteria. Not that it mattered. Whatever embarrassment Karen suffered had been paid back to Annie tenfold. Worst of all, they'd taken her clothes. She was alone and naked in the woods.

Annie picked up the doll and stared at it for a moment, then threw the small figurine as far into the water as she could with a choked scream.

She watched it flip end over end in the air before splashing into the middle of the pond and sinking from sight.

Karen's words echoed in her head. *If you think this makes us even, you're wrong. We're not even close.* She could only imagine what further torment awaited her the following week at school. Then there was Robbie. He wasn't in love with her. He didn't even know she'd come up here to be with him because he hadn't written those notes. He was, she realized with a sinking heart, still dating Lily. Not that it mattered. She could never face him again after this. Travis was sure to tell him what they'd done.

She wiped a tear from her cheek and looked around, hoping that Travis and Karen had left something, anything, with which to cover herself. They hadn't. They'd even taken her shoes. With no other choice, Annie started back toward the trail, and prayed she wouldn't encounter anyone on the way back to the parking lot.

The walk back felt much longer than the walk up to the pond. It was hot, and she was sweating, but at least the canopy of trees on the trail provided some shade, and for that she was grateful. As she walked, she found her embarrassment slipping away to be replaced by a cold, hard rage. Karen's words played in her mind on a loop, with their implied threat of further humiliation. The obnoxious bitch of a cheerleader was right. It wasn't over. Annie was going to make sure of that. If the spell book had worked once, it would work again, and this time she was going to do something her tormentors would remember for a very long time. There were spells she could use to put them in their place once and for all.

With a renewed sense of resolve, Annie forged ahead until she reached the parking lot. Travis and his buddies were long gone. As a parting gesture, they'd scattered her clothing across the parking lot. She found her shoes, blouse, and skirt. Her bra and panties were missing, no doubt kept as a souvenir by Travis. She could only imagine what plans he had for those, and she was sure it would be humiliating. But at least she could cover herself.

She put the blouse on, then her skirt, and finally, her shoes. She looked around, happy to see that her bike was still there. She inspected the tires and brakes, just to be safe, then cycled toward home. Her skirt flapped in the wind and she pushed it down, aware of her state of undress beneath.

Twenty minutes later, she arrived at the cabin. She dropped the bike in the dirt and ran up the porch steps, tearing into the house and heading for her bedroom with singular intent. From somewhere else in the cabin, her mother was calling her name, but she ignored it and slammed the door. Then she went to the bed, lifted the mattress, and pulled the spell book out.

# FORTY-TWO

ANNIE SAT on the bed with the book on her lap. She had no idea what to do with it, only that another stupid doll was not the answer. She needed something bigger. Something that would take care of Karen Leroux once and for all.

But what?

She thumbed through the pages, stopping occasionally to read a particular spell, but after an hour she was no closer to an answer than she was before. She slammed the book shut in frustration and leaned back with her head against the wall. Aunt Babette would have known what to do, just like she did all those years ago when she'd dispatched Annie's no-good father. She mouthed a silent prayer for guidance.

As if in answer, the book vibrated.

She opened her eyes, surprised, and looked down.

The book, which had been quiet and dormant only moments before, was now humming with energy. It was warm too. She could feel the heat under her palm. And it was getting hotter.

Alarmed, she pulled her hand away.

The book stopped vibrating.

Annie held her breath, wondering what would happen next.

Then the book flew open.

Pages fluttered as if some unseen hand was browsing them. She resisted the urge to fling the volume away and run from the room. Then, as suddenly as it had begun, the frantic shuffle of pages ceased.

Annie stared down, wide eyed.

An incantation stared right back at her off the page.

*A Spell of Transmutation to Conjure the loup-garou.*

Annie drew in a sharp breath. She knew of the loup-garou. Everyone did. It was an ancient Cajun legend, nothing more.

Except it wasn't.

And the spell that would summon the beast was right there, in her lap. The book had known what she wanted and presented her with the perfect solution. Karen Leroux and Travis Cox wouldn't ever mess with her again. Not after tonight.

# FORTY-THREE

ANNIE STUDIED the page the spell book had opened itself to with a growing sense of satisfaction. She memorized the incantation, repeating the three-stanza conjuration over and over until she could recite it back without the book.

But that was only part of it. She would need certain ingredients in order for the spell to work. Ingredients that must be combined and boiled down into a liquid, then drank. And there was only one place she could find those ingredients.

The swamp.

A tingle of apprehension wormed down her spine. It would be dark soon. Going out into the swamp at night was a bad idea. There were alligators and venomous snakes.

On top of that, there was her mother. She was bound to ask where her daughter was going and why. But maybe not . . . Emmylou had been cooking up a fresh batch of moonshine in her still out on the deck behind the cabin and had bottled it the previous afternoon. That meant she had a fresh supply of hooch.

Annie went to the bedroom door and opened it a crack, then peered out. Her mother had already started in on the alcohol. She was sprawled on the sagging and stained, teal-colored sofa they'd picked up from the side of the road years earlier, leafing through the pages of a months' old Better Homes magazine. A mason jar full of clear liquid—no doubt some of the freshly bottled moonshine—sat on the coffee table.

When she stepped out of her room, Emmylou Doucet looked up with dull glazed eyes. She met her daughter's gaze and picked up the mason jar, sloshing liquid onto her blouse as she put the jar to her lips and drank, then looked down at the magazine again.

The irony of her mother's choice in reading material did not escape Annie. She wondered if the magazine was merely a convenient prop, something for Emmylou to rest her eyes upon while she got quietly soused. Either way, it didn't matter. Her mother was far enough into the moonshine that she could escape without the usual third degree.

Annie stepped into the main room and went to the small area that served as a kitchen. In one of the drawers, she found a plastic shopping bag, which she stuffed into her pocket. In another, she found a flashlight.

At the rear of the cabin was a door that opened out onto the back deck. She slipped outside and hurried across the deck—stopping at the still long enough to grab an empty mason jar—then descended the steps and followed a narrow trail into the swamp, keeping her eyes peeled for predators.

As she waded through the brackish water, sweeping the flashlight's beam from left to right in slow arcs, her mind returned to the humiliation she had endured earlier that afternoon. Every time she thought about it, a fresh crackle of hatred rose from within the simmering anger that churned at the back of her mind. It drove her on as she moved further from the cabin, eventually coming to a small rise and a stand of clustered pine trees.

At the base of the trees, she found what she was looking for. A clutch of pale blue fungi. Indigo Milk Mushrooms, as her mother called them. She picked several and dropped them into the plastic shopping bag she'd brought for that purpose. Next, she scooped up a handful of rotting vegetation which also went into the bag. There were two more items on her list, and it didn't take her long to procure them. She needed a toad but was loath to catch a live one. Instead, she settled for a carcass she found floating in the water, legs stretched stiff, half its body gone, no doubt as a meal for whatever killed it.

The toad went into the bag along with the mushrooms.

Which left one more ingredient. And it would be the easiest to find because it was all around her. Swamp water.

She took out the mason jar and filled it, then screwed the lid back on, before hurrying back toward the cabin.

When she entered, her mother was asleep on the couch, loud snores signifying that she wouldn't wake up anytime soon.

Annie went to work in the kitchen, pouring the swamp water into a pot and bring it to the boil before adding the rotting vegetation. She chopped the mushrooms and dropped those in too. The last item to go in was the toad. Then she boiled the ingredients down for twenty minutes until the pot's contents became a thin brownish sludge.

At one point, the toad rose to the surface, its rotten flesh mostly gone now, then sank again. She almost gagged. Just the thought of drinking that vile concoction made her feel queasy. But it would be worth it.

The Kickoff Kegger would be starting soon. Karen had mockingly suggested that she show and give a reprise performance of her humiliating ordeal. Dance for them. Well, Annie had every intention of showing up, but she would do a lot more than dance. At least, if the gross swamp soup she had made actually worked.

There was only one way to find out.

After transferring the foul-smelling potion into a mason jar, Annie went back to her room, opened the spell book, and read the incantation one more time to make sure she remembered it right. Then she slipped out of the cabin to the sound of her mother's deep snores.

She mounted her bike and cycled toward Wolf Haven, veering off before she reached the town and heading up a narrow dirt road that meandered through the woods. When she was still half a mile from the road's terminus, a clearing in the woods well known among the residents of Wolf Haven as a party spot, she stopped and laid the bike on the ground. In the distance she could hear raucous laughter and faint strains of music. The Kickoff Kegger was in full swing. The entire football team would be there, including Travis. The cheerleaders would be there too. She imagined Karen, probably draped over her boyfriend with a beer in her hand. How surprised would she be when she saw Annie, or rather what Annie was about to become!

She stepped away from the bike and into the trees. It was almost 10 o'clock at night now, and the sky was jet black. The only light came from the moon hanging low on the horizon. Annie stripped naked for the second time that day. She folded her clothes and left them in a neat pile on the forest floor. She kneeled down and removed the top from the bottle of brown liquid she'd prepared back at the cabin. She drank deeply despite the earthy, foul taste that washed over her tongue and stuck in the back of her throat. She resisted the urge to spit the liquid out and swallowed the bottle's contents in three large gulps. That done she closed her eyes and recited the memorized incantation.

Crickets chirped in the undergrowth. A bird flapped out of a tree high overhead. Annie opened her eyes and waited for something to happen. She wondered if she had recited the spell incorrectly or collected the wrong ingredients for the potion. But just as she was about to stand up, a burning pain exploded in her stomach.

She gasped. Doubled over.

Her muscles exploded with pinpricks of searing agony that drilled all the way to the bone.

She whimpered and fell to her side, writhing on the forest floor. It was like being torn apart from within. Her legs, arms, even her head felt like they were being stretched and crushed in a vice, all at the same time. She wanted to scream, but when she opened her mouth, all that came out was a throaty, guttural howl. She writhed on the ground, desperate for relief, and wondered if she was going to die. Then, as quickly as the pain had descended upon her, it faded away.

Annie pushed herself up and rocked back on her knees, then climbed to her feet. She felt taller, more muscular. She looked down and was surprised to see that her thin, pale body had been replaced by thick leathery skin and bulging muscles. Her senses were keener. She could smell the football players at the kegger half a mile away. Could hear their beating hearts, calling her to them. Saliva dripped from her mouth as she anticipated how good they would taste.

If the creature that had recently been Annie could have smiled, it would have. The incantation worked. She had been transformed from a pathetic, weak girl into a powerful and deadly beast.

The loup-garou.

And now she would have her revenge. Annie dropped to all fours and raised her head, letting forth a chilling howl.

Then she took off in the direction of the Kickoff Kegger with one thing on her mind. Carnage.

# FORTY-FOUR

WHEN ROBBIE DECKER left the Wolf Haven Wildcats locker room Lily was already waiting for him next to his powder blue Mustang. He swept in and kissed her, adrenaline from the game still coursing through his veins. They had won easily. The Lagrange Bulldogs hadn't beaten the Wildcats in their last fourteen meetings, but this year had been a particularly bad rout, with the final score standing at 48-3.

"Come on, let's get up to the kegger," Robbie said, unlocking the passenger side door for her. "I'm pumped and ready to party."

"Robbie, you know I can't." Lily gave him an apologetic look. "My parents don't think it would be a good idea for me to go to a party in the woods, and they told me to come straight home after the game."

"That's ridiculous. The kegger's a wildcat tradition. Everyone knows about it."

"I'm sure they do. But we aren't from Wolf Haven. I didn't grow up here. All my parents see is a bunch of kids boozing it up in the woods and having sex." Lily climbed into the car and looked up at Robbie. "Maybe they'll let me go next year."

"We're seniors. There won't be a next year. We'll have graduated."

"I might not be able to go to the kegger, but we can still have some fun before you drive me home. My parents won't know when the game ended, so that gives us at least fifteen minutes."

Robbie rounded the car and hopped in the driver's side. He pushed the key into the ignition and started the engine, his foot pressing down on the accelerator so that the throaty 2.8-liter V6 roared. "I'm not sure how much fun we can have in fifteen minutes."

"I'd better show you then." Lily reached over and ran a hand up Robbie's leg to the inside of his thigh.

"Oh." Robbie grinned. "You think we should be doing that right here in the parking lot?"

"Heavens. Get your mind out of the gutter. I didn't mean *that*. I meant this." Lily leaned toward him. She put a hand on Robbie's shoulder and kissed him, her lips lingering on his. "See, isn't that fun?"

"I've done worse things." Robbie pulled her close and kissed her again, his hand roaming up her back and reaching her neck. His other hand rested on her knee.

Fifteen minutes was not long enough.

He drove her home, wishing he could turn the car around and take her up to Sullivan's pond instead. They could be alone there, and it would be much more fun than the stupid kegger. But he knew she would never agree to it. He pulled into her driveway instead. For his chivalry he received another quick kiss, more of a peck this time lest her father was peering out the window, and then she was gone. He watched her race up the front path and into the house, then reversed out of the driveway and drove out of town toward the party, which would by now, he was sure, be in full swing. He was disappointed that Lily couldn't accompany him, but he wasn't going to let that ruin his evening. The Kickoff Kegger was one of Wolf Haven High's most storied traditions, and this would be the last year he'd be able to attend.

He drove fast, pressing the accelerator a little harder than he should have. He was eager to get to the party and almost missed the turnoff, but then he saw it approaching on his right and slowed just enough to skate around the corner and onto the dirt road, then pressed the accelerator again, feeling the tires bite into dry earth. The car was flying along, kicking up dust. Robbie felt a surge of adrenaline and let out a whoop. A cry that quickly turned sour he saw something in the road ahead of him caught in the glare of his high beams.

A bicycle laying on its side.

He slammed a foot on the brake and swung the wheel hard to the left, knowing he couldn't stop in time. The car shuddered and slipped on the loose surface and then, just when he thought he could bring it back straight, the backend slid off the road into a tree.

The car came to a juddering halt with the engine racing. Robbie cursed and climbed out, slamming the door. He went around to the back of the car to inspect the damage. His wheel was fine, the tire still inflated, and that was something. But his rear wing hadn't fared so well. The metal was crushed in, the paint scraped and gouged. His bumper was dented, the chrome scuffed. A spider web of dark cracks meandering through the glass of his taillight.

It would cost a fortune to fix. Not to mention what his father would say when he saw it.

Robbie swore and kicked the tree. His foot bounced off, toes throbbing from the impact. He went around to the other side of the car and glared at the bicycle laying on its side in the middle of the road. Who in their right mind would leave a bike like that? How was it even there? Robbie picked it up and hoisted the bike over his head, then heaved it into the woods on the other side of the road with all the strength he could muster. He watched it fly through the air and crash into a dense thicket.

He stood for a couple of minutes, letting his anger subside. Who cared if there was a dent in the back of his car? He would just tell his father someone hit him in the school parking lot during the game. Better than saying he ran off the road, even if it was because of a stupid bike in his path. Pleased with his cover story, Robbie turned back to the Mustang and pulled the driver's door open. Then, just as he was about to climb in, he heard it.

A rising howl from somewhere off in the woods—doleful and chilling—that floated on the stirring breeze.

Robbie froze, half in the car, heart thumping against his chest. He looked nervously around, afraid of what he might see lurking in the darkness beside the road.

But there was nothing there.

Probably just a coyote.

Robbie lingered a moment more, listening for another howl. When none came, he climbed into the car, slammed the door, and continued on toward the kegger.

# FORTY-FIVE

BY THE TIME Robbie arrived at the Kickoff Kegger, his fury with whoever had left the bicycle in his path had receded to a mild annoyance tempered by the anticipation of a night of raucous partying. When he pulled the powder blue Mustang into the clearing and parked up next to the other cars, Travis came bounding over with a beer in his hand.

"Hey, man. I didn't think you were ever going to get here," the quarterback said as Robbie climbed from the car. He peered into the passenger seat. "Where's Lily?"

"Her parents wouldn't let her come." Robbie felt a pang of longing when he thought about Lily. It would be so much more fun if she were there by his side.

"That's too bad." Travis's eyes drifted to the car's rear quarter panel. "Yikes. What happened there? Let me guess. Her father went after you with a baseball bat for deflowering his little girl!"

"Not even close. And for your information, there hasn't been any deflowering, not that it's any of your business."

Travis shrugged. "Sure, buddy. I believe you."

"As you should." Robbie walked in the direction of the kegger. There was a bonfire in the middle of the clearing, the flames leaping high into the night air. Brightly glowing embers wafted in the fire's updraft, spiraling toward the heavens as they faded to ash. A mass of bodies clustered around the fire, football players and their girlfriends drinking and laughing in carefree abandon. "Where did you ever find a word like deflowering, anyway? Don't tell me you've been paying attention in English lit?"

"Like that's ever going to happen." Travis chuckled and slapped Robbie on the back. "I don't always have to be crude."

"No. But you usually are." Robbie stopped while they were still a little way from the bonfire. He turned to Travis. "Have you heard anything strange in the woods tonight?"

"Like what?" Travis looked confused. "You didn't hear cop cars, did you? They don't usually bother us up here, but there's always a first time."

"No. Not the cops. More like an animal."

"There're animals all over these woods, doofus."

"Not like this. I heard a howl while I was driving up here. It sounded like a wolf."

"It was probably just a coyote." Travis shook his head. "I bet they're bunches of them around. My dad claimed he saw one out on Miller Road a few months ago."

"I don't think it was a coyote. It didn't sound right. The howl was kind of long and drawn out, and low. I've never heard a coyote sound like that. Plus, it's a full moon."

"You're full of shit, man." Travis let out a nervous laugh. "The big bad werewolf's coming to get us."

"I never said it was a werewolf." Robbie started walking toward the group again. "It sounded odd, that's all."

"If you weren't saying it was a werewolf, why bother mentioning the moon."

"I don't know. I guess wolves and the moon just seem to go together."

"Not sure where you heard that," Travis said. "Besides it's not a full moon, it's a waxing gibbous moon. It won't be full for another two days."

"Holy cow. What's gotten into you? It's like you swallowed a dictionary or something."

"I saw it in the paper this morning, okay? I was checking the weather for the game tonight. I can't help it if I remember things."

"You better be careful, or people will start to think you're a nerd."

"Very funny." Travis nodded toward a red cooler sitting on the ground. "You want a beer?"

"Sure. I'll take an import if you've got one."

"Import? What the hell is that?" Travis started toward the cooler. "We have Budweiser, or we have Budweiser. We also have some wine coolers if you feel like switching sides and becoming a girl."

"I guess I'm having a Budweiser."

"One brewski coming up." Travis pulled a bottle from the cooler and tossed it to Robbie. He pulled a bottle opener from his pocket and held it out. "If you're done with talk of wolves running around in the woods, I'd really like to get back to partying."

Robbie shrugged, and cast a glance toward the trees, and the darkness beyond. When he looked back, Karen joined them. She sidled up to Travis and draped herself over him, her eyes shone with alcohol.

"We should go have a party of our own in the backseat of your car," she said with slurred abandon.

"Maybe later." Travis pushed her away. "How much have you had to drink, anyway?"

"I had a wine cooler." Karen hiccupped. She wrapped her arms around his neck and planted a kiss on his cheek.

"Yeah, right. One wine cooler." Travis looked at Robbie, a bemused smile on his face. "Maybe it's best that Lily didn't come to the kegger. I can only imagine what Karen's father will do if she doesn't sober up before I drive her home."

"Maybe you should take her to the car," Robbie said. "At least that way she won't drink anything else."

"Screw that. She's a big girl. I'd rather get buzzed myself than have to babysit Karen." He drained the last of his beer and tossed the bottle away, then reached into the cooler for another one. He was about to pop the top, when a strange sound rose over the music and excited chatter. He stopped and looked at Robbie, his eyes wide.

Other people had heard it too, and turned their heads toward the woods, nervous. Robbie felt a tingle of fear worm its way up his spine, because he recognized the strange sound. He'd heard it once already tonight, and this time it was much closer. A rising, drawn out howl that floated ominously on the breeze.

# FORTY-SIX

"WHAT THE HELL WAS THAT?" Travis glanced toward the woods, his jovial expression descending into a mask of fear.

"I told you there was something out there," Robbie took a step toward the fire.

The party had come to a halt, the gathered teenagers shocked into silence. Only the transistor radio continued to make a sound, emitting the dulcet tones of The Beach Boys as they sang about a little "Surfer Girl." People looked at each other with panicked expressions, waiting to see what would happen next.

Another howl split the night, this time from the other side of the clearing.

Karen stumbled back to Travis. She put her arms around his waist and stared out into the forest, sobered by fear.

"We should get out of here," Robbie said, glancing toward his car.

"It's just a coyote," Travis replied, but he didn't sound convinced. "I'm sure it will go away soon."

"That was no coyote." Robbie shook his head. "I really think we should leave."

"That's ridiculous, there's nothing dangerous in these woods. There can't be," Travis said.

As if to prove him wrong, a low, snorting grunt came from beyond the trees.

Someone screamed. One of the cheerleaders.

A football player—Robbie recognized him as Jordan Wright, who played left tackle—sprinted toward the cars with his girlfriend, Louise, close behind. He fumbled for his keys, drew them from his pocket, and reached for the car door.

Everyone watched the escaping teens, as if trying to gauge whether they should all be following or stay where they were.

Robbie saw a shape move against the darkness between the trees. There was another grunt. Then something extricated itself from the gloom and shot forward in a blur of speed.

The football player barely registered what was happening before it hit him. He swiveled toward the approaching menace; a look of horror frozen upon his face. Then he was flying backwards in a spray of blood, only to land in a crumpled heap a dozen feet distant.

His girlfriend turned to run, finding herself suddenly alone.

She didn't get far.

A large muscular animal landed in her path, skin leathery and brown, jaws open and dripping saliva. To Robbie, it looked like a creature from hell.

The cheerleader screamed and tried to change direction, but there was nowhere to go. The beast pounced upon her, its mighty jaws snapping closed.

There was a sound of bones crunching.

The scream was cut short.

For a moment, no one moved. The Beach Boys had finished singing their song and now a DJ was prattling on about young love and broken hearts.

The beast lost interest in the bloody rag doll that had been Louise only moments before, and turned to face the gathered throng.

Time ground to a halt. The crickets stopped chirping. The bullfrogs out in the swamp fell silent. Even the breeze dropped. Then, as if everyone at the party had come to the same conclusion through some kind of nonverbal agreement to flee, all hell broke loose.

People ran in all directions, stumbling and tripping over themselves in their haste to escape. The beast tilted its head back and let out a bloodcurdling howl, then leaped into the fray, knocking bodies in the air as it gnashed its teeth and snapped its jaws.

Travis dropped his beer and stared at Robbie, caught in a moment of terrified immobility. His mouth opened and closed even though no words came out. Then he pushed Karen away, and turned to run in his own bid for freedom. But the creature had seen him. It pounced forward with lightning speed and caught up to him. Travis turned to beat back his attacker, pounding his fists upon the beast's snout, but to no avail. It lifted a bloodied paw and opened his neck with one slashing swipe. Travis took a step backwards, then another. Then he toppled backwards onto the ground, his sightless eyes staring up at the moon.

Karen screamed. Her hands flew to her face, but she didn't run. Just like her boyfriend, she was frozen with fear.

"We need to leave, now." Robbie reached for her, grabbed her wrist, and tried to pull her toward his car even as the monster turned to face them.

Other cars were moving now, their headlights snapping on as the lucky few who'd escaped the creature's wrath managed to reach their vehicles.

Karen dug her heels in and refused to move. She stared at the wrecked and bloodied corpse of her boyfriend. A low warbling moan rose from her lips.

The beast skulked toward them, walking on its hind legs like a nightmare parody of a human being.

Robbie was caught between his urge to flee and desire to help Karen.

It stopped in front of them and in its eyes, Robbie thought he saw a flicker of intelligence. He saw something else too. Hatred.

Then, before Robbie could even register what was happening,

the beast surged forward and gripped Karen in its powerful hands. It lifted her from the ground and pulled her close so that their faces were inches apart.

Karen's lips trembled. She was making small sobbing sounds now. She made no attempt to free herself, but rather met the beast's gaze with what Robbie could only assume was fatal acceptance. Then, as if savoring the moment, it pulled one arm back, while still gripping her with the other. Robbie saw its claws, a set of deadly sharp daggers, in the brief moment before it plunged them into Karen's chest and ripped downward, opening her up like a ripe melon.

Robbie finally found the will to move. He stumbled backwards toward the fire; his own scream caught in his throat. The clearing was empty now. Everyone else at the kegger had either escaped already, or they were strewn around the clearing, dead.

The beast finally relinquished its hold on Karen. It dropped her limp body to the ground and advanced.

Robbie felt the bonfire's heat on his back. He wished he'd run earlier, because now there was nowhere to go. The beast was too fast.

It closed the gap between them, its breath coming in short ragged snorts. Robbie stopped and dropped his arms to his sides. He realized he was still holding the beer bottle, and let it go, then he closed his eyes and waited for death to find him.

The seconds ticked by.

Another song was playing on the radio now, providing a surreal juxtaposition to the horror of the last few minutes. The Chiffons were singing "One Fine Day".

Robbie opened his eyes, afraid of what he would see, but to his surprise the clearing was empty. The beast had disappeared. Then he noticed something else. The crickets were chirping, and the frogs had started their deep-throated croaking all over again.

# FORTY-SEVEN

THE BEAST STAGGERED through the woods. It stopped and leaned against a gnarly pine tree, breathing heavily. The change was coming. It could feel the humanity returning, flowing through its veins. It took a few more steps, raised its head to the skies, and gave one last triumphant howl, then dropped to its knees.

Its muscles tied themselves into knots. Its hide bubbled and rippled, malleable as unfired clay. A back leg popped from its socket with a sickening pop, soon followed by the other. Its front legs shriveled and twisted, even as its paws reshaped themselves into the knubs of fingers.

The creature crawled forward, gasping for breath. One agonizing step followed by another. Then toppled and writhed on a bed of fallen leaves. The sound of cracking bones and tearing skin echoed through the forest, accompanied by a guttural scream that erupted through lips part human, and part beast.

When the ordeal was over, after the creature had returned to its human state, it lay unmoving while the animalistic urges that had consumed it ebbed away into the ether. It was fragile now, nothing more than a waif-thin naked girl curled into a ball on the forest floor.

A while later, with memories of the beast's carnage still fresh in her mind, Annie Doucet stood up. She looked down at herself, at her grimy body, and the blood—not her own—that stained her breasts and stomach. She ran her tongue across her teeth and lips, relishing the tangy iron taste that lingered there.

Somewhere deep inside, a small part of the beast surged back.

Annie closed her eyes and savored the moment. Then, as if she didn't have a care in the world, she started back through the woods to the spot where she'd left her clothes, with her tormentor's dying screams ringing a sweet melody inside her head.

# FORTY-EIGHT

## BACK IN THE LIBRARY

DECKER WAS STUNNED.

He knew all about the slayings at the high school kegger out in the piney woods back in 1972. Everyone in Wolf Haven knew about them, even if it was before their time. It was an event he suspected would live on in town lore for as long as there was anyone around to tell the story. But as sheriff, Decker had access to the original police files and was able to gain a more intimate understanding of what happened on that fateful night out in the woods.

And everything in those files was wrong.

The official version of events listed a pack of rabid gray wolves as the culprit. Drawn by the sounds of music and laughter, they had descended on the party in a frenzied bloodlust, leaping into the fray and attacking anyone unlucky enough to be in their way. There were some problems with that theory. First, the survivors described a single beast, not a pack of animals. Second, the creature they described was bigger and meaner than any wolf. Last, it would have been highly unusual to find one rabid wolf wandering those woods, let alone a whole slathering pack of them.

The sheriff at the time, a man named Evan Barstow, suspected there was more to the killings, but all he had to go on were eyewitness accounts of a large wolflike creature—which a few of the survivors swore had walked on two legs more like a human than an animal—and the medical examiner's reports on the victims, which listed bite marks consistent with a powerful canine predator. Given the number of deaths, and the short timeframe, he came to the only conclusion that made sense—a pack of rabid wolves—even though it didn't sit well in his gut.

The conflicting eyewitness accounts bothered him, and he even said as much in his report, but in the end he concluded that the claims of a bipedal attacker were likely the result of panic and hysteria more than genuine observation.

Now, Decker knew it was no such thing. The medical examiner was right. The attacker was a canine. Except it was no Gray Wolf, and certainly not an entire pack of them. Instead, it was a humiliated seventeen-year-old girl striking out against her tormentors. Except this girl had just been given a powerful spell book that contained an incantation that turned her into the loup-garou. His hunch had been right. The killings in Wolf Haven when Annie Doucet was an old woman were far from her first. There had been blood on her hands almost from the minute Aunt Babette gave her that spell book.

He wondered if she really expected the incantation to work that first time. There was no way to know, but Decker suspected she used the spell book more as an outlet for her anger—a revenge fantasy that made her feel better—than out of any belief that the magic contained within those old and brittle pages was real. Maybe if there had been someone in her life she could go to, things would have played out differently. The loup-garou might have remained forever dormant. But her mother was hardly that person. She would more likely have punished Annie for sneaking out to meet Robbie Decker than defend her daughter's honor.

Which raised another question. Decker's father had been in the woods that night. He was at the kegger. Not only that, but Annie had almost killed him, holding off only at the last moment. Robbie Decker had looked into the eyes of the loup-garou decades before his son encountered that same beast and finally brought an end to the terror. Yet he had mentioned none of it to Decker.

Not a single word.

He didn't mention it to anyone else, either. There was no interview with Robbie Decker in the police files. Not a single mention of his name. He had clearly left the woods that night and stayed quiet about his presence at the kegger. And no one else at the party had mentioned him being there, either. Maybe the sheriff never asked who else was there, or maybe he could keep it secret because those that knew him best, people like Travis Cox and Karen Leroux, were all dead.

The question was, why?

Was it because he didn't want to admit what he'd seen? Was he afraid of getting into trouble for being out in the woods that night? Or was it because deep down, on a subconscious level, he recognized the girl he'd taken to the fair when he looked into the eyes of that creature?

It was a question Decker would never get an answer to, because his father was long dead. But it explained one thing: why the elder Sheriff Decker had been so obsessed after Decker's mother died. After his ordeal when he was a teenager, it must have felt like history was repeating itself.

Back when Annie Doucet was terrorizing the town, Decker had pulled out the box containing his father's old notebooks. The ones Robbie Decker had filled with wild theories and fevered ramblings. But there were two words that stood out. Words repeated more than once on the scribbled pages of those journals.

loup-garou.

Back then, Decker hadn't understood why his father had been so focused on an old legend. A mythological creature so ingrained in southern Louisiana folklore that they had even named the town after it. Wolf Haven.

Now it made sense because Robbie Decker knew that the loup-

176 ANTHONY M. STRONG

garou was real. He had watched it rip his friends apart when he was a teenager. It was only natural that he would zero in on the same creature when his wife met a similar fate.

Even after Decker came face-to-face with the creature inside the high school—a beast he now knew was the same one his father had barely survived—he had dismissed the notion that it had killed his mother all those years before. But maybe—just maybe—his father had been on to something.

Decker looked at the ghost waiting patiently for him to process what he had just seen—a past Decker had been blissfully unaware of only hours before—and asked one question. "Did the loup-garou kill my mother?"

His only answer was the faraway chime of a grandfather clock, somehow striking midnight yet again.

Decker ignored the clock and stepped closer to the ghost. "Tell me. I have to know."

The ghost refused to speak. Instead, she opened the book again and the library vanished, to be replaced by a humid summer night in 1972.

# FORTY-NINE

WHEN ANNIE STEPPED BACK into the cabin, her mother was sitting in a chair near the door, awake and waiting for her.

"Where have you been at such a late hour, young lady?" Emmylou Doucet demanded, except she mispronounced *have* as *hash*, and the last part of the sentence slid off into a drunken slur.

"Nowhere." Annie's gut clenched. She was in no mood to argue with her mother. After transforming from the wolf back into her true form, she had hurried back to the spot where she drank the potion earlier that evening. Her clothes were right where she left them, but her bicycle was missing. A swell of panic had gripped her. Had someone come along and stolen the bike? If so, it would take her at least an hour to walk back to the cabin, especially in the dark. She looked around, doing her best to quell the frustration that rose within her. Then, after fifteen minutes of searching that felt like an eternity, she found the bicycle tossed behind a thorny bush off to the side of the trail.

She had no idea how it had gotten there, and she didn't care. All that mattered now was getting as far away from the woods as possible.

And getting home.

Annie dragged the bike out, checked it for damage.

All good.

Then she took off as fast as she could back toward the cabin. She had hoped that when she got there, her mother would still be in a liquor induced stupor and she could sneak in unnoticed. Go straight to the shower to wash off the blood that she could feel mingling with her sweat to stick to her clothes. But now she would need to think up an excuse for why she was outside and hoped that her mother had only just woken up. "I was taking out the trash. It was full."

"Don't lie to me, girl." Emmylou tried to stand, wobbled, and sank back down into the chair. Through all of that, she fixed her daughter with an unfocused gaze. "You were out on your bike. I heard you lean it against the house. You were meeting a boy, weren't you?"

"No. I—"

Emmylou never gave her a chance to finish. "Who was it? That no good Robbie Decker? I can't believe it. My own daughter—a no-good hussy. Sneaking out to do vile things with boys."

"Mama, I wasn't meeting a boy." If only her mother knew what she had really been doing, Annie thought, Emmylou Doucet might not have been so brave. She might also have wished Annie really had been sneaking out to meet a boy.

"You're disgusting." Her mother spat the words. She tried to rise again, reached for Annie with grasping hands.

The anger surged back. That same anger that had coursed through Annie at the Kickoff Kegger when she opened Karen Leroux from neck to stomach with one swipe of her razor-sharp claws. She stepped forward, pushed her mother back down into the chair and towered over her. She felt the wolf deep inside, driving her fury, and for a moment she thought it might claw its way back to the surface. Then what would her mother do? Plead for her life? Beg for mercy? Annie could imagine how good that would feel, and for a second, she hoped the wolf would take over.

But it didn't, which was probably for the best, because if the loup-garou had its way, Emmylou Doucet would end up as nothing but a pile of raw, torn flesh. She clenched her teeth, hissed a warning at her mother. "Sit there and don't say another word, or you'll regret it."

Emmylou Doucet looked up at her daughter with wide eyes. The crazed look on her face was gone, replaced by one of fear.

"We'll talk about this in the morning," she mumbled, dropping her gaze.

"No, we won't." Annie left her mother in the chair and turned away. She stomped toward the back of the house.

In her room, she stripped off her clothes, taking a moment to study the filth and blood caking her body in the full-length mirror behind the door. Then she padded naked out into the hallway, not caring if her mother saw her or not, and went to the bathroom where she ran a shower.

Fifteen minutes and a good scrubbing later, the evidence of her murderous rampage was gone, washed down the drain. She stepped out, dried herself, and wrapped a towel around her torso.

When she stepped back out of the bathroom, the sound of the TV reached her ears. Her mother was still in the chair, only now she clutched a bottle in one hand and the TV remote in the other. She took a swig from the bottle, then flipped through channels with the remote, before downing another large gulp of liquor.

Annie stood in the doorway for a few seconds, watching her. The bottle was almost empty. Who knew how much of it she had consumed before her daughter came home. It was a miracle she hadn't passed out already. But Annie didn't care anymore. At first, when she saw her mother sitting there wide-awake, or at least awake enough to admonish her daughter, Annie's stomach had flipped the way it always did when her mother was in one of those moods.

But something had changed.

When she pushed her mother back down into the chair, when she actually stood up to her, it had felt good.

No. Better than that. It was exhilarating.

She suspected her mother would not remember much about their altercation come morning, but it didn't matter. Annie knew that Emmylou Doucet wouldn't be able to bully her anymore. She was stronger now, and she had a secret weapon.

The loup-garou.

Annie turned away and went back to her bedroom, closing the door quietly. She dropped the towel and pulled on her nightgown, then slipped into bed, exhausted.

She turned off the light and lay looking up at the ceiling. The wolf was still there, somewhere deep inside of her. She could feel it like a flickering candle in the darkness, slowly burning out. If she reached for the spell book, drank more of that foul tasting potion, it would roar back to the surface, she knew. But there had been enough killing for one night. By now, the cops would surely be at the clearing in the woods. They would be looking for whoever—or whatever—had caused such bloodshed. She couldn't risk discovery. The wolf must stay hidden. Besides, she needed rest, even if she couldn't silence her restless mind.

To her surprise, sleep came quickly.

# FIFTY

THE WOLF VISITED Annie while she slept. It stalked through the dark corners of her dreams, hungry to kill again. It whispered to her, reminded her how good it had felt back in the clearing when she was ripping and slashing. How Karen Leroux had cried with fear before the wolf ripped her open.

---

Annie sat bolt upright in bed, a scream on her lips, even as the nightmare image of Karen's torn, bloodied body faded back into her subconscious.

Her forehead was clammy.

A thin sheen of sweat clung to her skin, making her nightgown stick.

The first rays of dawn pushed through a gap in the curtains to cast a slender patch of light across the rough plank floor of her bedroom.

She thought back to the evening before, and her humiliation at the hands of Karen, Travis, and the rest of the football team. She had returned home angry and embarrassed. Looking for revenge. Anything to make them pay for what they had done to her. Which was why she turned to the spell book. Foraged for ingredients out in the swamp. Memorized that incantation. Then she went back out into the woods and drank the potion. After that, everything had a fuzzy dreamlike quality and at first, she thought that what came next must have been a dreadful nightmare. That she hadn't really transformed into the loup-garou and done all those terrible things at the Kickoff Kegger.

But then she saw her grimy clothes heaped in a pile on the floor and she knew it was all real. Because she remembered something else. Coming in and confronting her mother. Feeling the wolf lurking just below the surface as she put Emmylou Doucet in her place. Running a shower to wash away the blood of her tormentors.

Becoming the wolf had felt good. Even when she changed back, the feeling remained like an afterglow. She was a different person —powerful for the first time in her life—and she liked it. Except now that the glow had faded, Annie was horrified.

She balked at the terrible things she had done. Wished she could take them back. Karen and her friends might have been cruel, but they didn't deserve what the loup-garou had done to them. What *she* had done to them.

Worse, Sheriff Barstow would be looking for the killer. With so many dead teenagers, it would be the only thing he cared about. If he found out that Annie was responsible, came knocking on her door, she would spend the rest of her life in a prison cell. And she probably deserved it, but Annie had no intention of going to prison. Her life in Wolf Haven might be bad, but being locked up forever would be worse.

Her throat tightened.

Was there any evidence leading back to her? Had she left tire tracks from her bike out in the woods? Had anyone seen her cycling out toward the kegger?

A sob escaped Annie's throat. She half expected a knock at the door. For her mother to bring the sheriff into her bedroom and tell him to take her away forever. It was only a matter of time before the truth came out. Except . . . She wasn't herself when she killed those people. She was the wolf.

A glimmer of hope.

Sheriff Barstow wouldn't be hunting for a human perpetrator. He would think it was a wild animal. If the wounds on the bodies didn't convince him of that, then surely the eyewitness accounts of those who escaped the carnage would. And no one could have recognized her when she was transformed into the beast.

Annie breathed a sigh of relief. Maybe she would get away with it, after all. And even if she had to live with the guilt of what she had done for the rest of her days, it was still better than spending her life behind bars.

Besides, she had learned her lesson. There was no way she was ever turning back into the loup-garou. Not for as long as she lived. She couldn't bear the thought of what the beast might make her do next time. Also, it was too dangerous. Sheriff Barstow wouldn't be coming around to drag her away in handcuffs—didn't have a clue that his killer was a seventeen-year-old girl with a spell book—but he would not hesitate to shoot the beast if he crossed paths with it.

Annie slipped from under the covers and stood up. She lifted the mattress and retrieved the spell book from its hiding place. It weighed heavy in her hands. She placed it on the bed and stared at the old volume for a long moment. The only evidence of her crime was that book and the wolf incantation it contained. It had to go. Which was fine because she didn't want the book anywhere near her. Not after the trouble it had caused.

She should just take it and throw the damn book into the bayou behind the cabin. Let the swamp have it. But even as the thought crossed her mind, she knew that wasn't going to happen. Her aunt had entrusted her with the book, had said it was her heritage. She couldn't just destroy it. That would do her aunt's memory a disservice. But she *could* put it somewhere out of sight and mind. Somewhere no one would ever find it where she wouldn't be tempted to open it again on a whim. And she knew just the place.

184 ANTHONY M. STRONG

Leaving the book on the bed, Annie hurried to get dressed. She went to the bedroom door and opened it a crack, peeking out.

The cabin beyond was silent and gloomy.

She opened the door wider and stepped out into the corridor. There was no sign of life from the main room. The chair her mother had occupied the previous night was empty, just like she hoped it would be. The bathroom was also empty.

Turning to the only other door in the cabin, Annie listened. From the other side came a faint sound of snoring. Good. Her mother was out cold, no doubt sleeping off whatever she had consumed the night before.

Returning to her own room, Annie grabbed the spell book from the bed and hurried through the cabin to the back door. She glanced around, her gaze lingering for a moment on her mother's bedroom, then she opened the door and stepped outside, closing it softly behind her.

# FIFTY-ONE

ANNIE HELD the spell book close to her chest and crossed the rickety back deck. She stepped around the copper still her mother used to make moonshine and descended the back steps. The last time she had ventured out into the swamp was to gather the ingredients needed for the incantation that turned her into the loup-garou.

This trip was different.

It was daylight. And she wasn't looking for magical ingredients. Actually, just the opposite. She was putting the book somewhere where it could do no further damage. Where it wouldn't tempt her to open it. Because the book was alive—or if not actually living, it possessed some kind of force that allowed it to bind with its owner. Even now, as she clutched it tight, she could sense the book resisting. It didn't want to be put away. Hidden in some dark corner of the swamp, far from the cabin. It whispered to her, telling Annie of all the things they could do together.

But she didn't listen.

The book was trying to corrupt her. It had *already* corrupted her. She couldn't allow it to do so again.

Annie pressed forward, following the trail that led into the swamp until it petered out and she was forced to slosh through the brown and murky water toward her destination.

A splash came from somewhere to her left. She stopped and turned, heart leaping into her throat. Anything that made that kind of noise in the swamp was bad.

She was right.

A pair of reptilian eyes broke the surface of the water about ten feet away, near a tall cypress tree dripping with Spanish moss. Further away, the hump of the creature's torso was visible, the bony ridges of its back poking out of the water. Behind this, hidden by the murky swamp, would be a powerful tail.

An alligator. And it was a big one. At least eight feet long.

Annie suppressed a shudder. Alligators rarely attacked humans, preferring more manageable prey. But if she hadn't been paying attention, if she had passed too close to the skulking crea-ture—or heaven forbid, bumped into it—the beast might have snapped at her, anyway. And even if it didn't want to eat her, those jaws could easily crush her bones and tear her flesh.

She lowered her head and moved quickly on, giving the reptile a wide berth while keeping a wary eye on it.

Soon she came to higher ground. This was not the place she had collected indigo milk mushrooms the previous day. This was deeper into the swamp. Somewhere she had discovered many years before while exploring. The rise, which comprised more or less land depending on the amount of water in the swamp at any given time, contained a cluster of cypress trees similar to the one the alligator had been laying under, although these were not so large. Spanish moss hung from the branches like a curtain and when she parted it, a small shack came into view.

But this was not like the cabin that Annie inhabited with her mother. The structure had been abandoned for a long time, possibly because it was so difficult to reach. Whoever had built the shack and lived there, so far from civilization, must have valued their privacy.

Now, it was nothing more than a dilapidated pile of weathered boards held together by rusting nails. It was a place she visited to be alone. To escape her mother's watchful gaze. Annie had sometimes wondered if she was the only person on the planet who knew of its existence. Which made it ideal for stashing the spell book.

She pushed through the Spanish moss and walked up to the door. It wasn't locked. There wasn't even a way to lock it. She pushed the door open with a grunt, fighting the rusty hinges for dominance, then stepped inside.

The interior of the cabin was dark and muggy. A faint odor of mildew and rotten vegetation laced the stale air. Something skittered away as she moved toward the center of the room. A fat brown spider.

Annie ignored the arachnid and kneeled down, brushing slimy composted leaves and dirt from the ground to reveal wooden floorboards that had turned a silvery gray with age. And something else. A trap door.

She had discovered the hidden door not long after she first found the shack a decade before. She had taken a broom there one day to sweep away the detritus of abandonment that had piled up over the years. Leaves, rotten branches, and even the mostly skeletal carcass of a rat that had crawled in there to die. And once the floor was clean—or as clean as it would ever get—there was the trapdoor, just waiting for her.

She had pulled it open with a tingle of excitement, hoping to find coins, gold, or some other buried treasure lying beneath. But there was nothing in the shallow wooden box of a space beneath except some dead cockroaches and a leathery old snakeskin which she plucked out with a stick and threw into the swamp.

Now it would make a perfect hiding place for the spell book.

She heaved the door up and swung it back. There were still a few dead bugs inside, lying on their backs with tiny legs poking into the air, but no snakeskins this time, thank goodness. She pulled a plastic shopping bag from her pocket and slipped the book inside, wrapping the plastic around it and tying the bag's handles so it wouldn't come undone, then she lowered the book into the hole.

Her task complete, Annie went to shut the trapdoor. But then she hesitated.

The book had been a gift from her Aunt Babette. The old woman had entrusted her with it. It was the only thing Annie possessed that came even close to being called an heirloom. It felt wrong to abandon it in some ramshackle swamp shack.

Her aunt's words echoed in her head.

*The magic is strong in you. I can feel it like a pent-up tide.*

The old woman had said the book was her heritage. She had wanted Annie to use it. To embrace the magic contained within its pages.

The loup-garou could never come back. That much was obvious. But did she really have to abandon the entire book because of one bad incantation?

Annie lifted the spell book back out of the hole and unwrapped it again. Then she leafed through the pages until she came to the one containing the wolf spell.

Without allowing herself time to think, she tore the entire leaf out of the book.

Setting the rest of the volume aside, she rolled the torn page into a tube and put it into the bag, wrapping the plastic tightly enough around it to make sure the page didn't uncurl. Once she was satisfied that it wouldn't come undone and no moisture could get inside, Annie placed the rolled page into the secret chamber under the floor and closed the trapdoor.

She brushed leaves and dirt back over the floor, hiding the trapdoor, just in case someone else stumbled across the shack and got curious. Then she picked up the spell book, climbed to her feet, and headed back out into the sultry Louisiana morning.

# FIFTY-TWO

AS ANNIE DOUCET was picking her way back from the shack in the swamp to her cabin, Robbie Decker was sitting on his bed, staring absently out the bedroom window at a patch of pale blue sky.

It was Saturday, but even if it had been the middle of the week, school would have been canceled after the tragedy in the woods.

He hadn't slept all night. Every time he tried, he saw that beast again, stalking toward him with slathering jaws and those burning yellow eyes. He had been sure it would kill him. Tear him apart just like Travis, Karen, and the others. He closed his eyes and waited for death to find him. When he opened them again, the beast was gone. He was alone with the mutilated bodies of his friends.

He had stood there with the heat of the bonfire against his back for what felt like an eternity, dazed and terrified to move, but was probably no longer than a minute or two. The Chiffons finished singing "One Fine Day" and a more recent song took its place—the equally fitting "Alone Again" by Gilbert O'Sullivan. It was almost as if the radio was *trying* to be ironic.

But it broke his fugue and spurred Robbie Decker into action.

He took one last look at the surrounding carnage, then fled to his car and jumped in. Fifteen minutes later, he was out of the woods and speeding along the road to town, even as Sheriff Barstow flew in the other direction with lights flashing and siren wailing. Behind him was another car, equally lit up, and no doubt driven by his deputy.

Robbie ignored them and kept going. When he arrived home, he parked in the driveway and hurried inside as quietly as he could. The sound of a TV show—most likely the CBS *Friday Night Movie*—filtered from the living room, where his parents were no doubt curled up on the couch with a tub of popcorn.

He climbed the stairs, went to his bedroom and closed the door. At some point he was sure the sheriff or one of his deputies would show up to interview him. Robbie had made no attempt to call the them, but someone clearly had—most likely one of the other survivors—and when the cops asked who else was there his name would probably come up.

But there was no knock on the door. Not that night, nor the next morning. At least so far. And Robbie Decker certainly wasn't going to volunteer the information of his own free will. He figured he couldn't add any details beyond what the other kids who survived the slaying would already have provided, and even in his traumatized state he understood that being asso-ciated with what happened in that clearing might be a hindrance to his choice of career once he left school. Robbie wanted to be a cop.

Climbing off the bed, he went to the nightstand, where a picture of him and his friends sat in a small silver frame. It had been taken the previous year, in the fall, when they had all gone to the town's annual Halloween Haunting Festival.

He picked up the photo and studied it, staring into the eyes of people he would never see again, even as they looked back at him with blissful ignorance of their impending fate. Five of them, including Karen and Travis, all wearing cheesy costumes they had found at the five and dime store on Main. As far as Robbie knew, he was the only one in that picture who was still alive.

He put the frame back down and turned back toward the bed. At that moment, there was a knock at the front door.

Robbie went to the window and peered out, but he couldn't see the visitor because they were standing under the covered porch that spanned the front of the house. He swallowed. What if it was Sheriff Barstow, after all? What would he say?

Robbie hadn't explicitly told his parents he was attending the kegger but hadn't said he wasn't, either. It was a time-honored tradition, and as a member of the football team it was only logical that he would go. Maybe one of the other players on the squad had mentioned him being there, or maybe the sheriff was just fishing for leads and visiting every member of the team who was still alive to see what they knew.

Robbie briefly considered sliding the window up and climbing out onto the porch roof, then shimmying down the nearest post to the ground and making his escape. He'd snuck out that way many times after curfew.

But he didn't.

For one, it was broad daylight, and he was sure to be seen by whoever was at the door. Also, it would be pointless. It wasn't like he could hide from the cops forever. Eventually, he would have to come home, and they would be waiting.

Better to get it over with.

He pondered his options. He could lie and say that he wasn't at the Kickoff Kegger, but that would be just as useless. If someone had ratted him out, the cops would already know that he was there. He could say he left early, but again, he might back himself into a corner he couldn't get out of.

The best thing he could do was to be honest. Or at least, fudge the truth. He could say that he didn't know what attacked them. That it all happened too fast, and he didn't see it clearly. There was no need to mention that the beast had focused its attention on him. That he thought it would kill him. By that time, everyone had either run away, or they were already dead. Might as well salvage what he could from the situation.

He certainly wasn't going to say that he saw a seven-foot-tall wolf that reared up on its hind legs and walked erect, regardless of what anyone else said. Because he could think of only one explanation for what that creature was, and he wasn't sure he believed it himself.

Robbie sank down onto the bed and waited for the inevitable.

But when the expected knock came on his bedroom door, it wasn't Sheriff Barstow. It was a more welcome voice that called to him from the corridor, asking to come in.

It was Lily.

# FIFTY-THREE

WHEN LILY ENTERED THE ROOM, Robbie jumped up.
She rushed to him and threw her arms around him, kissing Robbie
on the cheek before pulling away.

"I would have come last night after I heard what happened, but
my dad wouldn't let me leave the house. He said it wasn't safe.
That there might be a killer on the loose." She went back and
closed the bedroom door. "Did you go to the kegger?"

Robbie hesitated. So far, no one knew his whereabouts the
previous evening, but that wouldn't be the case if he told Lily. Yet
she was his girlfriend. They had been dating ever since they first
met two weeks earlier at the fair. Since that time, they had been
almost inseparable, but it was still only two weeks.

"Well?" Lily sat on the edge of the bed and patted the
comforter for Robbie to sit down next to her. "Did you go?"

Robbie had to say something, and soon, or Lily might think he
didn't trust her. Which, he now realized, was not true. Despite the
short length of their courtship, Robbie thought he might be falling
in love with this flaxen-haired beauty. Besides, telling someone
might actually make him feel better.

He nodded.

Lily drew in a sharp breath. "Oh, my goodness. Were you there when—"

"I was there. I saw everything."

"You saw the killer?" Lily's eyes flew wide.

Robbie could tell what she was thinking—that he was lucky to be alive. And it was true. "It was horrible, Lil."

"I heard one of the sheriff's deputies talking at Cassidy's. They're saying it was a wolf, or maybe a pack of rabid coyotes."

"It was neither of those things," Robbie said. "At least, not the way they think."

"Then what was it?" Lily put an arm around Robbie's shoulder when she saw he was shaking. "What could have done such a thing?"

"You wouldn't believe me if I told you."

"Try me." Lily placed her other hand on Robbie's.

"It was . . ." Robbie hesitated to say the words because they sounded crazy, even to him. Which meant they would sound even more crazy to Lily, and he really liked her. What if she listened to what he had to say and thought he was nuts? What if she didn't want to see him again after that? He hung his head. "It doesn't matter."

"Hey. You don't need to worry about what I'll think," Lily said, almost as if she had read his mind. "You can tell me anything."

"Really?"

"Yes."

"And you won't repeat it, ever?"

"Cross my heart."

Robbie looked up and met her gaze. One glance was all it took for him to see that she meant everything she had said. He took a deep breath. "It was a werewolf, Lil. I swear to God, it looked just like a werewolf."

He waited to see if Lily would burst out laughing.

But she didn't. Instead, she squeezed his hand. "If that's what you say you saw, then I believe you."

"You do?" The tension drained from Robbie like water through a broken dam.

"One hundred percent." Lily bit her bottom lip thoughtfully. "Do you know why they named this town Wolf Haven?"

Robbie shrugged. "I figured because there used to be a lot of gray wolves around here or something. Or maybe they just couldn't think of a better name."

"That isn't it. I know the real story and it's much more mysterious. And scary!"

"How would you know that?" Robbie tried to keep the skepticism from his voice. "You've been in town for like a month, tops. I've lived here all my life, and I don't even know how the town got its name."

"That's because you never bothered to look. Am I right?"

"Maybe." Robbie shrugged again. "But they made us take some local history classes in middle school. That should count."

"It doesn't. There's no way the school would tell you such a grisly tale."

"But you know it."

"Because I went to the library and did some research. Figured I should know something about this town if I'm going to be stuck here."

"Really? I thought you were into cheerleading." Robbie knew instantly, from the look on Lily's face, that he'd said the wrong thing.

"Cheerleaders can't be smart?"

"I didn't—"

Lily cut him off. "They can't have an interest in things like history?"

"Hey. I didn't mean it like that. You just never mentioned being a book nerd, that's all."

"Because I didn't want to scare you away. You're on the football team. You're a jock."

"Now who's making assumptions?"

"Okay, fair point. I was afraid it might scare you off if you knew I was a closet nerd."

"Nothing would scare me away from you," Robbie said, his stomach performing a little backflip and momentarily easing the fear that writhed there. "I think I—" He stopped himself. Clamped his mouth shut.

"What were you going to say?"

"Doesn't matter." Robbie realized he had almost blurted out too much—told Lily how he felt about her, which might scare her away given the short length of their relationship, even if his tale of coming face to face with a werewolf had not. He changed the subject. "Finish what you were saying about the town."

"Okay." Lily gave him a strange look, then sighed. "Like I said, after I first got here, I wanted to learn about the town, so I went to the library. They have journals there going back over two hundred years all the way to when the first French settlers came to this area. They keep them in a private collection that you have to make an appointment to see. The librarian said I could look at them if I was really careful."

"Why would she do that?" Robbie asked.

"I don't know. Maybe they don't get many teenagers in there wanting to learn about history when it's not on some school test? Doesn't matter. She let me go into a room and look at the journals. Showed me the ones that contained the earliest written history of Wolf Haven."

"And?"

"They didn't name the town because there were a bunch of regular wolves roaming the area. The people who wrote those journals believed werewolves that fled France to escape being hunted down and killed founded Wolf Haven. That's how the town got its name. It was literally a haven for werewolves." Lily stopped to catch her breath. She studied Robbie for a moment, perhaps to gauge his reaction, before continuing. "Except they didn't call them werewolves. They had another name."

"What name?" The knot of fear in the pit of his stomach—the one that had been there since the night before—twisted tighter.

"The loup-garou." Lily said the words in a hushed tone. "So you see, it isn't out of the realm of possibility that you saw a werewolf last night. If you believe the people who wrote those journals, they've been among us for centuries."

Robbie said nothing. It all sounded like a tall tale to him. Nothing but Cajun superstition. But he couldn't refute the evidence of his own eyes. He had seen the wolf. It had been right there, standing in front of him. A nightmare conjured from hell itself.

"Hey," Lily said, resting her head on his shoulder. "What was it you were going to tell me just now when you clammed up? Please tell me."

"I don't think—"

"Please?" She caressed the back of his neck with her fingers. "I want to know."

"Just promise you won't run away."

"Never."

Robbie hesitated a second, then he put his arm around her and threw caution to the wind. "I think I love you."

Lily lifted her head, met his gaze, and in that moment, he thought it was all over. That he had scared her away, after all.

But then she smiled, her eyes alight with joy. "Me too."

# FIFTY-FOUR

JOHN DECKER STOOD in the corner of his father's bedroom —the same bedroom that would become his many years later— and watched Robbie Decker grapple with what he had witnessed at the Kickoff Kegger the previous night.

Sitting next to Robbie on the bed, doing her best to assuage his fears, was Decker's future mother, Lily.

It was strange to see his parents so young and not yet married. At this point in their relationship, they had only been dating for a few weeks. It would be another two years before Robbie Decker proposed, and one year more before they tied the knot.

Decker had seen photos of the wedding in family albums still sitting on a shelf in the house he had inherited after his father's death. An older version of the house he currently stood in. It was a strange sensation to see his parents looking just like they did in those photos. Young and vibrant, with their whole lives ahead of them. Knowing how those lives ended, cut short by tragedy, filled him with a sadness he could not shake. He wanted to go to them, beg them to alter the trajectory of their lives and avoid what lay in store, but it was impossible because he was nothing more than a ghostly observer from the future. He wasn't even sure if the ghost had actually taken him back in time, or if the events he was witnessing were nothing more than shadows of things that had already been. It didn't matter, because he had no ability to interact with these past visions.

Next to him, standing silent and still until now, the Ghost of All Things Past placed a hand on Decker's shoulder. "You've witnessed everything you need to in this era. It's time to move on."

"Wait," Decker said. He shrugged off the ghost's hand and stepped closer to his parents, standing in front of them and studying their faces. The last time he had seen his mother, he was ten years old, and it was not a good memory. He had glimpsed her cold, dead body lying on a mortuary table after she was killed. "Just give me a little more time with them."

"That is not our purpose here," replied the ghost, moving up behind him and placing a hand on his shoulder. "There are other things you need to see. Places we need to visit if you are to put the demons that haunt your past to rest."

"Please," Decker begged. "Just a few more minutes."

But it was too late. The room shifted and changed. It grew faint and then was gone.

Decker expected to find himself back in the library with the grandfather clock striking midnight yet again, but apparently the ghost thought he needed no such break between visions this time. Because instead of the ghostly house on Boston Common, an office with white painted walls and a large desk came into view.

Sitting on one side of the desk were his parents. On the other side was a bearded older man wearing a white lab coat with a pair of fountain pens pushed into the breast pocket. A doctor.

And they weren't in 1972 anymore either.

A calendar sitting on a shelf behind the doctor, surrounded by thick medical volumes, proclaimed the date to be Monday, September 14, 1981.

The year before Decker's birth.

# FIFTY-FIVE

## NEW ORLEANS, SEPTEMBER 1981

ROBBIE DECKER GLARED across the desk, not bothering to hide his frustration. "We've been trying to have a child for six years, and now you're telling us it's impossible."

The man on the other side of the desk, Dr. Brendan Lucas, spoke in a soothing voice that contrasted Robbie Decker's sharp tone. "I'm not saying it's impossible, Mr. Decker. I'm saying that it's unlikely. According to the tests we've run, your wife is suffering from—"

"We know what the tests said." Robbie leaned forward and placed his hands on the desk. "Now, how about you tell us what you're going to do about it?"

"I'm not sure you understand what I've been telling you." Dr. Lucas sat back in his chair and folded his arms. "We can run more tests, but they probably won't change anything."

"No more tests. I don't need you poking and prodding my wife anymore. You've been doing that for six months already, forcing us to drive all the way from Wolf Haven to New Orleans every time."

"Then I'm not sure what you want me to do."

Robbie clenched his jaw. "What I want is a solution. There has to be a treatment for her condition. Some kind of drug you can prescribe. A procedure."

"There really isn't. At least, not at this moment. There is a promising new procedure called IVF that Lily might benefit from, but it's still in the experimental stages right now. It would be prohibitively expensive even if it wasn't since your health insurance is unlikely to cover it."

"What you're saying is that we can't do anything." Robbie slumped back in his chair.

"No. What I'm saying is that you can keep trying to conceive and hope for the best, but regarding medical intervention, we've reached the limit of our ability to help you." The doctor slid open a desk drawer and withdrew a folded sheet of paper. He reached over the table and offered it to Robbie. "Here."

"What's this?" Robbie asked, taking the paper.

"It's a pamphlet. It explains certain things you can do to, uh . . ." The doctor cleared his throat. "Increase your odds of success."

"You just got done telling us we might as well give up."

"That isn't what I said. Your chances of conception are low. It's your choice whether to continue trying. But if you do, it can't hurt to try the techniques in that pamphlet."

"All those tests. All the time we've spent sitting in this office. A single piece of paper is all we have to show for it." Robbie looked down at the pamphlet. He felt like tearing it up, but instead he folded it and tucked the pamphlet into his jacket pocket.

"Robbie, it's not the doctor's fault," Lily said, speaking for the first time since they had entered the office. "He's only trying to help."

"I know." Robbie nodded. He understood Lily was right on an intellectual level, but on an emotional level, he felt let down. When they had first started trying for a child, he thought it would happen quickly, but as time dragged on and nothing happened, his confidence waned. He wondered if it was his fault. If there was something wrong with him, some defect that prevented them from conceiving, because it couldn't be Lily. She was perfect. Eventually, after it became apparent that nothing they did made any difference, Lily suggested they seek professional help. She even found a doctor. A man recommended by one of her coworkers at the library, where she had gone to work as a junior librarian after graduating high school. For the first time, Robbie felt hopeful. Maybe there was a way, after all. But now that he was sitting in front of Dr. Lucas, it was apparent he had been fooling himself. Still, that was no reason to lash out. He took a deep breath and looked at Lucas. "Sorry, I took my frustration out on you. I shouldn't have done that."

"That's quite all right, Mr. Decker. You wouldn't be the first." Lucas smiled. "My advice is to go home, take some time to think about this, and decide how you want to proceed in the future. If you conclude you don't wish to keep trying, there are other options."

"Like what?" Lily asked.

"You might wish to think about adopting."

"Taking someone else's kid?" Robbie rubbed the stubble on his chin. "I don't know about that."

"It's a valid avenue. Thousands of people every year adopt children and love them as if they were their own flesh and blood."

"I'm not disputing that," Robbie said. "It's just that . . . I always wanted a son. My own flesh and blood, as you put it."

Dr. Lucas didn't reply, at least not verbally. His gaze shifted to Lily.

Robbie went cold. He should have realized his words were insensitive before he uttered them. When he looked at Lily, the look on her face confirmed his fears.

"I'm sorry," he said for the second time in as many minutes. "I shouldn't have said that. I didn't mean it the way it came out."

"I know. Don't worry about it." Lily removed a tissue from her pocket and dabbed it under her eyes. She balled up the tissue and dropped it into a wastepaper basket next to the desk, then picked up her purse from beside the chair, setting it on her lap. "I don't think we have anything else to discuss here. We should go."

"Lily . . ." Robbie wished he could take the words back.

"I told you already not to worry about it. I know you want a child of your own, and I'm sorry I can't give it to you." She pushed the chair back and stood up. "I'd really like to leave now."

Robbie climbed to his feet and stepped toward the door, holding it open for her. He could see the secretary in the room beyond, watching them from the corner of her eye while at the same time trying to pretend that she hadn't overheard the exchange.

Lily brushed a wrinkle from her skirt. "Thank you for your time, doctor."

Dr. Lucas nodded. "Why don't you see Andrea on the way out. Let's make a follow-up appointment for a month from now."

Lily shook her head. "That won't be necessary, thank you. We won't be coming back."

Then she turned and walked through the door without giving her husband a second glance.

# FIFTY-SIX

THEY DROVE HOME IN SILENCE. Robbie almost said something a few times, but Lily sat in the passenger seat, turned away from him, staring out the window at the passing scenery. He hated himself for making her feel inadequate back in the doctor's office but could think of no words that would fix it.

When they arrived back in Wolf Haven, she climbed from the car and went inside without waiting for him. Robbie knew that her silence wasn't totally his fault. Lily was always broody after they left the doctor's office. But this time, it felt worse. After being subjected to so many tests, many of them degrading and unpleasant, it was only natural that she would react badly after being told that everything had been in vain. There was nothing modern medicine could do to help her conceive. Worse, Robbie had opened his big mouth and made her feel as if she had let him down. He chided himself for being such an insensitive idiot.

He followed her inside and closed the door. They had been booked for the last appointment of the day at the doctor's office, and the drive home to Wolf Haven had taken longer than usual thanks to heavy rush-hour traffic around the city. His stomach rumbled, reminding him it was dinnertime, but when he went to the kitchen, Lily was not there.

He found her upstairs in the bedroom, lying on the bed atop the covers and facing away from the door. She had kicked her shoes off and hadn't bothered to put them back on the shoe rack in the closet, which was unusual for her.

He approached the bed and sat on the edge. "Hey."

When she didn't reply, he tried again, touching her on the arm.

"I need some time alone right now," Lily said, finally responding.

"Why don't you come downstairs, and I'll make us something to eat. We can talk about this."

"There's nothing to talk about, and I'm not hungry."

Robbie stood up. There was no point trying to talk her out of the melancholy that consumed her. The best thing to do was give her space and wait. He went to the door, then turned back to look at her. "If you need anything, I'll be downstairs."

Lily mumbled a brief reply but remained facing away from him on the bed.

Robbie pulled the door closed, then lingered in the hallway for a minute, hoping she would call him back inside. When she didn't, he turned and went downstairs.

---

By the time Robbie reentered the bedroom at eleven o'clock to retire for the evening, Lily was back to her old self. At least, mostly. During the hours between, he had stayed out of her way, even when she had come downstairs briefly to make a sandwich. He had stayed in the living room and listened to her moving around in the kitchen. Fifteen minutes later, she climbed the stairs again, without looking in on him.

Now she was sitting propped up in bed, wearing his favorite red négligée—the one he had bought her for Valentine's Day two years before—and reading a magazine.

She lowered the magazine and watched him undress. When he headed for the bathroom, her gaze followed.

"I'm sorry about earlier," she said when he came out after showering and cleaning his teeth.

Robbie fluffed his pillow up and climbed under the covers. "You don't need to apologize. I know how hard this has been for you."

"Not just me." Lily still had the magazine in her hand. She placed it on the nightstand. "It's been hard for you too."

"I know. Which is why I think you made the right decision today."

"What decision?"

"Not to keep trying." Robbie yawned, covering his mouth with the back of his hand. "Why put ourselves through so much stress and heartbreak for no reason?"

"You think I decided to stop trying for a baby?"

"You told the doctor we weren't coming back. That sounds pretty definitive to me."

There was a moment of silence.

"I said I didn't want to go back to Dr. Lucas. I never said I wanted to give up completely."

"Then what? You want to find another doctor?" Robbie didn't think that was a good idea. They had already consulted three doctors during the past five years, and none of them had any answers.

"No. Not another doctor. I'm done with letting those people prod me in places I'd rather not let them see. That doesn't mean we can't continue trying on our own. You know, just do what we're going to do anyway and see what happens. No pressure. What harm could there be?"

"No pressure?" Robbie wasn't so sure. "Look, I'm all for keeping our love life alive, but doing it with the express intent of getting pregnant just feels like we're setting ourselves up for more heartbreak. You've been so down lately. I don't want you to keep feeling that way."

"I didn't mean we should keep trying, like we have been. I just meant that we don't shut the door on it completely. If it happens, then great. If not, I'm okay with that. I've accepted it."

"Have you?" Robbie glanced sideways at Lily. "Because keeping even a glimmer of hope alive will do more harm than good at this point. Every doctor we've gone to has told us the same thing—we're fighting a losing battle."

"Which is why I'm done with the doctors," Lily said. "But I'm not done with you, or our chance for a family. We put it out there, ask for what we want, and let the universe decide."

"The universe? That sounds mighty New Age. I wonder who *you've* been talking to."

Lily glanced toward the rotary telephone sitting on the nightstand. "I called Pam to tell her how we got on today."

"Pam Hodgkins. I thought as much." Robbie said, trying to keep the skepticism from his voice. "You know that she's certifiably nuts, right?"

"She's nothing of the sort."

"Says you."

"I *do* say. For your information, she's a smart businesswoman."

Robbie snorted. "She owns that weird Crystal Dreams shop downtown. They sell tarot cards and tinctures. She offers *spirit consultations*, for Pete's sake. Pretending she can speak with the dead hardy makes her Wolf Haven's businesswoman of the year."

"Don't be mean. Pam has been very supportive. She's a good friend. We meet every Wednesday for coffee at Cassidy's. You'd know that if you listened to half of what I say."

"I listen."

"Apparently not. For a deputy sheriff, you aren't very good at picking up on things."

"Big deal. I don't know who you're sipping coffee with at Cassidy's. I listen when it counts."

"Sure you do." Lily patted Robbie's arm. "Anyway, she suggested we try a more . . . spiritual approach."

"I don't like the sound of this." Robbie groaned inwardly. "Let

208 ANTHONY M. STRONG

me guess. She wants to tell our fortunes, so we'll know whether to
keep trying."

"Nothing of the sort. She suggested we go see one of her
customers who has a gift for helping people like us. She helped
Beth Lamborn and her husband when she couldn't conceive. A
month after consulting with her, they were pregnant."

"I'm almost afraid to ask, but who is this miracle worker?"

"Annie Doucet. She practices white witchcraft. At least, that's
what Pam told me. She lives in a cabin out in the swa—"

"I know where Annie Doucet lives." Robbie interrupted his
wife. "And I know all about her. Annie Doucet isn't a witch,
despite the town gossip. If anything, she's a lonely and deluded
woman who probably needs a dose of psychiatric help. I don't
want you anywhere near her."

"Robbie, what harm can it do?" Lily persisted. "Maybe she
doesn't have any special powers, but what if—"

"I said no." Robbie shook his head. Once, many years ago back
in high school, he had felt sorry for Annie Doucet. She had no
friends, and was picked on relentlessly, thanks to her living condi-
tions and crazy mother. He still remembered her nickname.
Swampy Annie. He had tried to help her. Even took her to the fair.
That was right before everything went to hell. Before the massacre
at the Kickoff Kegger. After that, Annie got even weirder. More
withdrawn. She dropped out of school, ostensibly to look after her
mother, who was an alcoholic. But Robbie wasn't convinced. There
was something else going on. A few years later, the rumors started.
That she was practicing witchcraft out at the godforsaken cabin in
the swamp she shared with her mother. People started going to
her. Asking her to help them. Sometimes they were satisfied. Other
times, they reported her as a fraud. He'd been out to that
ramshackle cabin at least eight times since becoming a deputy, and
it never went well. Now his own wife was pinning her hopes of
having a child on the damn woman. It was not going to happen.

"Honey, just hear me out."

"This isn't up for discussion." Robbie folded his arms. "We're not going anywhere near Annie Doucet, and that's my final decision."

"But—"

"No buts. This discussion is over." Robbie said. Then he reached out, turned off the light, and settled down in bed facing away from his wife.

# FIFTY-SEVEN

LILY DECKER WAITED for her husband to leave for work the next morning, then got dressed and left the house. She went to the garage and fetched her bicycle—Lily would have preferred to drive, but they only had one car which Robbie had taken—then set off to do something she probably shouldn't.

The night before, after Robbie had turned off the light, she lay in bed for a long while, unable to sleep. She couldn't understand her husband's resistance to trying a more unorthodox approach. It wasn't like it could hurt, and even if she didn't really believe in that stuff, southern Louisiana was steeped in superstition. Maybe the Cajuns knew something she didn't. At least, enough that she was willing to give it a go.

Which was why, before she fell asleep, Lily had made up her mind. What Robbie Dexter didn't know couldn't hurt him. When she woke up this morning, nothing had changed. Even if it meant going against Robbie, she was determined to follow through.

Annie Doucet lived far out of town on a meandering narrow road that gave up its pavement and turned to dirt a mile before the rundown shack she shared with her mother.

At about the same time as the paved road ended, the bayou began. Coffee-brown water bordered both sides of the trail. Bald cypress trees with conical bases of twisted roots rose from the murky stew. Higher up, Spanish moss dripped from the branches Like living sheets, blotting out the daylight.

For the first time since leaving Wolf Haven behind, Lily started to have second thoughts. The bayou was a scary place, especially when your mode of transportation was a bicycle. She kept an eye on the dark water between the trees, where she knew that alligators and snakes lurked, and pedaled as fast as she dared on the uneven road surface.

Finally, much to her relief, she saw the cabin up ahead. It sat alone on a patch of high land surrounded by yet more towering cypress trees. Lily had never been out this far into the swamp, but she knew it was the right place because she could see no other dwellings. And if that wasn't enough, the faded hand-painted name on the mailbox hanging from a crooked post clinched it.

*Doucet.*

Lily came to a stop and dismounted, then wheeled her bike closer to the cabin and leaned it against the porch railing next to another bicycle with a rusting frame and black tape holding the saddle together.

Now she got a good look at the building and its surroundings. To call the cabin rustic was an understatement. It looked like something out of another century, which was, Lily thought, probably about the same time it had last received a lick of paint. The warped shingle covering its exterior had weathered to a dull gray. The small amount of paint that remained was cracked and scaly, like the skin of some strange reptile. The front porch sagged in one corner where the support post had rotted through. The roofline also had a noticeable dip. A pile of firewood was stacked against the side wall, partially covered by a torn and stained tarp. Two signs hung on opposite posts. One read No TRESPASSING, while the other, daubed in a crude hand, proclaimed TAROT READINGS, POTIONS, AND TINCTURES.

Lily approached the porch steps warily. The contradictory signs —one warning people away while the other advertised Annie Doucet's services—gave her pause. She would have phoned ahead and made an appointment, but Pam from Crystal Dreams had informed her that the Doucet household didn't own a telephone. The cabin was far enough out that they were lucky to even have electricity. The only way to procure Annie Doucet's services was to make the trip out into the swamp and hope she was in a receptive mood.

Which was why Lily now hesitated at the bottom of the steps, her eagerness from the night before waning. She placed a foot on the bottom step, ignored the NO TRESPASSING sign, and started up toward the cabin's front door.

Her heart thudded against her ribs. If it wasn't for her over-whelming desperation, she might well have turned back already. But she had come this far, and if there was even a slim chance that the woman inside that cabin could help her, Lily intended to grasp it. Even so, she took an instinctive step back after knocking on the door.

Then she waited.

A minute passed.

She wondered if her trip had been in vain. That no one was home. But then, as she contemplated knocking again, the curtain covering the window on the left side of the door twitched and a pair of dark eyes looked out at her.

"Who are you?" A voice floated through the door. "What do you want?"

"I'm here to see . . ." Lily said in a faltering voice. Her throat was dry. Scratchy. She swallowed. "Pam from the crystal store in town said I should come here. I'm looking for Annie Doucet."

The eyes observed her a moment longer before the curtain fell back in place. A couple of seconds passed, then the door opened slowly inward.

The woman who stood on the other side was about the same age as Lily, but that was where the resemblance ended. Her hair— already streaked with a tinge of gray—hung over her shoulders in limp strands. Her skin was pulled so tight over her skull, her eyes so recessed in their sockets, that Lily briefly thought she was looking at a living skeleton until she realized it was nothing more than a trick of the light.

"Are you Annie?" Lily asked in a small voice.

The woman nodded. "I know you."

"You do?"

"You're Robbie Decker's wife," Annie said in a tone that sent chills running down Lily's spine. "Tell me why I should help you."

"I, um . . ." Lily glanced toward her bicycle.

"Speak up. Don't be afraid. I don't bite."

Lily wasn't so sure of that, but she had come this far. "I was told you have a gift. That you can help me. I want to get pregnant."

Annie observed Lily for a long moment, her eyes shrinking to narrow slits. Then she stepped aside. "In that case, you'd better come in."

# FIFTY-EIGHT

AFTER LILY STEPPED INSIDE, Annie closed the door, immersing them in the gloom.

She looked around, taking in her surroundings. The cabin was, in reality, a shotgun style shack with a small living room and open kitchen at the front, and a corridor that ran through to the back with what Lily assumed were two bedrooms. The last room, visible because the door stood open, was a bathroom. Next to this was another door that probably exited the rear of the building.

A musty scent hung in the air. An unpleasant combination of odors that smelled something like mothballs and rot. The furniture was in about the same condition as the rest of the cabin. Lily guessed that most of it had been salvaged from the side of the road.

Annie watched her with eyes that glinted from the light of a lamp standing in the corner. She motioned toward the torn and stained couch. "You might as well sit down. And be quiet. Mama's sleeping and I don't want to disturb her."

Lily looked at the sofa, almost said that she was fine standing, then gave in and sat down, perching on the edge and trying not to touch anything.

Annie crossed to a chair on the other side of the coffee table. "Your husband doesn't like me."

"I don't think that's true," Lily said, even though she knew better. Robbie's words from the night before echoed through her mind. His insistence that she keep her distance from Annie Doucet.

"He doesn't like me because we have history."

"Robbie's just doing his job," Lily said. Her husband hadn't explicitly mentioned it—he rarely talked about his work at home— but she was sure from his tone that the pair had crossed paths over the years.

Annie observed Lily for a moment, a slight smile playing across her lips as if she knew some deeper truth, but then she cleared her throat and leaned forward. "He doesn't know you're here, does he?"

"No," Lily admitted.

"That's what I thought." Another pause. "What makes you think I'd help you?"

"Because that's what you do, isn't it?"

"Sometimes. For those folks who aren't afraid of me." Annie leaned back in her chair. "Are you afraid of me, Lily Decker?"

"A bit." Lily shifted on the sofa, forced herself not to think about what she was sitting on. "Are you going to help me or not?"

"Are you going to tell your husband that you came here?"

"Probably not."

"Then I'll help you. It will be our little secret."

"Thank you." Lily sagged with relief. It had taken all her courage to brave the swamp and seek the help she and Robbie so desperately needed. To fail now would have been crushing.

"Don't thank me yet," Annie said. "Fertility spells aren't easy. There's no guarantee it will work. You must believe in the magic as much as I do. Are you able to do that?"

"I think so," Lily said. "I mean, yes, I can believe."

"Good." Annie stood and went to the kitchen. She came back with a Mason jar and a knife, which she held out.

216 ANTHONY M. STRONG

"What's this for?" Lily asked, eyeing the knife with trepidation.

"For the ritual to work, there has to be a blood connection."

"You want me to cut myself?" Lily recoiled.

"It's the only way if you want to have that baby."

"How much blood?"

"The more you give, the stronger the bond." Annie pressed the knife into Lily's hand. "Of course, if you can't do it, I'll understand."

"I can do it," Lily said quickly, even though she wasn't entirely sure. She pressed the knife into her palm. "Just a small cut."

"Barely more than a nick." Annie held the Mason jar beneath Lily's open hand. "Best to do it quick before you think on it too much."

That wasn't the worst advice. Lily gritted her teeth and pushed down on the knife, then sliced sideways across her palm. In her haste, she cut too deep, opening a gash from her thumb to her pinky.

"Yow." She cried out and jerked her hand up, almost dropping the knife as the blood gushed.

"Quickly, over the jar. I don't want any blood on the floor." Annie grabbed Lily's wrist and pulled it down. "Hold it there."

Lily nodded through the pain. She clenched her fist, letting the blood spill into the jar.

After a while, when the flow had reduced to a trickle, Annie pulled the jar away and screwed the lid on. "That's enough."

She took the knife and went back to the kitchen, leaving Lily to cup her injured hand to avoid staining the floor.

Annie returned with a rag and thrust it at Lily. "Here. Wrap your hand in this. It will stop the bleeding."

Lily took the rag and wrapped it gingerly around the cut, wondering just how many germs were on the torn piece of fabric. But it was better than the alternative. When she got home, she could clean the wound with disinfectant and bandage it properly. In the meantime, she tried not to think of what she had just done. "What happens next?"

"You go home and come back again tomorrow at the same time."

"What?" Lily could hardly believe her ears. "That's all you're going to do—just make me cut myself and then send me home?"

"Come back tomorrow. Everything will be ready by then." Annie placed a hand on Lily's shoulder and steered her toward the door. She glanced down at the injured hand. "And remember, don't tell your husband. He won't understand."

That much was right. After Robbie's reaction to her suggestion the previous evening, Lily had no intention of mentioning the day's events to him. She only hoped it would be as easy to slip away again the following morning.

"This is going to work, right?" she asked as Annie pushed her out onto the porch.

"I will do my part. The rest is up to you."

"What does that mean?" The way Annie spoke the words made Lily think there was more she would need to do than just have faith.

But if there was, Annie Doucet would not let on. She stepped back inside and closed the door without another word, leaving Lily standing alone on the porch.

# FIFTY-NINE

ANNIE WENT to the window and watched Robbie Decker's wife cycle back down the trail toward Wolf Haven. This was a curious turn of events, to be sure. After everything that had happened between herself and Robbie back when they were in high school—after what the wolf had done at the Kickoff Kegger— it was ironic that Lily Decker was now asking for Annie's help to create a new life.

She looked down at the Mason jar, and the thin layer of blood pooled in the bottom. She would do as Lily asked, even though she owed Robbie Decker nothing. He had led her on back then, made her think it was possible for someone like her to lead a normal life, and then cast her aside in favor of the woman who had just knocked on her door. If anything, Robbie Decker was the indebted one. She had spared his life at the Kickoff Kegger. He was only alive because of her.

But that was a long time ago, and Annie was not the same person now. She had cast black magic aside and focused on more wholesome uses for her powers. The spell that had transformed her into the wolf was still safely hidden under the floorboards in the secret shack out in the swamp. The book that Aunt Babette had given her, minus that page, was stored on a high shelf in her bedroom closet. She didn't open it because she was afraid of what else might tempt her within its covers.

Instead, she had collected a small library of less intimidating spell books full of white magic, mostly bartered for hard-to-find witchcraft ingredients that she collected from the swamp and took to Pam Hodgkins at Crystal Dreams. Other times, during high summer, when the occasional tourist from New Orleans found their way to Wolf Haven, she would give tarot and palm readings in the small room at the back of the shop.

It was to one of those books that Annie now turned. After placing the Mason jar in the fridge, she went to her bedroom and took down a thick leather-bound volume from a shelf next to the bed. She leafed through it until she came to the right page and started to read, even though she knew the spell well and had performed it many times.

Later that evening, as the full moon glowed overhead, she would take a flashlight and venture out into the swamp. There were ingredients she needed to gather, and they had to be fresh. Then, under the light of that same moon, she would combine all the ingredients, along with the blood she had taken from Robbie Decker's wife, and create a potion guaranteed to make fertile ground of Lily's barren womb. At least, if she opened her mind to the unknown.

Witchcraft worked best on believers.

Annie closed the book and returned it to the shelf, then stepped out into the hallway and went to her mother's bedroom.

Emmylou Doucet was lying on the bed, facing away. At first, Annie thought she was still sleeping off the previous evening's hooch, but at the sound of the door opening, she stirred and sat up.

"I heard you talking to someone," she said in a raspy voice.

"It was nothing, Mama. Just a young woman looking for my help."

"Looking for a witch, more like." Emmylou Doucet swung her

feet off the bed and stood on wobbly legs. "I've told you before, I don't want you doing that stuff under my roof."

"It's my roof as well."

"Then maybe you should find somewhere else to live." Emmylou made her way toward the door and pushed into the hallway.

"And what are you gonna do, Mama?" Annie asked, following her mother toward the kitchen. "You can't take care of yourself. We've had this discussion so many times."

Emmylou grunted and went to the pantry, where she took out a bottle full of clear liquid. Moonshine from the illicit still on the back porch. "I can take care of myself."

"No, you can't." Annie followed her mother into the living room and watched her flop down in the chair with the bottle cradled in her arms. "I wish you'd let me use my magic to take care of your problem. You don't need to be drinking that gut rot all the time. There's a spell—"

"I said no witchcraft, and I meant it. I'm doing just fine as I am. Now leave me alone."

Annie sighed. This was a battle she was never going to win. She had learned that lesson long ago when she was still a teenager. The spell books were the same. The only difference now was that she stood up to her mother. Wasn't afraid of her anymore. Of course, Emmylou Doucet wasn't the same woman she had been a decade ago, either. She still bristled at her daughter's choice of life-style, but knew better than to push her too far, so they had settled into an uneasy routine where they butted heads, had their arguments, and no one gave any real ground.

Which was exactly what Emmylou Doucet was doing now with the liquor bottle. She lifted it to her lips and took a swig.

Annie gave up and went to the kitchen, opened the fridge, and checked on the Mason jar containing Lily Decker's blood. It was unlikely her mother would move for the rest of the night now she had her moonshine, and when she did, it would be to stagger back into her bedroom and pass out. But Annie didn't want to take any chances. She moved the Mason jar to the back behind a pitcher of iced tea that her mother was sure to avoid, then retreated to her room, where she flopped down on the bed and waited for darkness.

# SIXTY

LILY CYCLED BACK to Wolf Haven as fast as she could. It wasn't easy with her injured hand, which stung every time she gripped the handlebars.

When she arrived home, she went straight to the bathroom where she washed and disinfected the cut, then dressed it with a clean bandage before throwing the bloodied rag in the trash.

She spent the rest of the day unable to concentrate on anything but what Annie had in store for her the following morning. She hoped it wouldn't be as unpleasant as slicing her palm open but wasn't going to hold her breath. Annie's lack of a reply when pressed on the subject was not lost on Lily, and she wondered if it was because the answer might be worse than not knowing. All things considered, it might be better to steer clear of Annie Doucet from now on, just like Robbie wanted, and forget the entire thing.

But even as the idea occurred to her, Lily knew she was going back. Because the doctors had failed her, and it was all she had left. Also, the woman already had her blood. Who knew what she would do with it if Lily didn't go back?

When Robbie came home that evening, the first thing he asked about was the bandage on Lily's hand.

"I cut myself peeling potatoes for dinner," Lily answered,

which was partly true. There was a pot of potatoes on the cooktop, and some carrots, which she intended to cook up and serve with a pork roast she had put in the oven before he arrived home.

Robbie accepted the explanation without question and went upstairs to change out of his uniform. By the time he came back down, Lily was hard at work in the kitchen, preparing dinner.

Afterward, as they settled down in the living room for the evening, Robbie revisited their conversation from the night before.

"I'm sorry I snapped at you last night," he said. "I know you've had a tough day, and it was wrong of me. I know you're just trying to explore every avenue before we give up."

"I still don't see how it could hurt," Lily replied, even though it already had. The cut on her palm was aching, and she hoped she hadn't sliced deep enough to require stitches. "But it's okay. I know you don't believe in this stuff."

"You be surprised what I believe in." Robbie put an arm around her. "But I still don't want you anywhere near Annie Doucet. She's not right in the head."

"Is that your official assessment as a law enforcement officer?" Lily asked.

"No. It's my personal opinion. My official assessment is that she preys on superstition to take people's money."

"Or maybe she gives them hope."

"False hope." Robbie rubbed his temples. "Look, I don't want to get into this again. And before you say it, yes, I do still want to have a child, but I don't think that grasping at straws is the way to go about it. All it will bring is more heartbreak when nothing happens."

"I understand," Lily said, letting the issue drop. She agreed with Robbie. There was no point in continuing to talk about it. He'd made up his mind, and she had done the same. Tomorrow she would go back to that cabin in the bayou and do whatever Annie Doucet asked of her. If it didn't work, then so be it. Robbie never had to find out either way.

The next morning, after her husband left for work, Lily made the trip out into the bayou for the second time. By the time she arrived at the cabin, butterflies swarmed in her stomach. She climbed the steps and knocked on the door.

But this time, it wasn't Annie who answered.

Instead, Lily found herself face-to-face with an older woman who looked back at her with a scowl.

"Didn't you see that?" she asked, pointing to the no trespassing sign nailed to the porch post.

"I saw it," Lily replied, taking a step back.

"Then what's the matter with you?" When the woman spoke, drops of spittle flew off her lips. "Don't you read?"

"I'm sorry. I have an appointment with Annie."

"Then you've wasted your time. Annie isn't here."

"Are you sure about that?" Lily glanced toward the rusting bicycle still propped up against the porch railing. She couldn't imagine it belonged to anyone else. "She told me to come back today."

"You don't think I know my own mind?" The scowl deepened. "Annie can't see you. Now get off my—"

"Mama." A voice spoke behind the old woman. "Go back into the bedroom and leave her alone."

Annie came up behind her mother and took her arm, tried to steer her back into the house.

The old woman shrugged off her daughter's touch. "We talked about this yesterday afternoon. I don't like you doing this stuff. Your Aunt Babette refused to stop, and it brought her nothing but trouble. She died alone and miserable."

"That's not what she told me," Annie said. "And she didn't die alone. We were both there with her when she went."

"And I wish I'd never taken you. Then she wouldn't have filled your head with such nonsense."

"That nonsense pays the bills, Mama." Annie managed to push

her mother toward the rear of the house. "And a good thing too. If it wasn't for me, we'd be sitting in the dark with an empty fridge. Now go back and lay down. We can talk once my business is done."

The old woman took one more look at Lily, still standing in the doorway, and shook her head. Then she shuffled off back toward the hallway and disappeared through the closest door, shouting loudly behind her.

Annie turned back to Lily. "Well, don't just stand there. Come on in. I don't have all day."

Lily stepped over the threshold. "I didn't mean to upset your mother. I'm sorry."

"Don't you worry about her." Annie went to the kitchen and came back a moment later carrying the Mason jar she had used to catch Lily's blood the day before. The jar now contained much more than blood. A greenish brown liquid sloshed within. She also carried a small cedar box, which she offered to Lily. "This is the first thing you need."

Lily took the box and opened the lid. Inside was a small, crudely fashioned doll made of twisted black twigs.

"What is this?" she asked, almost afraid to know the answer.

"That's a physical representation of your unborn child. It will draw the baby's spirit to you. You must place the doll under your mattress before you make love. Leave it there until you conceive, then remove it and burn the doll. Put the ashes back inside the box and bury them where no one will ever look."

"Is that all I need to do?" Lily asked, relieved. Hiding the doll under her mattress for a few weeks didn't seem so bad.

"No." Annie held out the Mason jar. "You must drink this. Both you and Robbie. Half each. Do it tonight while there's a full moon. Spells work better under the full moon."

Lily stared at the jar in dismay. There was a lot of liquid and it probably tasted as bad as it looked. Actually, she had a feeling it would taste worse. "How am I going to convince Robbie to drink that?"

"That's not my problem. But the spell won't work if you don't."

"Is there anything else?" Lily took the jar.

"Just drink the brew and put the doll under the bed. The rest will take care of itself."

Lily nodded. She wedged the jar under one arm and reached into her pocket with the other. "How much do I owe you?"

"I don't cast spells for a fee. I give my magic freely. That's the only way it works."

"Then how do you make money?" Lily was confused.

"You leave me a gift of whatever you can afford." Annie went to the door and opened it. "Place your offering under the mat, and I'll retrieve it when you've gone."

"Oh." Lily stepped outside. "Thank you."

"You're welcome. Don't forget. Drink the brew first, then put the doll under your mattress. And remember to burn the doll once you're done with it. That's important."

"I will." Lily wondered what would happen if she didn't burn the doll. She had no intention of finding out.

She waited for Annie to go back inside and close the door, then pulled a wad of folded banknotes from her pocket. Fifty dollars in total. She bent down and lifted the filthy mat in front of the door and slipped the money underneath, then dropped the mat back in place. That done, she descended the steps and went to her bike, placing the jar and the box into the basket attached to the handlebars. Then, as she cycled back toward Wolf Haven, she wondered how on earth she was going to get Robbie to drink Annie Doucet's foul-looking concoction.

# SIXTY-ONE

LILY SPENT the rest of the morning and early afternoon fretting over how she was going to convince Robbie to drink his half of the gross-looking concoction in the Mason jar. Just handing it to him wasn't going to work, but what other choice was there?

Then she had an idea.

She figured there were no more than twelve ounces of liquid in the jar or about the same as found in a bottle of beer. That wasn't too much when split between both of them, especially if she could disguise it. And there was no better way to do that than by making one of Robbie's favorite meals—gumbo.

The only question was, would mixing the potion with other ingredients stop it from working?

The obvious way to find out would be to ask the person who'd given it to her, but Annie Doucet didn't have a telephone, and Lily wasn't willing to cycle all the way back out into the bayou again. For one thing, there wouldn't be time to prepare the meal once she got her answer. Also, she didn't want to risk a second encounter with Annie's mother.

In the end, she decided to risk it. Annie hadn't explicitly told her that it couldn't be mixed with anything else, but she had impressed upon Lily the need to consume it that night, while the moon was still full. Which meant she would have to start preparing the gumbo right away, because it would need to simmer for at least two to three hours if she wanted enough complexity of flavor to mask the taste of Annie Doucet's potion. Even then, she wasn't sure it would do the job.

There was only one way to find out.

She gathered together the ingredients she needed, and went about making the gumbo, including chicken thighs and andouille sausage, the latter of which she cut into slices and browned in a pan before adding to the roux along with the holy trinity: Bell peppers, onions, and celery. The one thing she didn't add yet was the contents of the Mason jar. She decided to stir that in at the very end, right before serving, because she didn't want to risk any of the potion evaporating while the gumbo was cooking.

Three hours later, after simmering the roux on low heat until it thickened to a consistency she was pleased with—which was thicker than normal to account for the Mason jar full of liquid she would add later—Lily cooked the rice.

And not a moment too soon.

Robbie Decker walked through the door as she was laying the table.

He sniffed the air and broke out into a wide grin. "Gumbo?"

Lily nodded.

"You hate cooking gumbo. What's the occasion?"

"Can't I make something nice for my husband?" Lily replied, fending off his suspicions. It was true—she didn't like making gumbo. Lily hadn't grown up anywhere near Louisiana, having moved to Wolf Haven in her late teens when her mother took a teaching job at the local high school. She found the dish finicky, especially the constant stirring that was required to make sure the roux didn't burn. But in this case, it was worth it. Even if Robbie tasted Annie Doucet's potion, he probably wouldn't say anything so long as it wasn't too strong a flavor, for fear of putting his wife off from ever making his favorite dish again.

"Hey, I'm not complaining." Robbie headed toward the stairs to change out of his uniform. "Give me fifteen minutes to take a shower and then we'll eat."

Lily watched him go, then turned her attention back to the task at hand. She went to the fridge and took out the Mason jar before taking two bowls down from the cupboard.

From upstairs came the sound of Robbie showering. The water pipes groaned and whistled, like they always did when the hot water was running. After ten minutes, the pipes quieted down, a sure sign Robbie had finished and would be back at any moment.

Lily prepared two servings of the gumbo, adding the rice to the bowls first, then scooping generous helpings of the thick stew over the top, making sure to include lots of meat.

Now came the part she was dreading.

Lily picked up the Mason jar and unscrewed the top. She experimented on her own bowl first, gauging half the liquid and pouring it in slowly. She stirred the mixture and scooped some up with a spoon, then put it to her lips.

She held it there a moment, almost afraid to know if her work had been for nothing. If the gumbo tasted awful, she would be forced to find another way of getting the potion into her husband. She would have to consume her own bowl regardless of the taste because there wasn't enough of Annie Doucet's concoction left to do otherwise.

She had to know, either way, because Robbie was on the stairs now.

Taking a deep breath, she pushed the spoon into her mouth and swallowed the liquid.

To her surprise, it wasn't so bad. A little earthy, perhaps, but palatable.

She picked up the Mason jar and dumped the remaining liquid into Robbie's serving, giving it a quick stir even as he walked into the kitchen.

"I can't wait," he said, reaching past her and picking up the bowl. "I'm starving."

"That's good to hear," Lily said, glancing at the pot on the stove where the rest of the gumbo still sat. "Because there's plenty more once you finish that."

"Already on it." Robbie grabbed a spoon and tucked in before he'd even reached the dining room table. He shoveled a helping of rice and sausage into his mouth and smacked his lips. "This is tasty. Much better than the last time you made it. You find a new recipe?"

"Something like that," Lily said, overcome by a rush of relief. Then she grabbed her own bowl, joined Robbie at the table, and tried not to think about what might be in Annie Doucet's gross-looking concoction as she forced herself to eat every last bite of the potion-laced gumbo.

# SIXTY-TWO

LATER THAT NIGHT, while Robbie was sitting on the couch watching TV, Lily snuck upstairs with the cedar box containing the strange stick doll that Annie had given her.

She went to the bedroom and removed the effigy from its box, then lifted the mattress and pushed the tiny figure made of entwined twigs as far underneath as she could reach, before dropping the mattress back in place.

That done, she went to her dresser and opened the bottom drawer—where she kept her undies and knew Robbie would never look—and hid the box all the way in the back.

When she went back downstairs and joined him on the couch, he glanced sideways at her but said nothing, then returned to watching his show.

She sat with her hands in her lap and watched TV, but barely registered what was happening on the screen. All she could think about was the strange potion, and how Annie had told her to drink it while the moon was full. Did that mean that they also had to do other things while it was a full moon? Annie hadn't given her any instructions beyond drinking the potion and putting the doll under their mattress.

She didn't want to take a chance.

Which was why, when the show ended, Lily suggested they go to bed early. For a moment, she thought Robbie was going to protest because he liked to watch Johnny Carson on *the Tonight Show*, but when he saw the impish look on her face, he forgot all about late-night TV.

Not that it mattered.

Annie Doucet's potion and the doll hidden under their mattress didn't work that night, nor the next. In fact, it wasn't until almost two months—and a lot of early nights—later that Lily finally realized their long journey was over.

She was pregnant.

Robbie proclaimed it a miracle, especially since they hadn't been back to the doctor in all that time.

Lily knew better. It was all thanks to Annie Doucet and her white witchcraft. Which was why, at the first opportunity after she was sure, Lily retrieved the cedar box from her bottom drawer and removed the doll from under their mattress.

She took both items outside, then burned the doll in the backyard fire pit just as Annie had instructed her to do. After scooping up the ashes and placing them into the box, she buried it beneath the roots of a sprawling live oak in the corner of their yard where no one would ever find it.

Eight months later, in July, she gave birth to a healthy baby boy. They named him John.

# SIXTY-THREE

## BACK IN THE LIBRARY

JOHN DECKER REELED as the past faded away and the library came back into view. He could hardly believe what he had seen. "My mother went to Annie Doucet for help getting pregnant?"

The ghost of all things past nodded.

"She resorted to witchcraft?"

The ghost nodded again. "She was desperate. At her wit's end. They had tried everything else to have a child."

"Why did you show that to me?" Decker asked. "I don't see how it's relevant."

"Because everything is interconnected," the ghost answered. "Your father taking pity on a young Annie Doucet before he met your mother. Annie's humiliation at the hands of his friends, and the tragedy that followed. Your mother seeking Annie's help to conceive. The threads of fate run through them all like a winding river flowing toward the ocean."

"If those events are all connected, then what are they leading to?"

"The truth of your past," said the ghost, pulling another book from the shelf. "We have one more place to go."

"Where?" Decker asked, afraid that he already knew. "What is it that you want to show me?"

The ghost didn't answer. Instead, she opened the book as the grandfather clock struck midnight yet again.

The library shifted and faded from view even as the final peals from the clock rang out, to be replaced by a time and place Decker knew all too well. Wolf Haven when he was ten years old—a week before his mother died.

# SIXTY-FOUR

## WOLF HAVEN, HALLOWEEN NIGHT 1992

FERNDALE AVENUE WAS PACKED with ghosts and ghouls, zombies, killers in hockey masks, vampires, and even a couple of wizards gripping wands in one hand and plastic buckets to collect candy in the other.

Halloween was John Decker's favorite night of the year. He had been looking forward to it since summer ended. If the days had to get shorter, and the weather colder, then Halloween made it all worthwhile. And for the first time since he could remember, it fell on a Saturday, which meant there was no school to get in the way of his fun.

Even better, after turning ten years old a couple of months before, his mother had allowed him out with his friends unsupervised for the first time, so long as he promised to be home by eight, and not a moment later. He had also agreed to stay within three blocks of home.

Right now, he was about to break that rule. At least, if he ventured across Vail Street toward the row of homes that beckoned beyond and tempted him with the promise of even more goodies to fill his already overstuffed bucket.

236 ANTHONY M. STRONG

He hesitated, one foot on the curb and the other on the road, and glanced back toward Collier Street, where his mother would be waiting anxiously for his return.

"What are you doing?" Logan Olden asked, almost bumping into his friend as he stepped around him and crossed to the other side.

"I promised not to go too far from the house," Decker replied. "Why don't we try the other side of the street instead?"

"Because we've already done that, stupid," Beau Thornton said, punching Decker on the arm hard enough to elicit a yelp of pain. "We should keep going before the rest of the street gets picked clean."

"Yow!" Decker cried, pulling his arm away. He didn't much care for Beau Thornton. He was brash and pushy. Thornton also thought he was better than the rest of them just because his family came from money, and because he lived in an old plantation house on the outskirts of town. Decker wished that Beau had found someone else to go trick-or-treating with. He pulled his foot back from the road. "I'm not going any further."

"What's your problem?"

"You know very well what my problem is. My dad's the sheriff and he's been driving around all night. If he catches me too far from home, I'll be in for it."

"Fine," said the fourth member of their group, Tucker Williams. "We'll go back down the other side, but you better hope no one recognizes us. I don't have anywhere near enough candy yet." He reached into the plastic grocery bag his mother had given him instead of a bucket and pulled out a banana. "And someone gave me this. Gross."

"I got one too," Logan said, crossing back over to join them. "Figure I'll toss it in a trashcan before I get home, otherwise mom will make me eat it instead of the chocolate."

"Why did you even take it?" Beau asked as they crossed to the other side of the street and started back in the direction from which they came.

Logan shrugged. "I don't know. Mrs. Gentry gave it to me. She's really old, and all she had was fruit. I didn't want to hurt her feelings."

"Wouldn't have bothered me," Beau said with a snort. "If people don't know the rules of trick-or-treating, they shouldn't leave their porch lights on."

"Yeah, right! Like you'd have refused to take it."

"Sure I would. I'd have told the old hag to keep her rotten fruit, Then I'd have gotten some rotten eggs and plastered the front of her house with them."

"No, you wouldn't," Tucker said. "You're a chicken-shit. And where would you even get rotten eggs, anyway?"

"I don't know." Beau glared at his friend. "And I'm not a chicken-shit."

"Says you."

"Yeah. Says me." Beau climbed the steps of a shotgun house with plastic skeletons hanging from the porch railings. He went to a chair sitting next to the front door, upon which sat a large bowl. He looked down into it and pulled a face. Then he turned and stomped back down the steps. "It's empty. There's nothing left. I told you we should have kept going."

"It's fine," Decker said, looking down at his pumpkin shaped collection bucket, which was brimming with candy. "We've got plenty already."

"We could go to my place and watch a horror film," Logan piped up. "My dad rented the latest Freddie movie. I bet he'd let us play it."

"That's lame." Beau huffed and glanced wistfully toward the far end of the street, where other trick-or-treaters were quickly depleting what remained of the free candy. "Besides, I've already seen it and the movie sucks."

"Well, what else are we going to do?" Logan asked.

"We could sneak into the graveyard and make Beau go inside that crypt with the broken door and sit there in the dark," said Tucker Williams. "Since he's so brave and all."

Logan grinned, clearly amused by the idea. "Maybe he can take some rotten eggs to throw at the corpse if it wakes up and chases him."

"That's the best you've got?" Beau threw his arms up. "Let's go. I'll sit in that crypt all night if you want me to."

"Guys," Decker said. "I can't go to the graveyard. I have to be home by eight. Besides, it's such an obvious place to go on Halloween. My dad's sure to swing by there and make sure nothing's going on."

Logan shook his head. "He's right. I don't need Sheriff Decker taking me home in the back of his car. My parents will ground me for a year."

"Aw. That's too bad." Now it was Beau's turn to grin. "Guess you'll just have to take my word for it I'm not a chicken-shit."

"Not necessarily," Logan said. "Just because we can't sneak into the graveyard doesn't mean you're off the hook."

"What do you mean?" Beau's face dropped, just for a moment, before he regained his composure.

"Swampy Annie." Logan folded his arms, looking pleased as punch.

"That crazy woman everyone says is a witch?" Tucker shook his head. "What about her?"

"We should get our bikes and ride out to that old shack she lives in with her mother."

"And do what?"

"Dare Beau to sneak inside and steal her cauldron."

"How am I going to steal a cauldron?" Beau asked. "That's ridiculous."

"Fine. You have to sneak up to her door, bang on it, then wait for her to answer and ask if she eats toads."

"Why would she eat toads?" Beau didn't look impressed.

"Because she's a witch, dummy. They do that kind of thing."

"I don't think so." Beau grabbed a piece of candy from his bucket and tore the wrapper off, then popped it into his mouth and chewed loudly. "All your ideas are stupid. You really want me to prove I'm not chicken?"

"Yeah. We do." Tucker nodded.

"All right. We'll go out to Swampy Annie's place. But I'm not knocking on her door and asking about toads. I have a better idea."

"What?"

"You'll see. Go get your bikes and be at my house in fifteen minutes."

"Hey," Decker said. "I already told you; I have to be home by eight or else."

"Guess you can't come with us then." Beau unwrapped a second piece of candy.

"Guess not." Decker tried to look disappointed, but he was secretly relieved. The last thing he wanted to do was cycle out to Annie Doucet's shack in the bayou and cause trouble. And not just because he was afraid of being caught by his father, but also because Halloween was supposed to be fun, not mean-spirited. He didn't know if Annie Doucet was a witch or not—his father said she wasn't—but she didn't deserve to be harassed by the likes of Beau Thornton. "I think I'll just go home now."

"Suit yourself." Beau chewed the candy and swallowed. Then he turned to the others. "My house in fifteen, y'all. Don't be late."

# SIXTY-FIVE

ARE YOU SURE ABOUT THIS, GUYS?" asked Tucker in a breathless voice as they skidded to a halt on their bikes a little way down the trail from Annie Doucet's cabin. "I don't like it out here. It's dark, and I heard something splashing in the swamp. I think it was an alligator."

"Now who's the chicken?" Beau shot back. He dismounted his bicycle and slid a backpack off his shoulders. He placed it on the ground and unzipped the bag, pulling out a can of paint and a brush.

"I'm just saying we can go back." Tucker looked around nervously at the pitch-black Bayou that surrounded them.

"No one's going back until Beau does what he said he would." Logan hopped off his bike and leaned it against a tree at the side of the trail. Then he took off toward the cabin. "Come on."

Beau stepped past Tucker and followed. "You can stay here if you're too afraid."

"I'm not afraid." Tucker scrambled off his bike and lowered it to the ground, then ran to catch up with the others. "It's just kind of spooky out here, that's all."

"What did you expect?" Beau swung the paint can in one hand and carried the brush in the other.

"My dad said that the people out here can turn into wolves," Logan said, glancing up toward the full moon that hung low in the sky above the cypress trees.

"They don't need a full moon to turn into the loup-garou," Beau said with a derisive chuckle. "It's not like a normal werewolf. They can do it whenever they want to."

"I bet the loup-garou's out there tonight." Logan walked fast to keep up with his friends. "It is Halloween, after all."

"Would you shut up about werewolves?" Beau would have punched his friend in the arm—his usual method of punctuating whatever point he was trying to make—except that his hands were full. "There's no such thing as a loup-garou. Adults made it up to frighten kids into behaving themselves."

"Nuh-huh. It's real." Logan shook his head. "My dad said he saw one once out at a bonfire in the woods. Said it killed a bunch of people."

"Your dad's full of horse-crap."

"He *is not.*"

"Is too." Beau came to a stop. The cabin was in front of them now, and for the first time, he had second thoughts. It was even more ramshackle than he had imagined. The roof sagged, none of the walls were straight, and the porch leaned to the left as if it was about to collapse. It looked exactly like the kind of place where a witch would live. And Swampy Annie was obviously home, because one of the windows under the porch glowed a pale yellow behind limp curtains, and a curl of wispy smoke escaped the chimney. He almost suggested that they turn back, after all, but he could imagine what the others would say if he backed out now. He would never hear the end of it.

"Are you going to do this thing, or what?" Tucker said, as if sensing Beau's hesitation.

"Yeah. Do it," Logan echoed.

"I'm going to do it." Beau was gripping the paint can so tight that his nails dug into his palm. "Just give me a minute."

"What do you need a minute for?" Tucker asked. "It was your idea."

"I know." Beau set the paint can down on the ground and pulled a small pocketknife from his jeans. He opened the blade and used it to pry the lid off, then picked up the can again and took a tentative step toward the cabin.

"Holy crap. He's really going to do it," Logan said in an excited whisper.

"Hell, yeah!" Tucker gave Beau a shove in the back. "Hurry up. Before she sees us out here."

"All right, already." Beau said in a hushed voice. "I'm going."

He crept forward, trying to ignore the butterflies that swarmed in his stomach. The paint sloshed in the can, almost spilling over. He reached the steps and made his way up, wincing as they groaned under his weight.

When he reached the porch, Beau stopped and listened.

He could hear the low mumble of the TV somewhere inside the cabin. Who knew you could even get a television signal this far out in the swamp?

"What are you waiting for?" came a hoarse whisper from behind him.

Beau didn't know which of his friends it was, but it didn't matter. The longer he took, the more insistent they would become.

Beau took a deep breath and steeled himself, wishing he'd never let his friends goad him into this stupid prank.

Their expectant gaze drilled into his back.

*Come on, you can do this*, Beau told himself.

He set the paint can down and dipped the brush into it, loading the bristles with gloppy red paint. Then he put the brush against the cabin wall and brought it down in a long flowing stroke, then started upward, down, and up again, painting a crude letter 'W' on the siding.

He dipped the brush into the can a second time and loaded it with more paint, then went back to his task, spelling out the rest of the word in large letters.

The brush sounded too loud as it scraped against the house. He was glad for the TV noise, otherwise Swampy Annie might have heard him. Even so, he went faster, eager to be done with his friends' stupid dare.

When he finished painting the last letter on the wall, he slumped with relief and stood back to admire his work.

It wasn't perfect, but it got the message across.

W-I-T-C-H.

Now to make his escape.

He bent down and picked up the paint can.

At that moment, the porch light clicked on, bathing him in a harsh glare.

Beau yelped with surprise and let go of the can.

It clattered onto the porch deck, teetered for a moment, and tipped over, spilling its contents all over the boards and onto his sneakers. Then it rolled away toward the steps, leaving a trail of blood-red paint in its wake.

But that was the least of his worries.

The cabin's front door flew open.

Beau looked up as a figure emerged.

But it wasn't Annie Doucet. It was an older woman wearing a stained housecoat. She had wild gray hair, a face with lines so deep they could have been chiseled into her skin, and wide, frantic eyes.

"Crap. It's the witch's mother," said Tucker in a voice barely below a squeal. "Run."

Emmylou Doucet lunged forward with a howl, skeletal hands grasping at Beau and grabbing him on the shoulder. Her crooked fingers dug into the fabric of his coat and held on, even as she tried to pull him closer to her.

"Get off me," Beau screamed, overcome by raw panic. He twisted and bucked, trying to escape, but the old woman was surprisingly strong. She refused to let go.

In a last desperate attempt to free himself, Beau unzipped the coat and squirmed out of it, leaving Emmylou Doucet holding the slack garment like a trophy.

244 ANTHONY M. STRONG

Finally free, he backed up quickly lest she try to grab him again. In the process, he stepped right into the spilled paint. By the time he realized his mistake, it was too late. His feet slid out from under him a second before his back hit the porch railing.

The railing held for a brief moment—just long enough for Beau to think he had avoided serious harm—then it gave way with a splintering crack and sent him tumbling to the ground below.

He landed hard—the air whooshing out of his lungs. Then he scrambled to his feet—noticing with a flicker of irritation that his friends had already fled—and ran down the trail toward his bike, with Emmylou Doucet's curses ringing in his ears.

# SIXTY-SIX

ANNIE DOUCET SPENT the evening of All Hallows Eve out in the swamp collecting ingredients for her many tinctures, potions, and spells, just like she did every year. The ingredients worked better when collected at Halloween, almost as if they were imbued with extra magic. That it was also a full moon this year only heightened her expectations.

It was ten o'clock by the time she arrived back at the cabin, her basket overflowing with a variety of roots, mushrooms, tree bark, and even the discarded skin of a snake she had found hanging from a low branch. Later, after stashing her trove, she intended to head back out to find more items because midnight was always the best time to forage.

But she never got the chance.

She knew something was wrong the moment she stepped into the house. Her mother, who spent every night sitting in her favorite chair and watching whatever was playing on one of the three TV channels they could get with the antenna fixed to their roof, was pacing the living room and mumbling to herself instead.

At first, Annie thought that maybe the old woman had been at the hooch again. It was something that still happened regularly, although not as often as it used to, thanks to an addiction potion that Annie snuck into her mother's iced tea whenever she got the chance. It wasn't a perfect solution, and she felt bad using magic on Emmylou Doucet without her consent, but it was a necessity. Without the addiction potion to calm her cravings, the old woman would have drunk herself into oblivion long ago with the hundred-proof moonshine she had been cooking up out on the back porch ever since Annie could remember.

But Emmylou was not drunk.

That was obvious, not just because she was doing a fine job of pacing back-and-forth without stumbling, but also because the front door was flung wide open, letting in mosquitoes and swamp flies.

"Mama?" Annie dropped her basket and went to her mother. "What happened?"

"Devils," her mother replied. "Those little demons from town. They came out here causing trouble. I couldn't stop them."

"What devils, mama?" Annie knew that her mother was talking about kids from Wolf Haven. It wasn't the first time they had snuck out to the cabin on a dare, but usually they just snuck onto the porch and peer through the window, or knocked the door and ran away. This time, it felt different.

Emmylou ignored the question and leveled an accusation at her daughter instead. "You should have been here. Why weren't you home to protect me?"

"You know I go into the swamp on Halloween, mama." Annie steered Emmylou to a chair and coaxed her to sit down. "It's the best time to collect my ingredients."

"Always with the witchcraft. Shame you can't put a curse on those little brats."

"What did they do, mama?"

Emmylou pointed toward the door. "Go look for yourself."

Annie lingered a moment to make sure her mother wasn't going to get back up and start pacing again, then she went to the front door and stepped out onto the porch.

Her heart leaped into her throat.

There was blood spilled all over the deck boards. More blood had been daubed on the cabin wall, spelling out a single accusatory word.

**WITCH.**

She stared in disbelief, unable to comprehend who would be mean enough to do such a thing. To desecrate their home like that. But then she noticed something else. A paint can lay on its side at the bottom of the porch steps, and an abandoned brush.

She breathed a sigh of relief.

It wasn't blood, after all. It was common house paint. Not that it would be any easier to clean up. In fact, it would probably be harder. The paint on the deck was still tacky, but the words painted on the cabin wall had already dried.

Annie went back inside and shut the door. "I'll go into town first thing in the morning and see if I can find out who did this."

"No need. I already know who's responsible," Emmylou said, pointing at a garment draped over the back of the couch. "He left his coat behind."

Annie picked up the coat and opened it. There was a name handwritten in permanent marker on the label sewn into the back of the collar. Beau Thornton.

Annie read the name aloud, then dropped the coat back onto the couch.

"What are you going to do?" Emmylou asked, looking at her daughter with narrowed eyes.

"I don't know yet."

"No cops," said Emmylou. "We're not running to Sheriff Decker. He won't lift a finger to help the likes of us."

That went without saying. Annie had no intention of going to see Robbie Decker. The sheriff had never done anything to help them, even though he and his wife would be childless if it weren't for her. The only time Robbie Decker had ever graced their doorstep was to accuse her of ripping people off with her tarot readings and potions. Once, long ago when they were teenagers, she might have trusted him to help her, but not anymore. She glanced toward the door. "Maybe we should just clean up the mess and let it be. Anything we do will just bring more trouble down on us."

"He put paint all over our wall. Vandalized our home. The boy disrespected us. That can't go unanswered."

"I don't think we have much choice."

"You should put a curse on him."

Annie sighed. "I thought you didn't like me practicing witchcraft?"

"I don't. But if I can't convince you to stop, there's no point in wasting your gift. Not when we're under attack."

"I'm not putting a hex on the boy. I don't do that kind of magic."

"Some witch you are." Emmylou pushed herself up out of the chair. "Guess I'll have to take matters into my own hands."

"Please don't, Mama." Annie took a step toward her mother. "Promise me you won't do anything to make matters worse."

"Can't promise you nothing," Emmylou replied. Then she shuffled off toward the back of the cabin.

Annie watched her go, expecting to hear the slam of her mother's bedroom door, but instead, she heard the distinctive squeak of the door leading out onto the back porch. Then, before she could follow, the sound of Emmylou's beater of an old station wagon starting up. The same station wagon Arnie Temple, the town's only mechanic, had somehow kept running for almost three decades in exchange for regular crates of moonshine.

Annie ran to the front and flung the door open. But she was too late. Emmylou Doucet was already driving off down the dirt trail toward Wolf Haven, and revenge.

# SIXTY-SEVEN

AS ALL HALLOWS Eve ticked past midnight and became All Hallows Day, Beau Thornton lay in bed and listened to the branches of a big old live oak blowing in the wind and tapping against his window. The events of the evening ran through his mind in a constant loop. Especially the bit when Annie Doucet's mother had come lunging out of that cabin doorway, wild as a banshee, and grabbed ahold of him.

In that moment, as her fingers dug into his shoulder, he actually thought she was going to kill him. Or maybe drag him inside and let her witch of a daughter do something even worse.

His escape had been a minor miracle, and it was no thanks to his friends, who he was sure were already halfway back to Wolf Haven, peddling their bicycles like crazy, by the time he wriggled out of his coat, slipped on that paint, and went crashing over that railing.

That was the worst thing. He had lost his favorite coat, and when his parents found out, there would be hell to pay. They might have more money in the bank than pretty much anyone else in the town, but that didn't mean a thing. Wasting money was a cardinal sin in Beau Thornton's household.

Then there were the sneakers, now splashed with red paint that he was sure wouldn't ever come out. Which was why he had buried them at the back of his closet, where he intended to make sure they never saw the light of day again.

All things considered it had been a pretty crappy end to an otherwise fun-filled Halloween night. And all because Logan and Tucker had pushed him into that stupid dare. Well, he was going to make sure and tell them how he felt about that dare the next time he saw them, not to mention abandoning him to the clutches of that crazy old woman.

He rolled onto his side, facing away from the window, pushed his hand under the pillow, and tried to think of something else. Anything else. Like Wendy Baxter, who sat next to him in class. Only the previous Tuesday, she had flashed him a shy smile during second period, cheeks reddening. When he smiled back, she giggled and looked away.

His stomach flipped when he thought of that, but in a good way. Wendy Baxter was nice. She wouldn't have made him climb up onto that porch and do all that stuff just to prove he wasn't a chicken.

Great. Now he was thinking about Annie Doucet and her crazy mother all over again.

Tap. Tap. Tap.

The noise broke through his train of thought.

The wind was still pushing branches into the window, only now it sounded louder. Different. More like—he didn't even want to think about it—nails scraping slowly down the glass.

He focused on the closet next to his bedroom door—the same one hiding his ruined sneakers—and told himself that was a ridiculous notion. It was just branches.

But the longer he lay there, the more he was convinced it was no such thing. After a few minutes, he could take it no longer. He rolled back over and sat up, glanced timidly toward the window and was relieved to see nothing was there. No hag of a witch with a crooked nose and warts on her chin, floating outside his window and pulling her nails down the glass in a slow, drawn out scritch.

*Just those branches, tapping away in the wind,* he told himself.

Now he felt foolish for letting his imagination get the better of him. He realized he had been holding his breath. He let it out in a long exhalation, then he turned away from the window to settle back down under the covers.

That was when he saw it.

The bedroom door was slowly opening on silent hinges. Swinging inward all on its own. And in the hallway beyond, swirling blackness.

The fear lurched back.

Beau wanted to scream, but nothing would come out.

He pulled the covers up to his chin and bunched them in his hands as the door swung ever wider until the handle hit the wall and stopped its progress.

He stared into the murky gloom on the other side of the door, trying to tell himself that it was just his mother poking her head into his bedroom on her way back from the bathroom to make sure he was asleep.

But he knew it wasn't because she never opened the door that wide when she checked on him. She would just open it a crack, peek inside, and then close it again.

This was different.

Beau didn't want to see what might be lurking out in the hall-way. He let out a small whimper and sank down under the covers, pulling them over his head.

He hid there, straining his ears to hear any noise. The creak of a floorboard. An exhalation of breath. Anything that might indicate he was not alone in the room.

After a few minutes, when no sounds reached his ears beyond the tree branches and the whistling wind, he plucked up the courage to lower the covers and look.

And there she was, looming over the bed, grizzled face mere inches away from his.

# SIXTY-EIGHT

BEAU OPENED his mouth to scream a split second before the old woman clamped a leathery hand down over it.

"Don't you dare make a sound, you little shit," she hissed. "Are you going to keep quiet?"

Beau nodded and tried to answer but all that came out was a low mumble.

"Good." Emmylou Doucet lowered her hand.

"What do you want?" Beau asked in a voice barely above a whisper, which was all he could muster through his fear even though he wanted to scream blue murder and bring his parents running from their bedroom down the hall. "How did you get in here?"

"What? you think you're the only one who can sneak onto people's property and cause trouble?"

The old woman's breath so close to his face made Beau gag. "Please don't kill me."

"Give me one good reason not to." Emmylou touched Beau's chin with a bony finger. She scraped the digit across his jaw and down his neck to the top button of his PJs, her puss-yellow nail digging into his flesh.

"I'm sorry, okay? I'll come back tomorrow and clean it up, I swear. Just don't hurt me."

"I want you to do more than that. You're going to tell your parents what you did. You're going to confess and take your punishment."

"Uh, okay. Fine. Whatever you want." Beau had no intention of telling his parents that he had vandalized an old woman's house just for kicks. He would go back out there and scrub the porch, clean that paint off the cabin's walls, but he wasn't confessing anything to anyone. And Swampy Annie's mother would be none the wiser. She would never talk to them. If she wanted to do that, she would have done it already instead of breaking into their house and terrorizing their son in his bedroom.

"Don't you think about lying to me," Emmylou Doucet said, as if she had read his mind. "I'll know if you don't do as I say."

"Hu-how will you know?" Beau stammered, a cold sweat breaking out on his forehead.

"My daughter is a witch, remember? She has the power of second sight. You know what that is, boy?"

Beau shook his head.

"It means she can see what you're doing, no matter where you are. Like in a vision. Any time of day or night. And if you don't confess, then I'll have her put a hex on your family. You want her to curse your parents, boy?"

Beau did not want that. He shook his head.

"You want her to *curse you*?"

Beau shook his head again. "What kind of curse?"

"You'll just have to wait-and-see. Or you could just do what I say and never find out."

"I'll do it. I swear. Please don't curse us."

"That's a good boy." Emmylou Doucet grinned, revealing crooked, stained teeth that reminded Beau more of a wild animal than a person. She withdrew her finger and stepped back, much to his relief. "You stay quiet until I'm good and gone, you hear?"

Beau nodded.

"And don't you dare tell your parents I was here tonight. Understand?" She watched him with eyes cold as ice.

Beau tried to reply, but nothing came out except a strangled croak.

Emmylou Doucet obviously took that as a yes. She backed up toward the door and stepped out into the hallway beyond, then pulled the door quietly closed, leaving Beau alone again in his bedroom.

He sat there with the covers clutched to his chest, barely able to breathe as the minutes ticked away. He listened for any sign the crazy old woman was still there, lingering beyond the doorway, but all he heard was that tree, still tapping on his window— scratching like the old woman's bony fingers against the glass.

That thought pushed him over the edge.

Beau finally found his voice and screamed.

And when his parents came running, when his door flew open and they rushed into his bedroom, he told them everything. And that included Emmylou Doucet's nocturnal visit and the threats she had made, because in his terror, he just couldn't help himself.

# SIXTY-NINE

ANNIE DOUCET WAS in the kitchen making breakfast when the sound of someone knocking on the cabin door drew her attention. When she answered, Sheriff Robbie Decker was standing on the other side with one hand resting on the butt of his gun in its holster on his belt.

"Morning, Annie," he said, glancing at the word daubed across the front of the cabin in large, crude strokes, and the spilled paint on the deck beneath. "You have some trouble out here last night?"

"Nothing we can't take care of," Annie replied. "You know what people are like."

"Yeah, I sure do." Sheriff Decker rubbed his chin. "How's your mother getting on these days?"

"Has her good days, has her bad."

"She having one of those good days yesterday?" Sheriff Decker's gaze shifted briefly over Annie's shoulder to the interior of the house. "She go for a late-night drive into town, by any chance? Say around midnight."

"I don't know what you're talking about, Sheriff." Annie's gut clenched. She had been worried about getting a visit from Robbie Decker ever since her mother had returned in the early hours with assurances that the boy had been put in his place and everything taken care of.

"You sure about that, Annie?"

"I'm sure." What else was there to say? "She never left the house all night."

"See, that's where I have a problem." Sheriff Decker's gaze drifted back to Annie. "Because there's a terrified ten-year-old boy who swears your mother was in his bedroom last night. Says she threatened him. Told him that if he didn't clean this mess up and confess what he'd done, that you would put a curse on him and his family."

"Mama would never say that," Annie replied, although she knew full well that was exactly what her mother had said. "She doesn't hold with witchcraft."

"Maybe. But there's a big difference between saying something and doing it."

"Do you believe in witchcraft, sheriff? Do you really think I have the power to put a curse on someone?"

"This isn't about what I think. It's about your mother breaking into a house and threatening a ten-year-old kid."

"You have no proof she did any of that stuff," Annie shot back. "Maybe you should be arresting the person who did this to our home, instead of harassing law-abiding folk."

"And maybe I would be if you'd bothered to report it, instead of taking matters into your own hands."

"So the boy just gets away with it?"

"That isn't what I said. Beau Thornton's admitted to what he's done, and I've given him a stern warning regarding his behavior. His parents will pay for the damage he caused, and I'm sure they'll punish him accordingly."

"Yet you're here accusing my mother of a crime based on nothing but that little brat's word."

"It's more than just his word, Annie. I have a broken window at the Thornton house, where someone gained access. They left fingerprints behind. I also have muddy shoe prints on the kitchen floor and another in the flower bed outside."

"So what?"

"So if the fingerprints we lifted are your mothers, if those shoe impressions match her footwear, I'll have to charge her with breaking and entering, among other things." The sheriff hesitated for a moment, as if he were figuring out the best way to say what Annie knew was coming next. "I need to take Emmylou back to town with me, Annie."

"You can't do that. She's frail."

"Where is she, Annie?"

"I'm right here," said a voice over Annie's shoulder.

"Mama." Annie glanced back at her mother. "You shouldn't have come in here. I was handling it."

"The way you handled it last night? You weren't even here when that boy was desecrating our home." Emmylou pushed Annie aside and looked at the sheriff. "The boy had it coming. You can see what he did right here with your own eyes."

"Two wrongs don't make a right, Mrs. Doucet. I need you to come with me. We'll sort this out back at the Sheriff's office."

"She's not going anywhere with you," Annie said, stepping forward and putting herself between the pair. "You can just go ahead and get off our property right now. You're not welcome here."

"Careful, Annie." Robbie Decker folded his arms. "I'd rather not charge you with obstruction. Heaven knows, I don't need both of you in my cells."

"You're really going to lock her up? An old woman?"

"She's not *that* old, Annie. And yes, if those fingerprints match, I'll be locking her up, at least until you post bail. I won't have any choice."

"And just where do you think I'm going to get the money to do that?"

"That's not my problem." Robbie Decker placed a hand on Annie's arm and shifted her gently out of the way. Then he took hold of her mother and led her down the porch steps. "Come along, Mrs. Doucet."

"No. You can't do this. Get your hands off her." A furious rage burned inside Annie. She stepped forward but stopped short of actually engaging the sheriff. Even in her anger, she knew it would achieve nothing to get both of them locked up.

"Please, don't let him take me," Emmylou wailed in a warbling, high-pitched voice. She twisted back to look at her daughter as Sheriff Decker escorted her across the front yard toward the waiting police cruiser.

Annie rushed down the steps, overcome by a sense of helpless frustration. She started across the yard just as the sheriff reached his car. Then, as he was opening the back door to bundle her mother inside, it happened.

Emmylou's legs sank from under her. She stumbled, gave a frantic cry. Her face twisted in pain. A moment later, she crumpled to the ground.

"Mama!" Annie sprinted forward.

By the time she arrived at her mother's side, the sheriff was already reaching for his radio to call an ambulance. But Annie knew it was too late. Her mother was gone. She could feel her spirit taking flight, leaving the earthly plane, even as Robbie Decker assured her that help was on the way.

# SEVENTY

HER MOTHER WAS DEAD. Annie was now alone in the world. She sat in the cabin's cramped living room and stared at the wall, replaying the events of the morning over in her head.

The paramedics had tried to revive Emmylou after she collapsed. They rushed her to the hospital, where they tried again. But it had been pointless. She was gone before she even hit the ground. There was no coming back. Annie knew that before Sheriff Decker had even finished calling for the ambulance, because she sensed her mother's spirit crossing over. Going to wherever the souls of the dead went to spend their eternity.

No one had told Annie exactly what had killed her mother— that would be determined by an autopsy—but there had been mention of a heart attack, probably brought about by stress. They said she probably had a previously unknown condition— Emmylou hadn't exactly looked after herself over the years—and that it could have happened at any time.

Annie knew differently.

The cause of her mother's death was obvious.

Sheriff Robbie Decker.

If he hadn't come knocking on their door, hadn't tried to arrest Emmylou for doing nothing more than putting the fear of God into

260 ANTHONY M. STRONG

some spoiled brat of a kid who deserved it, then her mother would still be alive. Annie was sure of that.

Not that Beau Thornton was blameless. He was the one who set everything in motion. It was him who snuck up to the cabin. Wrote that word on their wall.

WITCH.

He spilled the paint and broke their porch railing.

But Emmylou had taken care of him. She had done what Sheriff Decker had failed, or was not willing, to do.

The thing that irked her most was that the boy confessed to his crime. There was no need for the sheriff to pay Annie and her mother a visit except to tell them that the situation was resolved. That Beau Thornton would get his comeuppance. Except instead, Robbie Decker had made Emmylou Doucet the villain of the piece.

His words echoed in her head. *Two wrongs don't make a right.*

Annie wasn't so sure she held with that notion. Sometimes it was the only way to get justice. The only way to prevent even worse transgressions in the future. Like at the Kickoff Kegger. She had made sure that Karen Leroux, Travis Cox, and the other kids who took such glee in tormenting her back in school weren't able to carry their spiteful ways into adulthood and do even worse things. She had made the world a better place, albeit not by much.

Was that wrong? She didn't think so.

Her only mistake was letting Robbie Decker live. She should have ripped his throat out when she had the chance. But she hadn't. She had taken pity on him instead. Let her feelings sway her judgement.

And look what happened?

It was proof positive that two wrongs *could* make a right. Because if she had done what she should have back then, her mother would still be alive now.

It made Annie want to howl.

It made her want to beat the walls and curse.

Why should Robbie Decker get to live when her mother didn't?

Why should he get to have a family, when there was no one left in Annie's life?

And the irony of the whole thing was that Robbie Decker wouldn't even *have that family* if it wasn't for her. At least, he wouldn't have a child. Lily Decker had come to her when they were trying to conceive, and Annie had made a fertility potion for her. Had told her exactly what to do if she wanted to get pregnant. And it had worked. She had given birth to a healthy baby boy.

And in that moment, a thought occurred to Annie. Maybe Robbie Decker shouldn't get to keep his family. Maybe she should even the score.

Annie stood up, not sure exactly what she was contemplating. She paced back and forth, focusing on the thought that had popped into her head.

She could put a hex on them, just like her mother threatened Beau Thornton that she would do to *his* family.

Then she dismissed the idea.

It was too subtle. Sure, Lily might get sick and die. The boy might ride his bike in front of a speeding car. But those things could be put down to bad luck. The hand of fate.

Robbie Decker wouldn't get the message.

Besides, hexes could be finicky. It could take months to achieve her goals, and even then, it might not work the way she hoped.

No. She needed something more certain. More definitive. Robbie Decker had to be sure, absolutely without a doubt, that he was paying the price for what he had done to her mother. What he had done to Annie.

And that was when it came to her.

An idea so simple in its execution, so beautiful in its simplicity, that he couldn't fail to understand.

The loup-garou.

He had come face-to-face with the wolf twenty years before at the Kickoff Kegger. He had stared into the face of the beast, and on some level, she was sure, had recognized Annie behind those eyes.

Had sensed her presence inside the creature, even if he didn't want to admit it.

The only problem was, Annie had sworn never again to release the loup-garou. Never again to let it take control of her and run wild through the bayou. She had torn the page containing the wolf incantation out of her Aunt Babette's spell book and hidden it out in the bayou—secreted it under the floorboards of that falling down and abandoned swamp shack—where no one would ever find it. Then she had put the book itself on a high shelf inside her bedroom closet, where it had gathered dust ever since.

After that, she turned away from the dark side of witchcraft and tried to use her gift for good.

Well, not anymore.

It was time for the loup-garou to have its vengeance once again.

Annie glanced toward the window. It was getting dark already; the sun slipping below the horizon and casting long shadows through the bayou. But she wasn't going to let that stop her.

Annie took her coat down from the hook next to the front door and put it on. She retrieved a flashlight from the cabinet under the kitchen sink. Then she stepped out the back door, made her way across the rear deck past Emmylou's liquor still that would never make another drop of moonshine, and entered the bayou.

Fifteen minutes later, she arrived at the abandoned shack—which was now in even worse repair than she remembered—and hurried inside. She lifted the trapdoor in the floor and removed the page containing the wolf incantation—still wrapped in the protective but now ratty plastic grocery bag—from its decades long hiding place. Then she started back through the swamp with one thing on her mind. Revenge.

# SEVENTY-ONE

WHEN SHE GOT BACK to the cabin, the first thing Annie did was go to her bedroom and pull Aunt Babette's spell book down from its shelf in the closet. She placed it on the bed and removed the missing page from the plastic bag.

She wasn't sure what to expect. The grocery bag was in a sorry state. It practically crumbled in her hands when she tried to unroll it, disintegrating into flaky pieces that littered the bed like plastic snow.

For a moment, she was overcome by a surge of panic.

Hiding the page out in the swamp had probably not been such a great idea. If the bag hadn't withstood the damp and humid environment, how could she expect the fragile sheet of paper to have done so?

But to her surprise, the page looked just like she remembered. There wasn't a splotch or a water stain on it. The paper was still bright and crisp, the words easily readable. It was almost like the ravages of time had been unable to touch it.

And maybe that was the case. Because Annie could feel a halo of energy surrounding the page. The air practically crackled with a charge of invisible electricity, almost as if the sheet knew its long and restless slumber was over.

And when she opened the book, turned to the place where she had ripped it out all those years before, and held the sheet against the jagged, torn edge, it knitted itself back together before her eyes.

Book and page became one again.

Annie stared down at the undamaged tome, hardly able to believe her eyes. She knew magic. Understood that it permeated the very fabric of existence. Earth, air, fire, and water. But this was something else. The book was powerful. More so than she had ever imagined. She had felt that power even when she was a teenager, but her gift was untamed back then. Raw. Now, after twenty years of honing her craft, she finally realized what had scared her mother so much about Aunt Babette's devotion to the black arts.

If white magic was a meandering river, then black magic was a roiling, storm-tossed ocean.

Annie took a quick step back, overcome by a sudden sense that she was going too far. That this was not a road she wished to tread again.

She closed the book and went back to the closet, then stood on tippy toes and reached up to the shelf, sliding it back into the place where it had rested for so many years.

As she did so, a final crackle of energy—which this time she swore she saw as a faint blue pulsing tendril—leaped across the gap toward her as she pulled her hand away, almost as if the book were trying to stop her from casting it back into darkness.

Annie yelped in surprise and took a quick step back. Maybe it had been a mistake to venture out into the swamp and retrieve that page. To make the spell book whole again.

She gripped the closet doors and slammed them closed. Then she ran from the room, ignoring the faint voice that whispered inside her head. A voice that told her to take the book back down and open it back up. A voice she knew all too well. The voice of the loup-garou.

# SEVENTY-TWO

FOR THE NEXT THREE DAYS, Annie did nothing. Aunt Babette's spell book scared her, much more than it had back when she was a teenager. She could feel its pull. Sense the book calling out to her, tempting her to open it and turn back to that page. The one that would transform her into the loup-garou.

Yet she resisted.

She even considered going back out to the abandoned shack in the swamp and hiding the entire book under the floorboards and leaving it there, where it could do no further harm. But she couldn't quite bring herself to do so, because then she would have no way of getting even with Robbie Decker.

Which was why, late in the evening on the third day, she went into the bedroom and took the book back down from the shelf. She placed it on the bed and opened it to the page containing the spell that would turn her into the wolf. The spell she had vowed never to use again all those years ago when she was a teenager.

All at once, the whispering inside Annie's head grew louder.

*Let me out*, the loup-garou coaxed her. *Set me free and we'll get our revenge together.*

The fear lurched back. Annie almost reached out and slammed

the book closed a second time. Almost threw it back on the shelf again.

But she didn't. Because the rage that burned inside her was only getting worse. She wanted Robbie Decker to pay for what he had done. Needed him to suffer just like she was. It had consumed her every waking moment over the past three days, and she kept coming back to the same conclusion.

She needed the loup-garou.

Which was why, under the cloak of midnight, she went out into the swamp to gather the ingredients. Later, when she returned, she followed the instructions from the spell book and boiled them down into a soupy mixture that she quickly transferred to a Mason jar. She placed the foul concoction in the fridge, mostly out of habit. Then she closed the spell book and carried it back into the bedroom.

But she didn't put it back into the closet. Not this time. Instead, she stripped off her filthy clothes smeared with mud from the swamp, left them in a heap on the floor, and climbed into bed without bothering to put on her nightshirt. Then she cradled the book in her arms, relishing the way it tingled and felt warm against her bare flesh, almost as if it were comforting her.

And as sleep overcame her, Annie smiled, because tomorrow she would take from Robbie Decker the same thing he had taken from her. Family.

# SEVENTY-THREE

TEN-YEAR-OLD JOHN DECKER was not happy. He wandered slowly home from school, wondering what he was going to do for the rest of the evening. Normally, he would be hanging out with his friends, but not today. In fact, probably not for a while. The weekend before, on Halloween, Logan Olden, Tucker Williams, and Beau Thornton had gone and gotten themselves grounded. And all because of a stupid dare.

Luckily, Decker couldn't have cared less about sneaking out to Annie Doucet's shack in the swamp and causing trouble. And much as he had been eager to see Beau put in his place, he hadn't wanted to break his curfew.

And it was a good thing. Because from what he'd overheard his father saying the next night when he came home from work, Annie Doucet's mother had collapsed and died earlier that day. He would have felt truly dreadful if he had been partly responsible for tormenting Annie and her mother on the old woman's last night on Earth. He hoped Beau felt suitably guilty.

But none of that helped his current situation. There were still a couple hours of daylight left, and here he was, all on his own, with nothing to do. It felt wrong to waste them. Especially as the clocks would go back in a few days, and then there would be hardly any daylight left. The last thing he wanted to do was to go home and spend the rest of the evening cooped up in his bedroom or sitting in the living room watching mindless television.

Then he had an idea.

The swimming hole out in the woods. Sullivan's Pond. During the summer months, when it was baking hot and all the kids were on break, it was too packed to even bother with. There would be teenagers swinging on ropes strung from tree branches and dropping into the cool blue water, or splashing around in the shallows, roughhousing with whoops of joy, and trying to impress girls. Later, at dusk, it was a popular make out spot far from the prying eyes of adults.

But not at this time of year.

Sullivan's Pond would be all but deserted. A private sanctuary where he could skip stones across the water's flat, calm surface or paddle at the water's edge. Maybe even swim or swing out over the water on those same ropes if it wasn't too cold. And even if someone was there, they would pay him no heed.

There was only one problem.

He was supposed to go home and tell his mother before going anywhere like that. But walking all the way home would waste valuable time. His house was in the opposite direction of the pond and every moment he wasted was less time to enjoy what remained of the daylight. In fact, if he went home first, his mother probably wouldn't even let him go to Sullivan's Pond. His father hated the woods. Did his best to discourage his son from going into them. Especially when he was on his own. Said they weren't safe. And with the rest of his friends grounded, Decker had no choice but to go on his own.

He came to a stop and mulled the situation over for a few minutes. If he went straight to the pond, he could still be back home before six. He might get away with that. He had stayed after school many times before, watching the older kids in football practice. Had even joined the art club for a while the previous year, although he was no good at painting.

So long as he didn't tell his mother exactly where he'd gone, he would be okay.

Satisfied that his plan was foolproof, Decker changed direction. Fifteen minutes later, he had left the town behind and was following a narrow and winding trail through the piney woods. Ten minutes after that, he stepped into a clearing with a cool, shimmering circular body of water in the middle.

Sullivan's pond.

Best of all, he had it all to himself.

# SEVENTY-FOUR

AT ABOUT THE same time as her son was sneaking off to Sullivan's Pond, Lily Decker was finishing a pot of gumbo in the kitchen of their home on the other side of town.

She was preoccupied.

Ever since Robbie had come home the Sunday before and told her what had happened out at Annie Doucet's shack, she had felt bad. She knew her husband wasn't responsible for Emmylou's death. He was only doing his job, and the old woman had left him no choice but to arrest her. She should have known better than to sneak into the bedroom of a ten-year-old boy in the middle of the night and threaten him, regardless of what that same boy had done earlier in the evening.

Kids played pranks, especially on Halloween.

Not that she condoned Beau Thornton's behavior. The kid was a spoiled brat with parents who let him get away with too much. But that didn't give Emmylou Doucet the right to break into his home and threaten him. As Robbie had grumbled to her that very evening, she should have called the police and let them handle it. That was why Wolf Haven had a sheriff's department. If people could just do as they pleased, anarchy would reign.

Lily turned the stove off. The gumbo was done.

She thought again about Annie, all alone out at that shack in the bayou, surrounded by mosquitoes and alligators. How lonely must she be now that her mother was gone? It almost made Lily's heart break. Annie had been good to her. Helped her with that potion when she was trying to conceive. Without Annie Doucet's fertility spell, she might not even have a son.

Lily glanced at the clock on the stove.

Robbie wouldn't be home for at least another couple of hours, and John was probably hanging out at the school doing some extracurricular activity.

There was plenty of gumbo. She always made too much because her husband liked to eat it as leftovers.

Annie probably wasn't eating at all right now, and someone should probably check on her. It was unlikely that many of the other townsfolk had bothered, if any. Annie Doucet had something of a reputation around Wolf Haven, and not in a good way.

But that didn't bother Lily. Not in the least.

What did bother her was the thought of that poor woman all alone and suffering out in the swamp.

Making up her mind, Lily went to the cupboard next to the sink and took out a glass dish with a plastic lid, then filled it with gumbo from the pot on the stove. The least she could do was offer her condolences and make sure that Annie had a hot meal inside of her.

She took the glass container and placed it into a plastic bag, then tied the top before heading out to the garage where she kept her bicycle.

As she cycled along Main Street with the gumbo safely cradled in a basket on her handlebars, she wondered if she should have left a note for John, telling him where she had gone and to go ahead and get a snack from the fridge if he was hungry. But that would mean going back, and if he was watching the high school football team practice—which he often did in the fall—then he wouldn't be home until at least five-thirty. Plenty of time for her to drop off the gumbo, give Annie her condolences, and get back.

And anyway, if she turned around now, if she went back and left that note, there might not be enough time to reach Annie's shack, do what she needed, and return home before darkness fell. And the last thing Lily wanted was to be riding through the bayou at night. It was bad enough during the day, but after dark it was just too creepy.

*No, better to just keep going,* she told herself. *The sooner you get this done, the quicker it will be over.*

# SEVENTY-FIVE

ANNIE DOUCET TOOK the concoction she had made the previous night out of the fridge. The spell book was on the kitchen table, open to the page containing the wolf incantation. The one that would turn her into the loup-garou.

She had been studying all day, memorizing the words just like she had done twenty years before on the night of the Kickoff Kegger. Now she had them memorized all over again. And this time, she was sure they would not fade from her memory, because she had no intention of letting the book sit unused for so long ever again.

She was done with white witchcraft.

Placing the Mason jar containing the brew on the table, Annie read through the incantation one last time, just for good measure. Then she undressed, draping her clothes over the back of the kitchen chair, before picking up the Mason jar again. Naked now, she walked to the door leading out to the back deck and stepped outside. The chill hit her immediately, raising goosebumps on her exposed flesh. The temperature had been in the mid-70s all day, but now, as dusk approached, it was falling fast and would probably drop at least twenty degrees overnight.

But Annie didn't care.

A few minutes from now, she wouldn't even feel that chill. She would be strong. Powerful. Unstoppable.

That thought made her smile.

She unscrewed the lid of the Mason jar and put it to her lips. The liquid inside gave off a rancid, pungent odor that rekindled a vague memory within her. She tilted her head back, tried not to gag, and drank the contents in several long gulps.

It tasted worse than it smelled.

Annie pressed her lips closed and fought a wave of nausea. The liquid rose in her throat, refusing to go down easily. She swallowed, fighting the urge to double over and expel the foul concoction from her body.

A flicker of panic washed over her.

She needed to recite the incantation but didn't dare open her mouth, let alone speak. If she couldn't say the words, she wouldn't turn. Then she wouldn't get her revenge on Robbie Decker.

Annie forced herself to stand tall. She closed her eyes and counted off thirty seconds inside her head, willing her body to stop resisting and her stomach to quit fighting back against the concoction.

By the time she reached thirty, the nausea had passed. At least, enough that she trusted herself to speak. She went to the middle of the deck, stared out into the bayou, and recited the incantation.

Nothing happened.

Annie waited, trying to remember how long it had taken her to turn the last time she had become the wolf. She couldn't remember, but it was pretty quick. She knew that much. So why wasn't it working now? Had she had done something wrong? Forgotten an ingredient or left the potion in the fridge for too long? Maybe she had forgotten a word in the incantation or said something in the wrong order.

Panic flared anew. She almost turned around and went back inside.

But then the pain hit, careening out of nowhere like a runaway truck.

It exploded from deep inside of her like a raging hurricane, consuming every inch of her body. She doubled over, sank to her knees, and cried out. Tears streamed down her face. Sharp pinpricks like a thousand needles tore at her flesh. Bones cracked and formed themselves into new shapes.

Annie dragged herself forward, rolled off the deck onto the soft mulch earth beyond. She clawed at the ground. Writhed and twisted.

She lifted her head and howled. Once. Twice. Three times.

And then she realized something. The pain was gone, replaced by a raw, animalistic power. And in that moment, even as her consciousness became one with the wolf, she wondered why she had kept the beast at arms-length for so long—why she had been afraid of it. She had been wrong. This felt good. It felt *right*.

Annie, or rather the creature she had become, raised itself up on powerful hind-legs and stood observing its environment. It sniffed the air, picking up scents so faint that even a bloodhound would have had trouble recognizing them.

And out of the thousands of smells that assaulted the creature's nostrils, it picked out one in particular. A scent familiar from the last time Annie had let the wolf roam free. The night of the Kickoff Kegger.

Robbie Decker.

Only it wasn't him. Not quite.

This scent was fresher. Younger. Sweeter.

The loup-garou tilted its head to the sky and howled again, giving fair warning to any creatures that might cross its path. Then it hunkered down on all fours and raced off through the bayou in the direction of the piney woods and Sullivan's Pond.

Annie would have her revenge. She had helped Lily Decker conceive. Given Robbie Decker a son. Now it was time to take that son away. Deprive him of everyone he held dear, just like he had done to her.

Come nightfall, the sheriff of Wolf Haven would know what it meant to be alone.

# SEVENTY-SIX

DECKER LINGERED at the water's edge with a small, flat pebble in the palm of his hand. He drew his arm back, and let the rock fly, watching the stone skip across the water in short hops until it finally sank beneath the surface.

He kicked the ground, looking for another pebble. Coming up to Sullivan's Pond hadn't been such a good idea, after all. He had the place all to himself, but there was a reason. The water, fed by a natural spring deep beneath the surface, was too cold to swim. He had kicked off his shoes and socks, and waded into the water, but soon changed his mind and scurried back out.

Now he was bored. Just as bored, in fact, as he had been earlier. Maybe he should have gone back home and watched TV instead. But it was too late now. He'd made the effort to come all the way out here, so he might as well make the best of it.

He found another stone. A round, flat pebble about the size of a silver dollar. He picked it up and weighed it in his hand, wondering how far he could send the disk before it succumbed to gravity and slipped beneath the surface of the water. If his friends had been there, they would have been competing to see who could throw their stone the furthest. Who could keep it above water the longest.

But they weren't, and if what Logan said was true—if he really was grounded until the following summer—he might be kicking around on his own for a while.

Decker dropped the rock, losing interest in the water skipping game. He turned back toward the woods and the narrow path that meandered down to a small parking lot. Beyond that was the road, and on the other side, another trail that wound its way back to town.

He took a step forward, avoiding an empty beer bottle with a faded label some inconsiderate person had discarded on the narrow strip of land circling the pond. Probably a teenager who had snuck up there to drink.

And then he heard it.

A rustle in the woods off to his left.

Decker froze. Not so much because he really thought there was anything dangerous lurking in the gloom between the trees, but more because his father had told him not to venture into the woods alone so many times, that it had almost become second nature to think of it as somewhere mysterious and forbidden. He had never understood his father's obsession with the swath of pine forest that surrounded Wolf Haven like a protective girdle, holding back the murky and much creepier bayou beyond.

A branch snapped from somewhere behind him—the sound sharp in the clear November air.

Decker spun around, casting his gaze across the tree line. His heart pounded in his chest. Whatever had stepped on that branch sounded large. Much heavier than the usual suspects that might be running around the piney woods, like raccoons, squirrels, foxes, or even a coyote.

Of course, there were also more elusive animals there. A wild hog could certainly snap a branch like that. And hogs were bad-tempered. They attacked without provocation. The last thing he wanted was to face-off against an annoyed feral pig with razor-sharp tusks that could easily slice him open.

Another crack, closer this time.

Decker clamped his mouth shut against a whimper. It was probably a bad idea to show fear. He didn't know if that piece of advice specifically worked with wild pigs, but he'd heard it enough times when his father was talking about bears. Don't run. Stand tall. Don't turn yourself into prey.

So that was what he did, even though he thought it unlikely to be a bear because it was too late in the year. They would all be in their dens where they would hunker down for the winter, wouldn't they?

Now that he thought about it, Decker wasn't so sure.

A rustle of leaves.

Decker's breath caught in his throat. He glanced toward the trailhead and summed up his chances of backing up far enough to make his escape without further agitating whatever was in the woods. What hadn't looked like a great distance before might as well have been a mile now.

He turned his attention back toward the woods, and that was when he saw it.

A skulking shape moving through the gloom between the trees. It was barely visible, just a darker black silhouette against the evening shadows. He couldn't tell exactly what he was looking at, but he knew one thing. It wasn't a feral hog. It was too big.

He backed away, trying his best not to let the panic overtake him. It wasn't working. He wanted to turn and run despite his father's advice, but he was afraid to look away. Terrified of what would happen if he took his eyes off that hulking shape.

As if sensing his fear, the unknown creature stopped and looked at him. Decker didn't know how he knew this because he could see no features. No eyes. Just a vague outline in the darkness. Then, as if it was completely unconcerned with him, the creature melted back into the woods and vanished from sight.

Decker stood there a while longer, willing himself to move, afraid of what would happen if he did. Then, finding his feet, he took off down the trail as fast as his legs would carry him back toward Wolf Haven, and safety. And by the time he reached home, he had convinced himself that it really was just a wild pig. Because what else could it have been?

Feeling better now that he had reasoned the encounter away, Decker went around to the back of the house and entered through the kitchen door, which was never locked during the day. When he stepped inside, he was surprised to find that he was alone. His mother was nowhere to be found.

# SEVENTY-SEVEN

THE WOLF RAN through the woods, and somewhere deep inside, the flicker of intelligence that was still Annie wondered why she had hesitated to kill the little Decker boy. He had been right there at the water's edge. Easy prey. Yet she couldn't bring herself to do it. Maybe somewhere, deep in her soul, killing a child in such a brutal fashion still felt wrong.

But now, as she ran through the piney woods with no clear idea where to go, or what to do next, she seethed. Her plan for revenge was falling apart before it even began. How was Robbie Decker going to know the sting of losing those he loved if she couldn't follow through when she had the chance?

She skidded to a halt, panting, and looked up at the dusky sky. The daylight was waning, and she could see the waxing moon hanging over the woods like a pale sentinel. She threw her head back and let forth a howl of rage that echoed through the trees and stunned the surrounding wildlife into silence. Then she took off again.

She knew where Robbie Decker lived. It was the same house he had lived in as a teenager when he flirted with her. When they had gone to the fair together. If she went there now, there might be another chance.

The wolf changed direction. Instead of heading back toward the bayou and her cabin, Annie went in the other direction toward the road leading through the piney woods to town.

It took no time to cover the distance. The loup-garou was powerful. Magnificent. She crashed through the undergrowth, snapping branches and crushing them underfoot, not bothering to hide her passage. All she could think about was reaching that house and redeeming herself. She might have hesitated to kill the child, but there was still Lily. Would Robbie Decker's pain be any less with only his wife gone instead of both his wife and child? She didn't think so. At least, not enough to make a difference.

But going to town was risky. Someone might see her, and given her reputation, that might bring people wielding pitchforks to her door. Folks were superstitious about these parts. They still believed in the old legends, and if they saw the wolf plain as day, it wouldn't be much of a stretch to connect it with the only witch they knew of within a hundred miles. Especially if that wolf had murdered the sheriff's wife.

Again, the wolf came to a stop. Despite her thirst for revenge, and her disappointment at having failed to kill the boy at Sullivan's Pond, Annie knew she couldn't risk being so easily seen. Better to retreat. Wait for a more opportune time. And that was the one thing she had plenty of. Time.

She turned to head south, away from Wolf Haven and toward the bayou. She could see the road through the trees. All she had to do was run parallel to it, and she would be back at her cabin in no time. Then she would head out into the swamp and collect more ingredients. Enough to turn into the wolf a hundred times if she had to.

But then, as she was about to take off, she picked up on a fresh scent, familiar and strange both at the same time. One she almost recognized.

At first, she thought John Decker was still out in the woods. Maybe he hadn't run as far or as fast as she thought. But soon she realized her mistake. It wasn't the boy that she sensed. This scent only carried the vaguest hint of the one she had picked up off Robbie Decker's son. It was someone else, but they shared a connection with the boy.

Curious, Annie turned and followed the scent until the road came into view. She stopped out of sight in the underbrush and waited, her heart hammering with anticipation inside the wolf's chest as the owner of the scent drew closer.

A bicycle with a wicker basket attached to the handlebars came into view.

Annie recognized the person riding it.

Lily Decker.

She could hardly believe her luck. After failing at Sullivan's Pond and deciding it was too dangerous to pursue her quarry back in town, here was Robbie Decker's wife, alone and vulnerable. Cycling along the road toward the bayou with no idea of the danger she was in. It was like the universe was giving Annie a chance to even the score despite her earlier weakness.

She wasn't going to waste that opportunity.

The bicycle was getting close now.

Lily Decker's scent was overwhelming. It assaulted Annie's senses like the aroma of a perfectly cooked steak, causing the beast to salivate in anticipation of what was to come.

The loup-garou hunkered down. Waited for the perfect moment. Then, as Lily drew level with its hiding place, the beast exploded from the underbrush in a fury of claws and teeth.

# SEVENTY-EIGHT

LILY HAD no time to react before the beast slammed into her, sending the bicycle careening sideways into a drainage ditch along the side of the road where it flipped and threw her over the handlebars. She didn't even see her assailant. Just a blur of movement, then a brief sensation of flying.

She hit the ground hard and tumbled down the bank, splashing into the muddy runoff at the bottom of the ditch a moment before the bike landed on top of her, pushing her under. Foul tasting water, silty and granular, rushed past her lips and hit the back of her throat.

Heaving the bike aside, she pushed herself up and emerged coughing and sputtering.

Her shirt was torn, sliced open below the shoulder, and she was bleeding from a nasty gash that quickly soaked the white fabric and turned it a bright shade of crimson. But strangely, she felt no pain. She wondered if it was adrenaline, or perhaps she was in shock.

She also wondered what had forced her off the road with such force.

Until she looked up and saw the beast crouched on the embankment above. A creature that observed her with sulfurous yellow eyes above a slathering jaw lined with sharp, glistening teeth.

Lily screamed.

She clambered to the opposite side of the ditch, kicking the bike frame away as it threatened to drag her down again into the murky water, and clawed at the bank.

She dug her hands into the soft earth, pulled herself up, then slipped back down again when it crumbled between her fingers.

From behind her, she could sense the beast watching. Waiting. As if it were toying with her. Savoring her terror.

She tried again, and this time found an exposed tree root that stuck out of the embankment like a gnarled arm. She gripped it tight with one hand and heaved herself up, using the other to feel around above the lip until she found another handhold to pull herself up and out of the ditch.

Then she ran.

She fled into the piney woods with no actual sense of where she was going, desperate only to escape the nightmare that had toppled her off the bike and into the ditch.

An image of the beast crouched above her flashed through Lily's mind.

It had looked like an enormous wolf. No, not a wolf. More like —she could hardly believe she was thinking it—a werewolf. Because the beast had been standing on two legs and regular wolves did not do that. Besides, she wasn't even sure if wolves lived in the piney woods.

But something did. And it was giving chase. She could hear it crashing through the undergrowth behind her.

She risked a glance over her shoulder. The beast was coming fast. It was almost on top of her.

When she looked back, there was a towering pine tree right in her path. She swerved at the last moment, barely avoiding it. Her foot caught on a thrusting root and she stumbled, flailing wildly, but somehow stayed upright.

It cost her valuable time.

She could sense the creature right behind her, could almost feel its hot breath on her neck. Just another second, and it would all be over. The beast would drag her down and tear her limb from limb.

Except it didn't.

Lily realized she could no longer hear the thump of its paws on the forest floor. The crack of branches and crunch of leaves as it barreled along behind her.

She glanced back over her shoulder a second time and was relieved to find the woods behind her empty.

The creature was no longer there.

She eased up and came to a stop, gasping for breath. She had no idea where she was, or in which direction the town lay. All she knew was that she had to get home and slam the door. Lock it against whatever horror was lurking out in the woods.

The obvious course of action was to go back to the road, pull her bike from the watery ditch, and cycle back to Wolf Haven as fast as she could. But that meant returning to the place where she was first attacked. Then again, if the creature had wanted to kill her, it wouldn't have given up the chase so easily. And her only other option was to carry on through the woods on foot, which was equally unappealing.

Making up her mind, Lily turned to retrace her steps.

Then she noticed the silence. It was *too* quiet.

The birds weren't singing. The crickets weren't chirping. Even the breeze had dropped. It was like someone had hit a pause button on the woods surrounding her.

Then she realized her mistake.

The creature hadn't given up. It was still out there. Watching. Waiting. Toying with her.

A sudden thought flashed through her mind. It actually wanted her to be afraid. The creature was basking in her terror, lapping it up like a cat drinking milk.

Lily swallowed a whimper. She would never make it back to the road and her bicycle. Of that, she was sure. But going forward, continuing to flee through the forest with no idea where she was going, might be equally deadly.

Lily stood frozen by indecision. Go back or keep moving forward? Or . . . stay right where she was and wait for Robbie to come looking for her. After all, she was still alive. The beast hadn't attacked. Maybe if she didn't move, if she showed no fear, it would leave her alone.

She considered that for a moment until she realized something. The sun was setting. It would soon be dark. The last thing she wanted was to be out in the woods at night with a dangerous predator. That left only one viable option. She would have to walk back to the road and hope that her bicycle wasn't too badly damaged.

She steadied her nerves and looked around, trying to pinpoint from exactly which direction she had run. When she saw the huge pine that she had almost careened into—recognizable because of the dirt and pine needles kicked up at its base when she tripped on the root—she took a step toward it. If she carried on in a straight line from there, she could retrace her steps all the way back to the road.

But before she could move, a low growl floated through the air. A growl that came from somewhere high above.

The breath caught in her throat.

She lifted her gaze from the forest floor and up into the canopy above. And there was the loup-garou, crouched on a thick branch ten feet off the ground, about to pounce.

Lily opened her mouth to scream. She never got the chance.

# SEVENTY-NINE

ANNIE STOOD over the body and looked down at the mangled lump of flesh that had once been Lily Decker.

The wolf was gone now, its bloodlust sated.

And so was Annie's need for revenge.

Let the boy live. Let him grow up without a mother, always wondering what cruel force of fate had ripped her from him so early. Let his father explain why Lily Decker had died. Why retribution had come down upon them. Because maybe that was a worse fate than taking away his entire family. Watching John Decker struggle with the loss of his mother, watching him deal with the grief, might be worse than if Robbie Decker had lost both of them.

Annie only had the weight of her own mourning to deal with. Sheriff Decker would carry the burden for two.

She smiled and licked a spot of blood from her lips, running her tongue across them and tasting the coppery tang that stirred a flicker of the loup-garou deep inside her.

She glanced toward the sky, alight now with the crimson hues of a fiery Louisiana sunset. It would be dark soon and she had a long walk home through the piney woods and into the bayou. The temperature was dropping too, and Annie had no clothes. Without the wolf's thick coat, she would feel the chill.

But it didn't matter.

What was a little cold? It wasn't like she would freeze. This was still Louisiana.

The bigger threat was navigating her way through the swamp at night when the alligators came out to hunt. But she wasn't worried about that, either. Not anymore.

She was the apex predator now.

The alligators would stay away, just like every other creature that crawled and slithered and skulked through the bayou. They would sense the creature that lurked within her, and it would scare them.

Annie took another look at the mangled remains of Lily Decker, relishing the thrill of the kill for a moment more, then she turned and started back through the woods to home.

# EIGHTY

## BACK IN THE LIBRARY

DECKER STOOD TRANSFIXED; the sight of his mother's mutilated corpse burned upon his retinas—a phantom image that refused to fade—even as the library shifted back into view.

"It wasn't my fault," he said, turning to the Ghost of All Things Past.

"No." The ghost's voice was soft. Almost tender. "The burden you've carried since childhood was never yours to bear."

"I always thought she was in the woods that day because I snuck out to Sullivan's Pond." A hard lump formed in Decker's throat. He remembered all too well what had happened in the hours and days after he ran home and found his mother missing— the house silent and empty. At first, after his dad came in from work, they had waited for her, figuring she must've stepped out to see a friend, or maybe went to the store. There was gumbo in a pot on the stove, so she couldn't have gone far. But when it got dark, and she didn't return, it became obvious that wasn't the case. By 9 o'clock at night, they were searching for her. Going door to door on their street and anywhere else they could think of looking. By midnight, his dad's deputies, along with officers from Bellows

Creek and three other nearby towns, were out on the streets of Wolf Haven and combing the woods behind their house. They found her the next morning, over a mile from home, lying torn and bloodied in the pinewoods close to Sullivan's Pond. The young Decker jumped to an obvious conclusion, even though he was too scared to say it aloud. "I thought she had gone looking for me because I didn't go straight home from school. I thought my mother died because of me. Even when everyone was trying to figure out why she went into the woods like that, why she was out there on her own, I never told my father where I was that evening because I was afraid that he would blame me. That I would lose him."

"Maybe if you had, he would have put your mind at rest. Told you it wasn't your fault."

"Maybe." Decker wasn't so sure. His father had latched onto any reason for his wife's death, even if it made no sense. Even without knowing of his son's transgression—of the young John Decker's trip to Sullivan's Pond—he had become distant and angry. Decker couldn't imagine how he would have reacted to the knowledge that his son had gone into the woods that day. Had ventured into the very place that Robbie Decker thought was unsafe and banned him from entering on his own. And his father was right. The woods were unsafe. And he would undoubtedly have viewed his son's disobedience as the catalyst for the misfortune that had befallen them. "But there was no way I could tell him. It would only have made things worse for me."

"You can't know that." The ghost looked at him with a soft expression, almost close to pity.

"I think I can." Decker had no doubt he would have become a focus of his father's obsession. That in his grief, and searching for blame, Robbie Decker would have latched onto that illicit trip. That would only have made his son's guilt all the more intense. The irony was that Robbie Decker knew the answer all along, even if he didn't know the reason. Years after his father took his own life, when Decker had returned to Wolf Haven and became sheriff in his own right, he had found the elder Decker's notebooks and files relating to Lily's death. At the time, he had dismissed the contents of those documents as the crazy ramblings of a fevered mind. Even when he came face-to-face with the loup-garou himself, Decker didn't quite believe that it was the same creature who killed his mother back when he was a kid. How could it be? Now he knew differently. Robbie Decker had been right back then. The loup-garou had killed his wife.

But none of that mattered now. Decker finally had an answer. He only wished his father were still alive to hear it. Especially now that he knew none of it was his fault. The loup-garou would have come after them, regardless. Annie Doucet was an unstoppable force hell-bent on revenge back then, just as much as she had been decades later when she went on the rampage that ended with Decker taking her life.

Decker felt as if a huge burden had been lifted.

He turned to the ghost. "I understand now. You can let us leave."

"No." The ghost shook her head. "There is more that you must see."

Decker was confused. "There's nothing left in my past to feel guilty about. I know the truth now."

"These are not the shadows of your past."

Now Decker understood. He knew the story of A Christmas Carol. If Charles Dickens had used this house as the inspiration for his book, then two more ghosts were waiting in the wings. "My present and my future."

"Yes." The ghost nodded, even as her form became wispy, and she faded from view. Like smoke dispersing in the wind. Her parting words hung in the air, echoing through the library. "My time here is over. I pass the torch to another."

Decker found himself alone. He wondered what visions the ghosts had in store for his present and future. Ebenezer Scrooge's premonitions had hardly been comforting when the ghosts had revealed what might lie ahead for him. Would his be any less disturbing? Decker feared what he would see but knew he had no choice in the matter, because when he went to the library door, it refused to open, no matter how hard he pulled on the handle. And even if he could escape the room, Decker thought, there was no guarantee he would be able to find Nancy, without whom he had no intention of leaving. His only option was to let the ghosts finish their task, and then maybe he and Nancy would be allowed to leave.

He was about to lift his hand from the handle when the grandfather clock gave a booming knell that reverberated from somewhere beyond the library.

Decker took a step back.

The clock continued to strike. Twelve peals in all. It was midnight yet again.

As the last knell faded, a voice somewhere behind him in the library spoke in a low baritone. "John Decker."

Decker turned, half expecting to find a jolly figure reminiscent of St. Nicholas sitting on a throne surrounded by opulent Yuletide morsels and carrying a flaming torch. But instead of this Dickensian representation of Scrooge's second ghost, he saw a more somber wraith-like figure dressed all in black with pallid flesh, dark hair that rippled as if touched by an unseen breeze, and coal-black eyes. In his hand was a book plucked from the library shelves.

The apparition observed Decker with a deadpan stare and said, "I am The Ghost of All Things Present."

Then the ghost opened the book, and they were in the library no more.

# EIGHTY-ONE

MINA WAS in her suite of rooms occupying the third floor of the 19th-century mansion that made up one wing of CUSP's island headquarters off the coast of Maine when there was a light knock at the door.

Adam Hunt stood on the other side.

"Where's Lucas?" he asked, referring to Mina's valet and body-guard, who would normally have answered the door.

"I gave him the evening off. I wanted to be alone," Mina replied. "Besides, it's late. I was about to turn in for the night."

"Sorry." Hunt flashed an apologetic half-smile. "I've been trying to catch up with you for days. You've been elusive."

"I've been off island. My presence was required at the Pentagon. If we want to keep on the establishment's good side, keep them turning a blind eye to our activities, we need to pamper them once in a while. Remind them just how much better we all are when they stay out of our way." Mina yawned. "I only got back this morning. But that doesn't explain why you're here at such an ungodly hour?"

"No choice. I was in a briefing all day and most of the evening. Came as soon as I could when I heard you were back."

"Trouble?"

"Not sure. There's a situation in the Lombardy region of northern Italy. Several people are going missing under strange circumstances. Possibly abducted. An eyewitness to the most recent incident mentioned a winged creature that looked part human and part bird swooping down from the night sky and snatching the victim up. Carrying them away."

"A harpy?"

"That would be my guess. Roman mythology is rife with them. Maybe there's a grain of truth in it."

"You think we need to get involved?" Mina asked, stepping aside to let Hunt enter.

"Not yet. The eyewitness was returning home from a meal out where they consumed a bottle of wine, which makes them hardly credible. We'll monitor it and see how the situation develops."

"Which means your briefing could have waited till morning. Why the rush to come up here tonight?"

"Because I'm not here about that. At least, not directly," Hunt said. "But if there really is a harpy terrorizing rural towns in northern Italy, it would be nice to have John on hand to deal with it. You know, given that he's our resident monster hunter. I hear you paid him a visit the other day. Tried to talk him into coming back."

"Ah, so you want to know if I was successful?"

"Something like that . . . were you?"

"What do you think?" Mina led Hunt into the spacious living room and went to an antique drink cabinet. She ran a hand across the cherry-colored wood as if it were an old friend. "Clarence Rothman left this to me in his will, among other things."

"I know." Hunt lingered near the doorway with his hands in his pockets.

"He gave up his bohemian ways and took over the family business after his brother's death. Used what was left of the money and became a philanthropist. He was also a generous benefactor to the fledgling CUSP. Provided us with funding in the early days. Even allowed us to requisition Singer Cay during the war, although I suspect he was happy to get rid of that particular piece of property given its history." There was an almost wistful tone to Mina's voice. "It was his money that bought this island."

"He was grateful for what you and John did for him," Hunt said, stepping further into the room. "You saved his life."

"And he helped John return to the present, which was repayment enough."

"Speaking of which . . ."

"John doesn't want to come back. He thinks we recruited him solely to keep the timeline intact."

"That's not quite how it works, at least according to Rory. If anything, it was the other way around. The timeline only happened the way it did *because* I brought him into CUSP. It was my decision, not yours. When you sent me to Shackleton, I had no idea how important he was to CUSP's past, because you never told me."

"With good reason. You had to recruit him for his skills, make the decision on your own, which was how it had to be for everything to fall into place. The fact that I already knew what would happen was neither here nor there."

"What are you going to do now?"

"Keep trying. We need him back."

Hunt narrowed his eyes. "Because you know something else that I don't? Please tell me you haven't traveled into the future too."

Mina chuckled. "I haven't traveled into the future. Trust me, it's as much a mystery to me as it is to you, which is a nice feeling. We need John back because he's one of our best operatives."

"And because he's your friend," Hunt said.

"Yes. That too. I miss him." Mina opened the drink cabinet and withdrew a half-empty bottle of scotch with a faded label. "Clarence sent this to me for Christmas in 1937."

"You've made it last well." Hunt raised an eyebrow.

"Not so much. He actually sent me two full cases, which are now mostly gone. Some of Howard Rothman's last import liquor stock. The stuff Clarence managed to hide during prohibition. Aged fifteen years in oak casks and bottled in 1912."

"The same year you saved him."

"Yes. Would you like a glass?"

"Hundred and thirty-year-old whiskey?"

"Give or take."

"I'm not sure I can afford to drink it."

"Consider it a bonus." Mina took down two cut crystal tumblers, poured a dram into one, and offered it to him.

"I think I shall politely pass," Hunt said. "At least for tonight. If we get John back, then maybe the three of us can toast his return."

"*When* we get John back. Not if." Mina lifted the glass to her lips and sipped the whiskey. "Are you sure? It really is rather good. The caramel notes are divine."

"I'm sure." Hunt nodded. He went to the living room door, then turned and looked back at Mina. "You know, John might not come back. This might be as much a part of the timeline as anything that went before."

"Immutable."

"Yes."

"I don't accept that. We need John. CUSP is his home. We're not whole without him."

Hunt shrugged. "It's not our choice to make."

"I know."

Hunt lingered in the doorway a moment longer, then he turned and walked to the front door, stepping out wordlessly and closing it behind him.

When he was gone, Mina stared down into her drink. It wasn't just CUSP who needed him. She needed him. Despite everything that had happened, the unageing decades that had passed for her as she took the long way back to the 21st-century, she still viewed him as a mentor. The closest thing to a father she had ever known.

It filled her with sadness to think that he might be lost to her forever.

She sipped the whiskey, savored the burn as it went down her throat. Then she put the glass down and sighed.

"Come back to us, John," she said to herself in a voice barely above a whisper. "It's not the same without you."

# EIGHTY-TWO

MINA'S WORDS rang in Decker's ears even as the ghost transported him back to the library. He had been wrong. That much was clear. Mina had meant every word she said when she came to see him the day he resigned from CUSP. He wasn't being manipulated. Wasn't merely a necessary pawn to keep the timeline on track. Adam Hunt hadn't been aware of the full situation when they first encountered each other in Shackleton, even though it was Mina who sent him there. She knew that with the players where they were meant to be, the pieces would fall into place on their own.

And maybe he had known that all along. He just didn't want to admit it because he felt slighted. He had carried such guilt about what happened in Whitechapel—Mina's brush with death and subsequent transformation when she absorbed Abraham Turner's life-force. He resented the older version of Mina because she let him struggle with his guilt for so long when she could have intervened and told him the truth. Only he now realized that she couldn't. Knowing the future would have influenced his actions, which would have caused a split in the timeline. Even if she had tried to tell him, it wouldn't have mattered, because the original reality would have continued unabated.

He turned to the ghost, expecting the apparition to remove another book from the library shelves. "Where are you taking me next?"

But the ghost shook his head. "There is nothing more for you to see in the present. You have all the information necessary to face your future."

"So that's it?" Decker asked. "We're finished?"

"My time with you is over, but your future remains to be seen." With those parting words, the ghost turned and walked away, growing fainter as he went until only a vague and barely perceptible outline remained, hanging in the air. Then even that faded, leaving Decker alone in the library.

At that moment, the grandfather clock struck again, its peals somehow deeper and more ominous than those that had come before.

And then he saw it. The Ghost of All Things Yet to Come.

A featureless dark form full of black shadows that writhed and seethed. A wraith whose shape undulated between human and something more demonic. It reminded Decker more of death than of the future.

He recoiled, a shiver of fear running up his spine.

The ghost advanced upon him in silence, moving more like mist than a solid entity. Then it raised an arm, lifted a finger, and pointed toward a book high upon the library shelves.

The world around Decker fractured. He endured a momentary sensation of gut-wrenching movement, as if he were lurching violently forward. He closed his eyes against a sudden wave of dizziness. When the feeling passed, he opened them again, and he was somewhere else entirely.

Adam Hunt's office.

The same office he had visited only days before to hand in his resignation. But the man sitting before him—Adam Hunt's future self—looked nothing like Decker remembered. There were bags under his eyes. He hadn't shaved. He looked disheveled. Something had happened in this version of Decker's future. Something bad. He had a feeling he was about to find out what.

# EIGHTY-THREE

I GOT YOUR MESSAGE. What's wrong?" Mina burst through Adam Hunt's office door without bothering to knock.

Hunt was staring at his laptop. He closed the screen and looked up as she approached his desk. "There's been an incident. It's not good. You might want to sit down."

"Just tell me." Mina hovered over the desk; concern etched on her face.

"You remember the conversation we had last month about the disappearances in Italy?"

"Sure. The suspected Harpy. We were going to monitor the situation."

"That's right." Hunt massaged the bridge of his nose between his forefinger and thumb. "Another eyewitness came forward last week with a similar tale to the previous one. Naturally, the local police dismissed his story of a winged creature carrying people off in the dead of night. But I found it credible enough to warrant further investigation, so I dispatched a team to Italy a couple of days ago."

"And?"

"They found the creature in a cave surrounded by the remains of its victims and cornered it. The situation got out of hand. They underestimated the creature's strength. There were fatalities."

Mina remained silent for a moment, absorbing this information. When she finally spoke, her voice carried a hard edge. "They should have called in the Ghost Squad," she said, referencing the specially trained paramilitary unit CUSP employed when dealing with extreme threats.

"They did. A unit was on standby. But by the time they got there, it was too late. The Harpy had killed two of the original team members, including the team leader."

"Who did you send?"

"You won't like this."

"Just tell me."

"Colum O'Shea. I sent him to lead the local team assembled in Italy."

"So what you're trying to say is that . . ." Mina trailed off, not willing to voice what she suspected out loud.

"I'm trying to tell you that Colum is dead."

There was a moment of stunned silence as Mina absorbed this information. Then she took a deep breath and composed herself. "You're sure about this?"

"Quite sure. I spoke to the leader of the Ghost Squad personally and he confirmed it." Hunt grimaced. "Honestly, if John hadn't resigned, I would have put him in charge of the team and Colum might still be alive. He's the best that we had."

Mina sank into a chair, her face ashen. "You can't know that."

"I appreciate you trying to make me feel better, but I'm sure of it. John had a knack for these things. Almost like a sixth sense for danger. Regardless, it doesn't matter. What's done is done. Now we have to deal with the consequences."

"And the Harpy?"

"Eliminated. The ghost squad took it down and mopped up the damage. There won't be any blowback."

Mina nodded. "Colum knew the risks just like everyone who works for CUSP."

"Doesn't make it any better." Hunt looked at Mina with searching eyes. "How have you done this for so long? Dedicated so much of your life to the Order of St. George, and then to CUSP. There must have been so much heartbreak."

"More than you could ever imagine." Mina glanced down so that Hunt wouldn't see the moisture brimming at the corners of her eyes. "And it never gets easier. I've lost more people than I care to think about in the last hundred and fifty years." She wiped away a tear. "What about Celine? She and Colum had become close."

"I haven't told her yet," Hunt said stiffly. "I only got the news from Italy a couple of hours ago."

"I'll tell her." Mina said through clenched teeth.

"No. I'm the one who sent Colum on this mission. I'm the one who got him killed. I should be the one to tell her."

"I appreciate the sentiment. But I really think it would be better to come from me. Woman to woman."

Hunt shrugged. "As you wish." A flicker of relief passed across his face. "We'll need to tell John. He and Colum were close."

"That's not a conversation I look forward to," Mina said. "He would have led that team had he not resigned. There's no way that won't cross his mind. He'll blame himself as much as you do."

"Maybe he should." Hunt clenched his fist and slammed into the table. "He turned his back on us."

"Adam. That's not fair."

Hunt composed himself with visible effort. "You're right. I just wish this turned out differently."

"Me too." Mina pushed her chair back and stood up. "Is there anything else I should know?"

Hunt shook his head. "I'll prepare a full report. You'll have it on your desk by morning."

"Make sure that it is." With that, Mina turned and strode from the room, pulling Hunt's office door closed behind her. Out in the corridor, away from prying eyes, she leaned against the wall. And then she allowed herself to weep, just for a few minutes.

# EIGHTY-FOUR

DECKER STOOD in the corridor outside Adam Hunt's office and watched Mina grieve. Next to him, hovering near his left shoulder, was the Ghost of All Things Yet to Come.

He turned to the wraith. "These events haven't happened yet. They're in the future, correct?"

The ghost said nothing.

"Speak to me. Tell me I can change this." Charles Dickens had written that the visions Scrooge saw in his future were merely shadows of what might come to pass. That they were not set in stone. Decker had no idea how closely Dickens had relied upon his own experiences inside the phantom house when crafting that narrative. "Can I save Colum?"

The ghost remained silent, and Decker wondered if his words were even being heard.

"Answer me, dammit."

The ghost still didn't respond.

A sudden anger rose inside Decker. Why would the ghost show him events if they couldn't be altered? There would be no point. He turned his attention back to Mina, who was still leaning against the wall, wiping tears from her cheeks. Hunt was right. If he had been there, things would have worked out differently. He was sure of that.

"I'm sorry, Mina. This is all my fault," Decker said, taking a step toward. But she wasn't aware of his presence. He might as well have been as much a ghost as the specter that stood beside him.

Instead, she took a deep breath and pushed herself away from the wall, then started down the corridor, walking past Decker so close that had he possessed a corporeal form they would almost certainly have collided.

Decker watched her go, then turned to the shadowy wraith. "I've seen enough. You've made your point."

But instead of transporting him back to the library, the ghost shook his head and laid a hand on Decker's shoulder.

And as he did so, the scene in front of Decker changed. It morphed and shifted into another place he knew all too well. Somewhere he had already visited with the Ghost of All Things Past.

The piney woods outside Wolf Haven. The place where his mother had died at the hands of Annie Doucet. It was night. The moon hung low over the woods, bathing everything in a pale silvery light. It reminded Decker of a similar evening many years before, when his father, along with deputies from the surrounding towns, had gone out to search for Lily Decker.

But this was not a vision from his past. That part of his journey was over. This could only be his future, which confused Decker, because he could not imagine why he would ever go back there.

Except he knew it must be true, because if the ghost had brought him here, then it had good reason to do so. Which could only mean that at some point in the future, he would end up right back where the nightmare began.

But why was he in the woods?

Decker didn't have to wait long for an answer.

Someone was coming, crashing through the undergrowth to his rear. Decker turned in time to see his future self appear out of the darkness. He stumbled along, almost tripping at one point, before casting a quick glance back over his shoulder.

*I look terrified*, Decker thought to himself, even as it occurred to him that there would be only one reason why he would be running through the woods like that. Someone, or something, was chasing him.

It soon became clear what that something was.

From behind his future self, Decker saw a blur of movement. A shape leaped forward, sinewy muscles rippling under dark fur. Yellow eyes blazing.

The loup-garou.

Decker could hardly believe his eyes. Annie Doucet was dead and buried, and so was the wolf that she had become. He had killed the creature himself after it went on a rampage in the high school while a hurricane raged outside.

Yet here it was. Alive!

Sensing the creature close behind, the future John Decker veered left and tried to evade the attack he surely knew was coming.

He wasn't fast enough.

The loup-garou slammed into his back, sending Decker tumbling to the ground. It kept going, carried forward by its own momentum, but not for long. Digging its heels in, the creature skidded to a halt and turned, rearing up on two legs.

Future John Decker pushed himself up onto his knees. Saw the creature blocking his path. He reached for the gun sitting in a holster at his hip. But it was too late.

The creature flew forward, arm raised, and slashed at its prey, sending the gun flying from his grip. A moment later, it was upon him. Ripping and tearing in a frenzy of bloodlust.

Then, mercifully, the woods faded from view and the library came back into focus, even as his future self's dying screams echoed in his ears.

# EIGHTY-FIVE

## BACK IN THE LIBRARY

DECKER WAS STUNNED. He could hardly believe what he had just witnessed.

"The loup-garou killed me," he said, almost as much to himself as to his spectral guide.

The ghost observed him in silence.

Decker wished it would say something. Anything. He wanted confirmation that the events he had witnessed—Colum dying on a mission because he wasn't there to alter the outcome, and his own demise at the hands of the wolf—could be changed. "If I go back to CUSP, will the future you just showed me be averted?"

The ghost's only answer was to raise its arm and point at the library door, which clicked open and swung wide to reveal the entrance hole beyond.

And there, waiting for him, was Nancy.

Decker rushed forward and flung his arms around her. He pulled her close, desperate to make sure she was real and not just another vision.

Somewhere deep in the house, the clock had gone back to striking twelve again. It was like no time had passed at all.

Decker released Nancy and looked back into the library, but it was empty now. The shadowy dark wraith—the Ghost of all Things Yet to Come—was gone, as if it had never existed. He was tempted to go back and look at the shelves, pull down one of the books chronicling his own future and see if it changed, but he knew it was pointless. He had tried that already when he was visited by the first ghost. The pages had been blank, and he was sure they still would be. Only the wraiths could read the history that lay upon them.

He turned toward the front door. "Come on, let's get out of here before we end up trapped inside this house forever."

Nancy hurried behind him. "You won't get any arguments from me."

When he got to the door, Decker placed a hand on the knob, but then he hesitated. What if it was locked? What if they weren't meant to escape? But that was ridiculous. Why show them visions of their past, present, and future if all the house wanted to do was trap them forever? Besides, Dickens had escaped and written an entire book about what happened to him inside this house, albeit fictionalized.

He turned the handle.

To his relief, the door opened.

Beyond it was nothing but swirling whiteness. The same strange fog that had forced them into the house hours before.

"John!" Nancy gripped Decker's arm.

"It's fine," he replied, even though he wasn't exactly sure of that. "Stay close to me." Then he stepped across the threshold and out of the house.

As he did so, Decker cast one last glance back toward the wall of portraits upon which hung the paintings of himself and Nancy —the latest additions to the strange gallery. He wondered who the ghostly house would trap within its walls next, and if they would look at those portraits in wonder. Then he pulled his attention away and waited for Nancy to join him before shutting the door behind them.

They descended the steps back down to the sidewalk.

The fog swirled around them.

Decker took Nancy's hand and turned toward their hotel, even though he could see nothing of the surrounding landmarks. Not Boston Common. Not the apartment buildings and brownstones on the other side of Beacon Street. None of it.

But as they walked, the fog cleared, and the city came back into view.

Decker cast a glance back over his shoulder toward the phantom house, but it was gone. The building and its occupants had disappeared back into the ether as if they had never existed. All he saw was the grassy expanse of Boston Common falling away into darkness, even as the last wisps of mist curled into nothingness.

They had made it back from whatever strange plane of existence within which the house and its ghosts existed.

Beside him, Nancy slumped with relief.

She glanced sideways at him. "I saw the past."

"I know," Decker replied.

"You came back for me." She took Decker's hand in hers. "You came to the diner with flowers. I saw it."

Decker nodded.

"But you left again before I saw you."

"You were with Tommy Broussard. What else was I going to do?"

Nancy came to a stop and turned to Decker, tears glistening in her eyes. "You could have let me decide who I wanted to be with."

"I know that now." Decker knew very well what had happened in the months and years after he walked away from the diner. Nancy and Tommy Broussard hadn't worked out. They broke up the following summer and she eventually married a man named Lenny Snider who had a quick temper and a drinking problem. The pair had a child together, Taylor, but it didn't take long before he'd had enough—of both his wife and his kid. In the end, he abandoned Nancy and Taylor. Walked out on them and left her to run the diner and raise the child alone. Decker could have saved her from all that, if only he'd given her the choice. "I was just a 19-year-old kid. Seeing you in the diner that day . . . it hurt. I figured you'd moved on. Are you mad at me?"

Nancy shook her head. "No. If anything, I'm relieved. After you left, I thought you didn't care about me anymore. That you didn't love me. That's the one thing that has bothered me all these years. Now I know differently. I can't change our past, but I can change my perception of it. You came back for me, even if I never knew it at the time."

"I never stopped loving you."

"Why didn't you tell me? When you came back to Wolf Haven and we started dating again, why didn't you tell me?"

Decker shrugged. "I guess I couldn't see much point in stirring up the past. Especially a past full of so many missed opportunities."

Nancy looked into Decker's eyes. She smiled. "It doesn't matter. I know now, and that's all that counts."

Decker held her hand as they started walking again. "What else did you see in the house?"

"Nothing of any consequence," Nancy said, in an almost offhand manner. "What about you? What did the ghosts show you?"

Decker stiffened. He wished she hadn't asked. An image of his future self being torn apart by the loup-garou flashed through his mind. But he wasn't sure that telling her about that, or about Colum's death, was a good idea. At least, not yet. He wanted time to absorb it. Process what he had seen. Instead, he told her about his father's relationship with Annie Doucet, going back before Decker was born, and his mother visiting her and using witchcraft to get pregnant. He told her about his mother's death, and the huge weight of guilt that been lifted from him now that he knew it was not his fault.

"What about your present and future?" Nancy asked as they left Boston Common behind.

"There's not much to tell," Decker said. Up ahead he saw a diner—the OPEN 24 HOURS sign flashing a neon red. He steered her toward it. "I know it's late and we've had a weird night, but let's get a coffee. There's something I need to say."

"John?" Nancy looked suddenly worried. "What's wrong?"

"Nothing," Decker lied, holding the door open for her. After they settled in a booth at the back with two steaming mugs of coffee, he reached across the table and took her hand. "I don't think we should wait to make new plans for our wedding. I think we should get married right away. Like, in the next few weeks, even if no one else can come. What do you say?"

Nancy looked at him across the table, her expression unreadable. "I think that would be for the best."

# EIGHTY-SIX

THEY LEFT the diner and walked back to the hotel in silence. Decker could only imagine what was going through Nancy's mind. He knew she was holding back about her experiences in the house but was loath to press her given his own omissions.

After they climbed into bed and turned out the lights, Decker lay awake for a long while, unable to forget those slathering jaws and the sound of his own dying screams. Eventually though, exhaustion overcame him, and he fell into a fitful sleep, where he dreamed of ghastly creatures prowling through the darkness, and of Colum, scared and alone, with no one to save him as the monsters closed in.

He awoke to weak sunlight streaming in through a crack in the room's curtains, and the insistent ring of his phone.

The clock on his nightstand read 7:42AM.

He fumbled for the phone, almost dropping it as he struggled to banish the last remnants of slumber and answer.

"John?" The voice on the other end—someone he thought he would never hear from again—cut through him like a knife. "Please don't hang up on me, okay? It's Chad. Your old deputy from Wolf Haven."

"I know who you are." Decker *was* sorely tempted to hang up, but the tone of his ex-deputy's voice was enough to give him pause even though the man had betrayed him and taken his job. "Kind of hard to forget. What do you want?"

"Well—" Chad sounded like he would rather be doing anything other than calling his old boss. "Is this a bad time?"

"I was sleeping, so what *do you* think?"

"Sorry." Chad sounded genuine, which surprised Decker. There was a brief hesitation. "I know we didn't exactly part on the best of terms, but I need your help."

Decker didn't know how to respond, so he waited for Chad to elaborate.

"Are you still there?" Chad asked, perhaps wondering if Decker really had hung up.

"I'm here." Decker sensed Nancy move in the bed beside him and raise herself up on her elbows. "What's wrong?"

"It's back, John." Chad's breath sounded loud and ragged over the phone's speaker. In short, he sounded stressed. There was a brief hesitation before he spoke again. "I don't know how, but the loup-garou is back."

# ACKNOWLEDGMENTS

Fourteen books and one prequel ago, when I started writing What Vengeance Comes I had no idea it would turn into such a long series, and give John Decker so many adventures. I just wanted to write a creepy pulp-horror style tale about a fascinating werewolf legend local to New Orleans, where I lived at the time. The loup-garou. When I wrote that book, I gave John Decker a cross to bear that foreshadowed the events of the main storyline. The killing of his mother by an unknown creature in the piney woods when he was a ten-year-old boy. I never truly revisited that part of Decker's past, or explained how his mother's death tied in with current events.

Later, several books into the series, I wrote another short prequel called Blood Moon, which I gave away at the end of What Vengeance Comes, to people signing up for my mailing list. It filled in some back story, focusing on John Decker's father, Robbie, and his dealings with a teenage Annie Doucet. But it still didn't explain how or why Lily Decker, John's mother, died that day out in the woods.

With Night Wraith, I saw a chance to put that right. Decker has always carried emotional baggage surrounding his mother's death, and the Dickensian theme of the book, loosely based as it is on A Christmas Carol, gave me a chance to revisit Decker's past. Like Ebenezer Scrooge before him, our hero gets to witness the terrible events that shaped his life and come to terms with them thanks to the ghosts of past, present, and future—the names of whom I changed slightly for the purposes of my book.

I hope you enjoy Night Wraith, and for those who have read Blood Moon, I apologize for including it in this book, but without it, I could not have told the full story of Annie Doucet's lifelong influence over Decker's life, which began years before he was born.

It also brings us full circle. The next book in the series will be called Wolf Haven. I won't say any more than that, but rest assured that Decker is far from done, and I have many new adventures planned for him.

And now I would like to thank my fantastic beta readers who were so generous with their time, and found all the snafus I made writing this book. I am so grateful for your dedication, and love for these weird tales. Thank you, in no particular order, to Dawn Hills, Tim Meehle, Marilyn Rubin, John Carlson, Pete Stapleton, Karen Padgett, Barbara Gorman, Paul Dinsdale, Sigourney Welborn, Emily Haynes, Alan Cobb, Cat Blyth, Leslie Farfour, and EJ Ruddier. Your help is, as always, invaluable.

And now it's on to writing the next John Decker adventure!
Anthony

# ABOUT THE AUTHOR

Anthony M. Strong is a British-born writer living and working in the United States. He is the author of the popular John Decker series of supernatural adventure thrillers.

Anthony has worked as a graphic designer, newspaper writer, artist, and actor. When he was a young boy, he dreamed of becoming an Egyptologist and spent hours reading about pyramids and tombs. Until he discovered dinosaurs and decided to be a paleontologist instead. Neither career panned out, but he was left with a fascination for monsters and archaeology that serve him well in the John Decker books.

Anthony has traveled extensively across Europe and the United States, and weaves his love of travel into his novels, setting them both close to home and in far-off places.

Anthony currently resides most of the year on Florida's Space Coast where he can watch rockets launch from his balcony, and part of the year on an island in Maine, with his wife Sonya, and two furry bosses, Izzie and Hayden.

Connect with Anthony, find out about new releases, and get free books at www.anthonymstrong.com

Made in the USA
Las Vegas, NV
23 November 2023

81368880R00184